THORNWYN

LAURENCE TODD
THORNWYN

THE CHOIR PRESS

First published in the United Kingdom in 2016 by
The Choir Press

ISBN 978-1-910864-48-7

For Karen, Caitlin and Ryan, who make it all possible.

Thanks to those who helped, encouraged, advised and criticised (you know who you are), and to Harriet (for the guidance and wisdom).

ONE

Friday

THE INEVITABLE OUTCOME of the trial had been the only topic of discussion in the office since the jury had returned its verdict. Yesterday, at the Old Bailey, Commander Neville Thornwyn, a much decorated and senior police officer, had been found guilty of several charges relating to bribery and corruption whilst in pursuance of his sworn duties as an officer of the Crown. This had included accepting payment not to arrest a suspect, conspiracy to pervert the course of justice, and receiving money from criminals to allow them to continue with their illegal activities, notably dealing class-A drugs such as heroin and crack cocaine. Thornwyn had been found guilty after a trial lasting eight days, and the jury had taken only one day to deliver its verdict on all charges, such was the weight of the evidence against him.

The trial judge, His Honour Mr Justice Lincoln QC, had said this was the most distressing case he'd had to adjudicate and, in all his many years of experience at the bar and now as a high court judge, he could never have believed he'd ever have to preside over a trial where a senior police officer in this country had acted so heinously in dereliction of his sworn duty. Rather than pass sentence immediately, the judge had remanded the defendant whilst he reviewed reports concerning the likely sentence, though he did stress a custodial sentence of many years was a very real likelihood.

I was remembering the sense of shock when news had first come through several months previously. The Yard had been burning with unsubstantiated rumours about someone very senior being investigated and about to be arrested on charges of bribery and corruption. Several candidates had been mentioned, none of which I or anyone in Special Branch could credibly believe. But then the news had come through, stating someone had come forward and offered incontrovertible evidence, in the form of detailed ledgers containing dates and names, of suspect payments being made to someone holding the rank of commander. The commander had been suspended from duty with immediate effect whilst the allegations were investigated and he had eventually been arrested and charged.

I was aghast when I heard the name of the man arrested: Neville Thornwyn. Because of his seniority in the force and the charges being brought, the arrest was headline news in the national media, though, of course, whilst still *sub judice*, only the outline of the charges could be given. Frankly I didn't believe the allegations and I wasn't slow in claiming it must all have been a mistake of grievous proportions, given the seriousness of the charges and Thornwyn's reputation as a good cop, which was stratospheric. I didn't even expect the matter to come to trial, but I was proven wrong and the evidence proved I was very wrong in my belief as to his innocence. The case did indeed go to trial and Thornwyn was found to be demonstrably guilty. There could be no arguing against the weight of evidence presented against Commander Thornwyn.

Everyone in Special Branch knew or knew of the defendant, whether personally as a friend, by reputation (which up to the trial had been stellar, given his thirty-three years' service and his achievements) or, like myself, through having served in his team before moving from CID to Special Branch.

After promotion from being in uniform to becoming a detective constable in CID, I'd been assigned to the team run by Thornwyn. He was then fifty-three years old, a DCI and a legendary figure in the Met, having been an outstanding police officer for many years. He'd refused promotion to commander a few years previously as he said he was happy out in the field taking down criminals rather than accepting a promotion which would see him become largely office-bound. His record of arrests was extremely impressive and included a number of major criminals who'd been taken off the streets after Thornwyn's team made it their business to put an end to their nefarious activities.

I'd only been in his team a few months when I had a part in arresting a gang of violent criminals attempting to hijack a juggernaut lorry from a car park in East London; we'd intercepted them in the process after a tip-off from one of Thornwyn's informers, of whom he had a veritable army. This was the first occasion I'd ever come up against hardened criminals using firearms, though only a couple of shots were fired and, happily, none in my direction.

The trial had made nationwide news because of the notoriety of two of the robbers, one of whom was an escaped convict with a very violent disposition, and Thornwyn had received a commendation for bravery after successfully disarming him and bringing him down when attacked with a machete.

I'd served with DCI Thornwyn for just over three years when he finally took the promotion he'd been offered to the rank of commander, up there in the stratospheric heights of the Metropolitan Police and rubbing shoulders with the great and good of the force, as well as with top political figures in the Home Office. He'd ultimately joined the ranks of those to whom senior Government figures would defer when it came to converting policy aspirations into workable and enforceable legislation. At the same time as his elevation to such rarefied heights, I too had been promoted, to the rank of detective sergeant, and I'd transferred over from CID to Special Branch.

Since his promotion I'd only seen him on two further occasions, and one of those was when he passed me in the corridor and just nodded at me as he didn't have time to stop. The other time was at the Old Bailey when he was

———◆◇◆———

giving evidence in a case, where we'd managed a quick word before he had to go into court.

The only other time I'd seen him after this was in court number one of the same building a few days back, when the trial judge was completing his summing-up to the jury and instructing them to retire and carefully consider their verdict. I'd not waited around for the verdict as the likelihood of his being acquitted in the face of overwhelming evidence of his guilt was roughly that of the USA ever forgiving al-Qaeda for 9/11. I was positive he was about to be convicted of the serious offences he'd been charged with, which would ensure him a custodial sentence for a significant number of years. I remember leaving the court feeling bewildered by the range and scale of Thornwyn's extra-curricular activities.

I'd spent some of last night watching *Newsnight*, which had devoted almost a third of the programme to the outcome of the trial. One of the participants, an eminent professor of law from an Oxford college, had raised the issue of lack of accountability and supervision at the top of the police, and had raised the pertinent question of how a top police officer could have got away with such blatant illegality for so long. He'd wanted to know the extent of the discretion allowed to senior officers like DCI Thornwyn and who was responsible for regulating and controlling their activities, but the answers given by a recently retired chief constable hadn't satisfied him.

This morning I'd read a detailed account of the trial and the background to the case in the *Independent*, which had devoted three pages to the trial and its implications for policing. The case was no longer *sub judice*, so the media were now able to present far more details of the case against Thornwyn; they presented stories of significant cash payments being made to ensure evidence was lost in transit or confessions retracted before they could be acted upon.

A few of these allegations had been made at earlier trials

involving arrests made by Thornwyn or one of his team, but they'd not been admitted into evidence and thus not allowed to be made known whilst the trial was ongoing. One person had come forward with a story about how he'd been forced to plant incriminating material, stolen property, on someone Thornwyn wanted off the streets because it hadn't been possible to arrest him through following normal police procedures. Thornwyn had justified his actions by reference to what's known and justified in certain police circles as *noble cause corruption*: rules being bent or broken because, whilst the defendant might not have been guilty of this particular offence, he was known to be guilty of *something* of at least equal seriousness, so the ends, getting a working criminal off the streets, justified the means.

Despite all this, for me the most harrowing story was one of a confession being obtained by force from a man charged with attempting to defraud HM Revenue & Customs on behalf of a company known to be a long firm. This man, though aged twenty-four, had a mental age of only eleven and was being interviewed without a competent and independent adult being present to act and advise in his best interests, contrary to the Police and Criminal Evidence Act 1984. It was obvious even to a blind man the defendant didn't have the mental faculties to plan and engage in such a crime, yet an attempt had been made to charge him of this.

The clear impression I was left with was that Commander Neville Thornwyn was now almost the dictionary definition of police corruption. His proud and distinguished record, as well as a stellar reputation accrued over so many years, was now in tatters.

The *Independent*'s story hadn't made particularly pleasant reading. None of the other broadsheets that had covered the trial had anything good to say either. The *Guardian* had also devoted almost three pages to the case and I'd stopped reading after a few paragraphs. Even fervently right-wing papers like the *Daily Telegraph* and the *Daily Mail*, which would normally be reluctant to ascribe any blame to police misconduct, had little good to say about the case.

What was worse, for me personally, was the loss of a hero, a man I'd looked up to as a role model upon becoming a detective, someone I'd respected and admired as I was beginning to move up in the force. As a young detective learning the ropes, soaking wet behind the ears but keen to learn, I'd been very impressed watching DCI Neville Thornwyn in action; the cool and methodical manner in which he assessed evidence against suspected criminals; the way he organised raids and deployed his teams across London for maximum impact; the fact he never panicked under pressure and, most importantly, the fact he almost always got the desired results. Sadly, I'd just discovered some of the ways in which these results had been obtained.

I remembered his team talks as we were about to go into action on dawn raids, about the importance of what we were about to do and how we'd be making London just that little bit safer when those we were about to nick were taken off the streets. He had a way of succinctly summing up how and why the streets would be safer once we removed the persons we were about to arrest. It was almost "*For St George and England.*"

Previously, I'd been particularly impressed with his record of arrests and convictions, stretching back many years, and seeing him in action I could see why he had such a stellar record. However, after recent events, I was now wondering, along with others in the police, how many of these convictions were now likely to be re-evaluated upon what would very probably be a spate of appeals. Several lawyers had already come forward after the trial, stating to the media they would now be considering whether clients they'd represented had grounds for an appeal as their clients may have been convicted on tainted evidence or perjured testimony. I suspected some were already salivating like hungry dogs at the thought of so

————◦————

many potentially lucrative briefs shimmering like a heat haze on their horizon.

Concentration was almost impossible in this febrile atmosphere. The whole office was in a state of, if not shellshock, then certainly amazement. Thornwyn's reputation had descended into the gutter almost as quickly as Jimmy Savile's had when news of his escapades with young children and teenagers had been made known and he'd gone from being a national treasure to a disgraced pariah in the same time it takes me to blow my nose.

I'd read the same page about four times and had taken little in. I was preparing to attend a meeting about this topic soon, something about psychological preparedness when about to undergo hostile questioning in court, and I was not looking forward to it. Not only had someone with a sadistic streak scheduled it for a Friday afternoon, but it was likely to be about as interesting as a wet January Thursday night in Scunthorpe.

The head of Special Branch, my boss DCI Smitherman, entered the office and saw me at my desk. He came over and sat down. My newspaper was opened at the trial report, and he picked it up and glanced at it for a few seconds, then put it down. Given his political persuasion, it was an eye-opener watching him look through the *Guardian*. I resisted the temptation to take a picture on my iPhone.

"I've been hearing whispers about this bastard for some years." He nodded at the paper.

Smitherman, as a good churchgoing Christian, swears with the same frequency I wear Laura Ashley frocks, so, when he does, it has symbolic meaning.

"You know the old saying, *if something looks too good to be true, then it probably is*?" he asked. "I keep thinking of that. Thornwyn's helped put a lot of people away, including several big names in major gangs, and it's made me wonder if this is how he did it. There were always whispers up on high" – he looked upwards – "about his methods and the results he obtained, but nobody believed them. Looks like they might have been on to something."

I knew what he meant but didn't want to think about it. The bad publicity that police and public relations were about to endure would last some while, it would be demoralising and every serving police officer would feel the impact.

Smitherman sat still for a moment, nodding to himself. He looked like he was tensing himself in the dentist's waiting room. Finally, he spoke.

"You served with Thornwyn, didn't you? You were part of his team until he went upstairs, weren't you?"

Why was he asking me this? He knew the answer. I agreed I'd served under Thornwyn before his promotion to commander and my becoming a DS and transferring to the Branch.

Smitherman nodded. "I remember you saying recently, when he was first charged, you didn't believe any of it. You were convinced of his innocence. I remember you saying this quite clearly. What's your view now?"

"What's there to say? Evidence looks pretty conclusive, doesn't it? He didn't deny much of what was thrown at him, did he? Looks like I got it wrong."

"Could it have been, subconsciously, you didn't want it to be true?"

"Might have been." I shrugged. "I mean, I enjoyed my time in his team. He was a good squad leader. Maybe I was hoping it wasn't true because it's all pretty damning."

"Stretches credulity to believe some of this could have been going on right under people's noses, though, doesn't it? *That's* what I don't get." He paused again. "Did you ever suspect anything like this was happening whilst you were in his team?"

"God, no." I was emphatic. "As I said, when I was with him, Thornwyn was a good team leader, a good boss to work under. I didn't see much else, certainly none of this." I nodded towards the paper. "I suppose I should be asking if I'm just blind or too stupid for my own good."

Smitherman tensed, about to speak, then stopped. He was clearly absorbed in something. He paused for a few moments.

"Come on up to my office." He said this in a way which made me think it wasn't because he wanted a chat about the weekend's football.

I followed him. He closed the door behind me as I took my usual seat in front of his desk, but then he surprised me by, rather than going behind his desk, sitting across from me on the same side, too close for comfort and with a serious expression on his face, which could only mean one thing. He wanted to look me right in the eyes from close range. There was something serious on his mind.

"You're aware of what Thornwyn's been found guilty of, aren't you?" He wasn't asking.

I told him what I knew about the circumstances relating to his arrest, which wasn't much as I'd largely gleaned what I knew from the media or in-house gossip.

"Many of his arrests were by the book, absolutely righteous. No one disputes that," Smitherman began confidently. "However, several, it seems, were only obtained because of either falsified evidence or perjured testimony. He probably won't be the last to go down either, once the perjury trials begin, and it'll be quite something if they don't. Lawyers are going back over some of their old cases as I speak. I wouldn't be surprised if several officers who've served on his teams over the years were already misplacing their notebooks about now so they can't be tripped up on what they did or didn't say."

"What do you think'll happen to him now?" I asked. Despite what he'd been convicted of, I still had a soft spot for my old boss. I'd learnt a lot about the realities of policing in Thornwyn's team, and I still couldn't get my head around thinking of him as a convicted criminal on his way to a lengthy stretch inside.

"Now? He's been remanded for psychiatric reports, probation reports and the like. MI5 will also want a word with him 'cause he's a commander, in possession of some quite sensitive information about operations involving both CID and MI5. Unofficially, that's one main reason why the judge deferred sentencing. Once MI5's satisfied he's not sitting on anything they need to know, or that could cause any damage if it came out, the judge'll decide how long and where. But he'll go down, that's a certainty. It's just a question of how long the judge gives him."

"Yeah," I sighed. I'd liked working under Thornwyn, but his list of transgressions was as long as my left forearm and had made wretched reading. I briefly wondered what Richard Clements had made of the trial and the verdict. I'd seen him around the Old Bailey a couple of times and once inside the courtroom. We'd nodded but hadn't spoken.

"The unspoken thing, of course, is the issue of putting a police officer in prison, especially someone of his rank and distinction. You know what happens when police get put in prison, don't you? His offences are too serious for an open prison to be a possibility, so it'll be the real thing for Mr Thornwyn, and that'll raise concerns about his safety. They'll be looking at where's the safest place to put him, but there's no guarantees there either. It could be he ends up spending a lot of time in solitary as he may have to be kept isolated, if for no other reason than his own safety."

Putting a convicted police officer in prison for any length of time poses a real dilemma for the authorities. Prisons are populated by people with long stretches ahead of them and even longer memories. Prison is a jungle and the grapevine reaches everywhere inside the system. Even if Thornwyn ended up in a prison where no one he'd arrested had been placed, the chances were good there'd be someone who knew someone whom he'd helped put away, and *ex parte* reprisals against him were a very real possibility. The future for Commander Neville Thornwyn was not one he'd be looking forward to. If he'd ever thought he was on his way to a long and leisurely retirement in some sunny clime, he could forget it.

"Anyway, I've asked you here because I wanna talk to you about your stint in Thornwyn's team." He paused, still staring at me directly.

I was starting to feel uncomfortable.

"I've been looking at the record about your time with Thornwyn. You were in on several notable arrests, and you testified in a few trials involving them, didn't you?" Again, this wasn't a question.

"Yeah, I did." I was confused and wondering where this was going.

"Lawyers are already re-examining a number of trials involving people he arrested. That'll mean arrests and trials you were involved in will also be scrutinised and, because you were a DC in his team, any testimony you gave will be scrutinised, almost line by line, to ensure there are no inconsistencies with the facts as now known. Lawyers are gonna go after anyone who gave evidence in trials where Thornwyn or his team were involved in the arrests. You were on his team, which'll mean they'll also put *you* and any evidence you gave or any statements you made under the forensic microscope."

Smitherman adjusted his posture in his seat and fixed me with an almost inscrutable stare. He leaned forward.

"You were part of the team who arrested Max George, weren't you?"

Max George was a particularly vicious criminal who was part of a large North London crime family, the Chackartis, and he'd been responsible for collecting protection money from small businesses, usually run by immigrants who'd borrowed money from dubious lenders and couldn't afford to obtain insurance in the usual manner. I agreed I'd been part of the team.

"His brief was screaming intimidation and fit-up all the way to the appeal court. I heard earlier this morning his lawyers are already looking at a fresh appeal. He wasn't the only one, either. One shylock claimed to have documentary evidence he was making payments to police to keep operating, and he said two of Thornwyn's team were also in on this. He was asked to produce this evidence of corruption and he did, and the evidence he produced was what got the case against Thornwyn started. He produced files detailing payments to police officers going back several years. You remember what the media made of all this?"

I nodded. Allegations had been made about miscarriages of justice in the broadsheets and it had made for some very unpleasant media stories for a while.

"But, whatever, the fact is you're on *my* team now, so never mind about what the IPCC want; *I* need to be sure about what occurred when you were with Thornwyn in cases such as this." He took a deep breath. "So I want you to look me in the eye and give me your solemn *word*" – he jabbed his right index finger on the desk, his eyes almost boring into my soul – "the IPCC won't discover any fraudulent testimony given by you, or anything at all relating to *your* conduct at *any* trial you gave evidence at."

Was *I* under suspicion of something? The bewilderment must have shown on my face. I was silent for a few moments, but then Smitherman raised his eyebrows and nodded, indicating he wanted an answer.

"I'll stand by everything I ever said in open court," I said firmly.

"You never knowingly gave perjured testimony to get a conviction?"

"No." I shook my head.

"You ever give testimony where you couldn't honestly say

———◄○►———

12

whether the evidence was true or not? You just said what you did to get a conviction?"

"No, I didn't."

"Off the record, strictly between you and me, did Thornwyn ever tell you to embroider any testimony you gave? You know what I mean: the evidence isn't exactly over-whelming, so tart it up a bit, exaggerate a little, distort it somewhat, make sure the jury gets the idea what the defendant's been charged with?"

"No, he didn't."

"Never?"

"Never."

"No implied pressure to do so? No nods or winks implying *you know what to do*?"

"No." I shook my head.

"You're certain?"

"Absolutely."

"Did *anyone* in Thornwyn's team, a DS, a DCI, ask you to do anything like this?"

"No, they didn't."

He seemed satisfied for the moment. He then continued, "When you wrote up your arrest reports, were you under any pressure to distort the facts or embellish the circum-stances to help ensure whoever was arrested drew the more serious charges? You know what I mean: saying a burglar was carrying a weapon or used violence against a home owner, or inflating the value of any property stolen?"

"No, I wasn't. Everything I wrote up was as I saw it."

Smitherman nodded sagely. "Okay. Next thing: again, I want your solemn word, when the fraud squad subpoenas your financial records, as they most certainly will, they won't find any large deposits, cheques, cash, whatever, you can't adequately account for or justify."

"My bank manager would love to find a few of those; so would I." I grinned. Smitherman didn't; his face looked like it was carved from stone and his stare was almost hypnotic.

———◦———

If I looked at his eyes long enough, I'd lapse into a trance. "No. They'll find no large deposits and no movements of large sums into and out of my account, apart from the small fortune the police pay me every month," I stated, calmly but with a smile on my face.

"Anyone who's served with Thornwyn over the last decade is going to have their finances looked at going back several years. They'll turn your accounts inside out looking for cash deposits or any evidence of abnormal or unusual financial activity. You know the kind of thing: a large cash deposit or a big cheque and then a withdrawal of the same amount a few days later once it's cleared. You comfortable with this? Should I be worried?"

"No. I'm not worried." I sat back in the chair.

"This'll include looking at your credit card spending as well. So, if you've put an American holiday or a brand new car on your credit card but paid it all off in one go soon afterwards, that'll also get them asking questions. You see what I'm saying?"

"You seen that piece of crap I drive?" I laughed. "Also, my last two holidays were in Southern Ireland and North Wales. Quite the jet-setter, aren't I?"

"Have you made any substantial purchases in the last few years? *Substantial* in the sense of costing a four-figure sum."

"Only my car. I bought it from a reputable Volkswagen dealership and put it on my card. You can check that on my Visa statements."

"How much?"

"Four and a half thousand. I'm still paying it off."

He nodded. "Was any money paid into your *partners'* accounts for you?"

"No."

"Any money paid into the accounts of *any* member of your family or friends?"

"No."

"You've no offshore accounts anywhere?"

"Only the one in the Cayman Islands, and even then it's only used for tax purposes." I smiled.

"This is serious, DS McGraw." Using my surname indicated this wasn't an informal chat and I should be aware of this. He nodded. He wanted an answer.

"No. I've no accounts offshore anywhere."

"I know you've been positively vetted and all that, but to operate in Special Branch you've gotta be *seen* to be above board and beyond reproach. I can't have anyone out there" – he nodded at the window – "who I don't have complete trust in."

He paused for a moment, sighed, then continued. "So, is there *anything* at all that happened when you served in Thornwyn's squad I should be in front of where you're concerned? The IPCC is very likely going to examine several cases where you were involved. Everyone who served with him can expect to be looked into after some of the evidence presented against him, because it's obvious he couldn't have done all this on his own. Someone has to have helped him frame defendants and testify everything was done right-eously, by the book. The IPCC's just following standard procedure after cases like this. But have they got *any* reason to go over *your* time in Thornwyn's team and expect to get a result?" He was emphatic.

I held Smitherman's stare. "No, they haven't. On my mother's soul, hand to God, I swear there's nothing for them to find, except my overdraft, and they're welcome to that."

He seemed satisfied for the moment. I noticed my heartbeat, which had increased somewhat when Smitherman had first started firing questions at me, was slowing down and approaching a normal rhythm again.

"Did you ever see anyone getting a confession forcibly extracted from them by the use of or the threat of violence?" he asked. "Someone signing a statement under duress, anything like that?"

"No, I didn't."

"Never?"

"No, never. I mean, a couple of people were assaulted in the process of being arrested. We'd go to arrest someone, they'd come at us swinging and we swung back, if you know what I mean, but any force used was reasonable. I've no doubt there was the odd punch or kick now and then that probably wasn't Queensbury rules," I said, raising my eyebrows to indicate he'd know what I meant, "but nobody went over the top."

Smitherman gave a dismissive shrug. Accepted police wisdom was, if someone swung at you and you swung back, the victim deserved what he received, so long as it was not excessive. "And you personally, did *you* ever use force to get a confession from anyone? Can anyone come forward and say they only admitted guilt because you used violence or intimidating behaviour or the implied threat of violence?"

"I've wanted to," I admitted.

"Haven't we all, but it doesn't answer the question. Have you *ever* used violence in any form to secure a confession or an admission of guilt?"

"No, I haven't."

Smitherman kept me transfixed in his forensic gaze. "You're not lying to me, are you? If the IPCC tell me they've found something against you, and it turns out you've been lying to me . . ." He didn't have to finish the sentence. I knew exactly what he was implying; I'd be a dead man career-wise.

"Everything I've told you is the whole truth."

Smitherman kept me fixed with his iron stare for a few more moments. Then his expression changed to one of relief, and he relaxed.

"Good." Smitherman smiled and sat back in his chair. "I knew all this anyway, but I had to be sure. I had to be certain there were no twinges of conscience and you weren't thinking you'd got away with something untoward after what's become of your old boss."

I must have looked surprised. "Huh?"

"Up to his trial, you were adamant he couldn't possibly be guilty, weren't you? You were so sure of that. Everyone who asked, you said he was a good cop and couldn't have done what he'd been charged with, so I wanted to know if that was because you were in on it *and* because the evidence was buried so deep it couldn't possibly be found."

"No, it was nothing like that."

"So, as I said, Thornwyn's arrest record is being investigated and anyone who's served under him can expect to be investigated by the IPCC as well as the fraud squad. So I had to be *absolutely* certain you weren't feeling *there but for the grace of God go I* about Thornwyn's fate."

"I'm not."

Smitherman got out of the chair he'd been sitting in and went around to sit behind his desk. This was the distance I preferred him to be from me. Having a desk between us was much more comforting, much less scary. My heartbeat returned to normal.

"If you knew all this, why were you asking me about it?" I wondered aloud.

"As I said, I had to be sure. If the IPCC found evidence of police misconduct, and there was some suspicion about what you'd said in court, or anything wrong with pre-trial procedure, you'd be looking at the wrong end of a disciplinary hearing, and you know what that'd mean."

I did.

Smitherman grinned, almost evilly. "But I also wanted to be sure because Thornwyn's asked to see you," he said casually.

"*Me*? Why's he wanna see me?" I was baffled. I wanted to see him about as much as I wanted to catch a sexually transmitted disease. I still had some warm feelings for my ex-boss, but I didn't want to spend any time with him.

"He needs to open up about a few matters before he's sentenced. We think he knows a few things he ought to share with us before he goes down. He's agreed to talk but said he'll only talk to someone he trusts, and he specifically asked for you."

"Aren't *I* the lucky one?" I said with more than a hint of irony.

"He was initially told by IPCC he couldn't see anyone in his old team because of the suspicion of colluding to pervert the course of justice, but he said you could be trusted because when you served with him you were the only person in the squad whose honesty he was 100% certain of and who wasn't in the Fund, and the IPCC have accepted that."

"*The Fund*? What's that?"

"You didn't know about it?"

I shook my head. "No."

"Thornwyn and two others in his team were skimming money from drug dealers and others, splitting it between themselves. They'd opened accounts under different names and you'd not believe how much was found in the bank accounts of these three; ran into *hundreds of thousands*. This was *the Fund*." Smitherman said this in a disbelieving tone. "They also had other scams on the go. As you heard at his trial, a couple of shylocks only operated because Thornwyn gave them his blessing in return for a share of the proceeds. They were actually *paying* him to operate." Smitherman shook his head. "Some of the allegations made against Thornwyn in earlier trials were true, it seems. Apparently you weren't invited to become part of the firm within a firm, so to speak, because you were considered to be too honest. They didn't trust you." Smitherman smiled.

I wasn't sure if this was a compliment or an insult.

"Two detectives are currently suspended from duty pending inquiries into their role working with Thornwyn," Smitherman said.

I was trying to remember who else had been in Thornwyn's team and who might be the two Smitherman was alluding to. There were several candidates I could think of.

———◄○►———

"I know what you're thinking but, before you ask, unless and until charges are brought, I can't tell you the identities of the two detectives in question. IPCC is looking into the entire squad and some of its activities. That'll include you."

"What about the rest of the team?" I inquired.

"A few of them thought they knew something shady was going on but didn't know exactly what and didn't take any part; turned the other cheek, if you like. You know how it goes; see no evil, and all that."

This was understandable. Unless it involved sex with young children or farm animals, no police officer in any team was going to rat on other squad members. Teams like the one I'd been part of, going after violent criminals, depended on total cooperation, trust and an unspoken willingness to go the extra mile for each other when the situation demanded. This means every member of the team had to trust others in the team would have his back should the situation require. No one wanted to risk being on the outside looking in because you were suspected of disloyalty to the team. I briefly wondered what I'd have done had I known of Thornwyn skimming money from drug dealers. Would I too have seen no evil?

"What sort of evil, exactly?" Was I being naïve here?

"You name it; evidence planted where it could be found, putting undue pressure on a defendant's family if he won't cooperate. In some cases they knew money was being paid but, even though they didn't take anything themselves, they turned a blind eye to it. Things like that. They mentioned one case where someone wouldn't cop to being part of the team turning over a number of warehouses in North London, kept maintaining his innocence, said he had nothing to do with it. Thornwyn got someone he knew in the Social Security office to have the benefits for his whole family stopped. His daughter, who was a single mother of two kids, had her family allowance and housing benefit stopped. The family had their housing benefit withdrawn.

——◦——

The suspect's jobseeker's allowance was suspended. This person ended up admitting guilt and, almost immediately, benefits are paid out again."

I was taking this all in. It was chilling to realise a team of eleven detectives and some uniformed officers I'd served in for three years, and had good memories of, was now being perceived as wholly corrupt. Despite what Smitherman had said, would any of this stick to me? It was a daunting thought.

"So, as I said, Thornwyn wants to see you and has vouched for you as someone who wasn't a member of his inner circle and who, so far as he's concerned, was clean. That's been investigated and found to be correct. I'd have you out of the Branch if it wasn't, trust me on that." He glared at me again. "So the powers-that-be have given permission."

"Meaning what?"

"Meaning you're off to sunny Belmarsh to talk to him in a moment; find out what you can from him, anything that hasn't come out yet but we ought to at least be aware of. He's agreed to talk and we need to know what it is he has to say."

I backed up a little. "So I've already *been* investigated?"

"Yes, you have," Smitherman agreed. "That's why the questions. You served with Thornwyn, so of course IPCC's going to look into you, but don't worry; you came out clean. No suspicion against you whatever. As I said, *I* wanted to be satisfied you had no skeletons deeply buried for IPCC to find. They're not going to let Thornwyn see anyone suspected of being corrupt." He then gave me a very serious look. "*I'd* suspend you myself, this very second, if I thought you were lying to me just now. If I'd got the impression you thought you'd got away with something."

I didn't doubt this was true. *Integrity* was Jack Smitherman's middle name.

"But if I have to go talk to Thornwyn, that'll mean I'll miss this afternoon's meeting, and I was *really* up for it as well," I said facetiously. Smitherman ignored it.

I considered everything that'd been said so far for a few seconds. Smitherman was as straight as a die and as honest as a summer's day was long, and any notion there could be corruption inside the force he loved almost produced physical pain for him.

"You know," Smitherman reminisced, "I joined the police straight from the army in the late seventies. Up to that time, the British police were routinely seen as the best in the world. That was what the public saw out there on the street. But there was *so* much corruption and intrigue beneath the surface. I take it you've heard of Sir Robert Mark?"

"Yeah, 'course I have."

Being a London copper and not having heard of Sir Robert Mark was like being a football fan and never having heard of Pelé. He might have been before your time, but you knew who he was, what he'd done and why he was feted.

Robert Mark had become the Commissioner of the Met in the early 1970s and he'd been appalled at the levels of corruption he'd found in the organisation, especially near to the top of the force. He had taken drastic steps to purge the police of those officers he'd thought were more crooked than those they caught. Whole squads were disbanded or merged with others, long-time detectives in one squad were transferred to other squads, and several who were suspected of corruption but against which nothing could be proven to the standard required by a court of law were virtually forced to retire early or resign from the force if they refused to go back into uniformed service. In the space of a few short years he'd transformed the entire culture of the monolithic Metropolitan police and produced a far more effective force in the process. Despite initial horror at some of the revelations which emerged, the public had been solidly behind Mark's changes and the reputation of the force was re-established in the eyes of the public. The Met in 1980 was a much different and cleaner force than it'd been a decade earlier.

"He aimed to create an environment where crooked cops

couldn't flourish out in the open any longer, and he largely succeeded. People like Thornwyn are now the exceptions rather than the norm. You wouldn't believe how endemic corruption was back then. Some top coppers openly boasted about how much Soho pornographers were paying them to let them operate unhindered. It's not like that any longer and I don't want the likes of Thornwyn bringing it back either."

I remembered a Politics course I'd taken at King's entitled *Britain in the 1970s*. One strand of the course had been about policing as this was the decade where major demonstrations became regular sights, political and industrial militancy having become the norm by this time. Police strategy and tactics had been the subject of much contention, particularly after events like at Saltley in 1972 where sheer weight of numbers had forced police to accede to requests to close a coal depot after thousands of miners and their sympathisers, in pursuance of furthering their industrial claims, had blockaded the gates and prevented lorries leaving with coal to help bring pressure on the National Coal Board. In this instance the police were seen as victims, as nobody had foreseen the vast numbers arriving at the gates at Saltley. But this had also been the decade when the extent of police corruption had finally been made public and where senior officers had gone to prison after having been found guilty of bribery and corruption in, amongst other things, allowing the porn trade in Soho to continue unmolested in return for sizeable cash favours. It was also the decade when TV shows like *The Sweeney* had shown the reality of police life in more graphic detail, suggesting that PC George Dixon was receding into mythology.

A popular piece of graffiti found on London walls at that time read: *A good police force arrests more criminals than it employs.*

For an honest young man like Smitherman, to have joined the police in the midst of all this controversy and societal turbulence had to have been a real eye-opener. That he'd survived and risen to his current exalted position in the force was testament to his honesty and integrity.

"So he wants to spill his guts; so what?" I asked. "Why does he want to speak to someone in Special Branch? Can't IPCC or someone else handle it? I don't particularly want to see Thornwyn."

"Well, he's asked for you, and I've agreed to it. I agreed because one of Thornwyn's cases touched on something the Branch was investigating," Smitherman said, almost airily, "and I want you to talk to him about it. Get his side of the story." He smiled wickedly. He knew I'd sooner fall down stairs than see Thornwyn.

"Huh? He was CID, wasn't he?"

"True, but this case crossed over into something we had an interest in, and I don't think we ever got to the bottom of it either."

"Which case was that?"

"You remember the controversy about the resignation of that parliamentary under-secretary to the Home Secretary a few months ago, Paul Sampson?"

I did. Paul Sampson had suddenly stood down from the Government and, soon after, caused an even bigger stir when he'd resigned his seat as an MP, citing health as well as personal reasons. The media had taken a keen interest in this because Sampson was only forty-three and seen as a rising star in the Conservative party, and his out-of-the-blue resignation had taken the political establishment by surprise and provoked much comment in the media about the real reasons behind his departure. Within a month of his resignation and standing down, though, he'd committed suicide by swallowing three quarters of the contents of a bottle of strong sleeping pills, as well as most of a half-bottle of cognac to keep them company. His wife had stated he'd been suffering from deep depression and had seemingly lost all interest in everything.

———◇———

"I remember reading about it," I said. "Interesting case. It never did come out about why he really stood down, did it? I only know what I read in the press, but he seemed a bit too young to jack it all in like that."

"He was. Unofficially, there were whispers from above." Smitherman nodded upwards. "Sampson was pressured into resigning to keep the lid on something, and it was suspected Thornwyn had something to do with that, but that was never established because Sampson wouldn't talk about it, and now can't as he's dead. Any undue interference with the duties of a minister is a serious offence. We need to know if the whispers are true."

"How could Thornwyn get a minister to resign?" I was puzzled.

"We don't know if he did, so you're off to talk to him and find out."

"Is that it?"

"No. There's something else as well. I can't be too specific at present, but the media have somehow got wind of an ongoing investigation into possible breaches of the ministerial code of conduct. The suspicion was someone in the Government wasn't playing by the established rules."

"They have a *code of conduct*?" My sarcasm was evident. "When did *that* happen?"

"Yes, they do." Smitherman looked sternly at me over the top of his glasses. I thought his faith in the integrity of those at the top was somehow touching. "Anyway, one of the MPs concerned was a senior member of his party. He was in Government when the coalition was first formed in 2010 and, before becoming an MP, used to work for a leading arms manufacturer supplying weaponry of all kinds to the armed forces. He was supposedly lobbying on the manufacturer's behalf for orders to be put its way. The rules state they can't do this whilst in office, and it's a clear violation of the ethics of the office held. The thing is," Smitherman said, matter-of-factly, "he was probably lobbying because the coalition was continuing with policies the last government had inherited from the previous one, one of which was selling arms and weaponry and other military equipment to countries the UK officially does no business with, especially not selling them weapons."

"What sort of weapons?"

"Firearms mainly; rifles, pistols, things like that."

"Which countries?"

"That's classified, I'm afraid."

"Let me guess; Paul Sampson's the MP concerned."

"Yes. Suffice to say none of this was ever intended for public consumption, but someone's leaked it to the media. Government was trying to hush this up and clear it up without it making the press, and the media's now making waves, asking questions Government doesn't want to answer just yet. The last thing it wants is for the public to know a minister who committed suicide was involved in selling arms to hostile countries."

"So, what's actually being looked into and who's doing it?"

"Customs and Excise is investigating the issue of exporting of weapons to places they shouldn't have been going to, and I believe the House Intelligence and Security Committee was going to be investigating as well."

"Thornwyn was involved in this?"

"That's what I want you to find out. It's known Thornwyn and Sampson were seen together a few times, so I wanna know what Thornwyn knew about this and whether the whispers we've heard about blackmail are indeed true. Also, anything else he knows about Sampson and his activities on behalf of the firm he used to work for."

"Sounds like I've got a fun afternoon, doesn't it?" I stood up.

"Fun? You work for *me* and you expect *fun*?" He flashed a sardonic smile.

*

Belmarsh Prison. Thornwyn had been remanded here because it had the appropriate facilities to keep him away from those whose spiteful resentment of the police might easily spill over into the dispensation of violence against a senior representative of the state agency they held responsible for their incarceration. Belmarsh was also equipped to hold high-security prisoners on remand or detain those found guilty of serious terrorist offences. It would be easier to keep him confined here whilst he waited for whatever sentence the judge was mindful to give him after considering all the reports currently being prepared for his perusal.

I'd visited Belmarsh not too many weeks before when I'd come to talk to Simon Addley about matters I was investigating, and it had been no more inviting then. The atmosphere was still austere and psychologically inhibiting, as though once inside, all possibility of returning to the outside world any time soon should be forgotten as quickly as possible. What would it be like to work in such a place? How did prison officers deal with their own feelings about the people here, several of whom had committed disturbingly violent offences? Was it different here from anywhere else, given that many inmates in Belmarsh were unlikely ever to be freed?

I'd assumed I'd be going to the same block where I'd spoken to Addley, and I very vaguely toyed with the idea of an unannounced visit because it was a safe bet he hadn't just popped out for the day, but, just as I decided I'd sooner have toothache than spend any more time with him than I had to, I was taken in the opposite direction. I was escorted into a different block by the prison officer who'd checked my credentials at reception. We engaged in some small talk along the way about prisons, the police and our respective roles inside them but, once he found I'd come to Belmarsh to talk to Commander Thornwyn, he let loose with a stream of invective about him and how he'd like to leave him unattended in the prison yard for ten minutes when some of the most violent and homicidal offenders were exercising. He looked at me with a satisfied smirk as his rant finished. He unlocked the door to the interview room. I stood face on to him, close enough to hear him breathing.

"I don't remember asking for your opinion about Commander Thornwyn," I said calmly. "I don't give a fuck what you think about him. Keep your fucking opinion to yourself. Okay?"

"I'm just saying," he said defensively.

"Don't," I snapped back. "You know the consequences if anything happens to Commander Thornwyn whilst he's on remand." I stared at him as I entered.

"Nice. We bend over backwards looking out for some corrupt cop, and then we have to take shit from other police officers as well." He looked at me with evident displeasure. "I suppose you think he deserves four-star treatment?"

"How about just doing your job, eh?" I muttered. I walked over to an armchair and sat down. The prison officer looked at me for a few moments with what I assume he thought was an aggressive stare and left the room.

Compared to the room where I'd interviewed Simon Addley, this room was almost palatial. The pale blue walls looked as though they'd recently been painted. There were two soft armchairs, a shag pile carpet and a table with four chairs, none of which was secured to the floor. There were two framed pictures on the wall, views of Belmarsh taken from the air. There was even a window letting in the sunshine, making the room appear bigger and brighter, and with a view of the main road. I was taking all this in as I sat back in one of the soft armchairs waiting for Thornwyn's arrival.

I didn't have long to wait either. A minute later the door opened and a senior prison official, someone I recognised as having seen on television recently talking about penal reform policy, led Thornwyn into the room with another prison officer behind him.

I looked at my ex-boss. He still cut an imposing figure; immaculately turned out, with his silver-white hair stylishly groomed, a jacket carried nonchalantly over his shoulder, smart but casual trousers, a white shirt and a tie slightly loosened at the collar. He looked like he was on his way for a night out and carrying himself as though he didn't have a care in the world. If I'd not known where we were, I'd have assumed he was still on duty as a ranking officer. Had I been expecting a broken man after the outcome of his recent trial, I'd have been very disappointed.

The official whispered something to Thornwyn, which seemed to amuse both men, and then left the room with the other officer. I was alone with probably the most reviled man inside the British police force.

I remembered the respect I used to have for him when I was a new DC in his section, and now I wondered whether I'd been taken in by the illusion he perpetrated and the patrician aura he undoubtedly radiated. He carefully hung his jacket across the back of one of the chairs, then sat in the armchair opposite and pulled it closer to the table. At that moment I think he realised I was actually in the room as he finally acknowledged my presence.

"DS Rob McGraw," he said in a knowing manner. "How are you, son? Long time no see." He still had the faint trace of a northern accent despite his years in London. Henry Higgins could probably have placed exactly where in the north. He extended his right arm to shake hands with me. I didn't reciprocate.

"Commander." I nodded, acknowledging his rank.

"You're still working for Smitherman, then."

"Yeah."

"Must be quite a culture shock working for someone as uptight as him after being in my team for a few years, eh?" He laughed. "You like it?"

"Working for Smitherman? Yeah, he's a good bloke. Could have done worse."

———◦———

"You like Special Branch?"

"I do, yeah. I like what we do. We make a difference." It felt like *I* was being interviewed.

"You think so, eh? Don't you think you made more of a difference in CID, helping get the *real* scumbags off the streets and behind bars, where they belonged? *That's* where the difference gets made, son."

"Don't call me *son*. I didn't come here to be patronised." I didn't like his sneering tone.

"Hey, calm down, Rob, no one's patronising you." He sat back in his chair.

At that moment the door opened and a prison officer entered carrying a tray with a pot of coffee, two mugs and a plate of biscuits, which he placed on the table. He poured coffee for Thornwyn and me, then left. At the door I could see the officer who'd escorted me looking disgusted at what was occurring.

When the door was closed, Thornwyn passed a mug of coffee to me. "So, you drew the short straw, eh? You're the one Special Branch sent over to talk to wicked old uncle Neville about his wrongdoings, eh?"

"I was told you'd specifically asked for me." I was surprised.

"That's true, I did. I just never expected them to agree to it. I wasn't sure you'd want to, either. I told them I wanted to talk to you because you're straight."

He stared directly at me. I wasn't sure how to respond, so I didn't.

"No, seriously, Rob, I'm not bullshitting you or doing you down. When you were in my team, you were probably the *only* one I could be certain wouldn't have accepted any of the money we were raking in. That's why there were a few arrests we didn't take you along on and a couple of interrogations you were kept away from, because we weren't sure whether you'd blow the whistle on whatever went down. You know how carefully we had to tread around you?" He laughed. "It wasn't easy, trust me."

———◇———

Was I being patted on the back or sneered at? I wasn't certain what to say in response to this, so I said nothing.

"You could have made yourself some easy money, Rob, you really could." He sounded as though he was sorry for me.

"I could also be sitting where you are," I replied.

He smiled again. I sipped my coffee, which was surprisingly good. Only the best for the prison service hierarchy. I was looking longingly at the biscuits but didn't take one.

"This'll sound familiar to you," he said. "You know how sickening it feels, *really* feels, to spend seven months working on a case against a violent drugs gang who're pushing bad stuff onto innocent and willing dupes, putting several of them in hospital 'cause of what they mixed in with it? And then, when you finally get enough evidence to arrest them, finding a few *millions* in cash" – he emphasised the quantity – "stashed away inside a hold-all in a lock-up garage, more money than you and I'll ever earn in an honest working lifetime. You ever seen that much money in one place at one time? It's quite some sight, I can tell you."

He sat forward and put his mug on the table. "But then you get to see them walk because of some slip-up in procedure? An *i* not dotted or a *t* not properly crossed, or a jury of *Guardian* or *New Focus* readers acquitting them, and they sail away laughing their fucking heads off at police as they go straight back to doing it all over again, and you have to start building a case all over again, whilst all the while you know what they've done and you know they're as guilty as hell? That's what happened to me when I was a rookie in the drugs squad in the late eighties. We nailed those bastards righteously, but they still walked. Not too long later a teenage girl haemorrhaged and died because of the poisoned crap these people were pushing."

He paused for a moment. "So I thought to myself, there's gotta be a better way of ordering things if the law's not gonna do its job. So, from that point onwards, I was determined to

———◦———

30

see the scum go down, lawfully if I could, but if that wasn't possible, or if I thought they could be more use to me on the outside, then paying for what they do, so long as the taking of life wasn't involved."

He paused again, staring at me to ascertain if I was listening. He continued. "When I became a DCI, over a period of years I slowly built up a small, dedicated team who went after villains with a vengeance, people who were largely in tune with how I thought, and we put a lot of them away."

"With or without evidence," I said, only semi-facetiously.

"You judging me, Rob? You my moral arbiter now?" He looked quizzically at me. "Did Smitherman send you here to refocus my moral compass, is that it?" He didn't speak for a few seconds. "There was *nobody* went down who didn't deserve what they got. I'll challenge you to find me *one person* who didn't deserve it. They might not have committed the actual offence they were sentenced for, I agree, but look at it in the wider, and I'll give you a true story. Some young slag commits several aggravated burglaries whilst he's coked out of his brain. Causes a lot of distress, does a lot of damage. We know it's him but we can't prove it." He shrugged. "So, I get someone good to enter his place and plant something incriminating. We act on a tip-off, raid his place, find the evidence. The slag goes down. Justice is done. We get the result we deserve, he gets what he deserves." He said this with a degree of finality, as though nothing he'd said could possibly be disputed.

"That was the case with Max George as well, wasn't it?" I remembered what Smitherman had said earlier. "He was fitted up, wasn't he?"

He drained his coffee and poured another. He looked at me as though I were a particularly dumb student, slow on the uptake. "What if he was? You really saying the victims of what these bastards did aren't going to be pleased at their being taken off the streets? I'm no political philosopher and prison may or may not work, but what I *do* know is, whilst

---

they're inside, they're not committing any crimes against those who don't deserve to be victims. George was a violent scumbag and, because victims were too scared to testify against him, we stitched him up and he goes down." He looked pleased.

"*That's* what I mean about CID making a difference, Rob. We serve people where they live, on the streets where their houses are and where they park their cars. We're not Special Branch; CID doesn't deal with abstract concepts like *state security*, whatever that means." He laughed again. "The overwhelming majority of people out there" – he nodded at the window – "are only concerned with their daily reality, not abstractions. I've been a copper over thirty-five years, so I know it's true. As long as people feel safe in their homes, they'll support whatever police do in their name. Someone breaks into their house, nicks their car or tries raping their daughter? Society wants these people put away, Rob. It's not interested in judicial abstracts like *the right to a fair trial* or criminals having their fucking *human rights* protected." He poured scorn on both terms. "People want them put away, locked up and out of sight, preferably for as long as possible. *That's* what people care about. *That's* what I gave them."

There was plenty I could have said in response about rules of natural justice not being abstractions, but rather the foundation of any functioning democracy based upon respect for the rule of law, but this wasn't the time or place. Thornwyn had been convicted and was waiting for sentencing, so there was nothing to be gained from debating the rights and wrongs of what he'd done.

There was an awkward silence for a few moments.

"But you didn't come all this way to listen to my proselytising, did you, Rob? You sat through all this at university. You want to know about specifics, don't you?" he said in a light tone. "Such as how I might have trodden on Special Branch's toes."

"Yeah." I sat forward and looked directly at him. "We're

interested particularly in what led to that MP, Paul Sampson, suddenly standing down and no real reason given. Word on the street has it you know the score here."

"Special Branch were interested in Sampson?"

"He was involved in something with a connection to other things being investigated, and also there was no explanation for his sudden departure."

His expression changed to one of smug satisfaction, as though he knew some priceless secret he was keeping from the world. He looked up at the window for a few moments whilst he gathered his thoughts.

"Sampson," he said. "Interesting case, and one I fell into almost accidentally."

Without asking, he refilled my coffee cup and offered the biscuit plate. I took four coconut cookies as a reward for my patience.

"Couple of years ago, two blokes were caught *in flagrante delicto* late at night in a car park somewhere, don't remember where exactly. Some woman walking past with her dog, the dog runs over and cocks its leg against the wall behind a car. She's aghast, runs over, tries to shoo the dog away. There's people in the car and, from the positions, she thinks she's disturbed a couple having it off. What she actually sees in the car is the back of some bloke's head who's sucking another bloke's dick." He grimaced whilst saying this, as though swallowing something bitter. "She dials 999, a patrol car in the vicinity was on the scene pretty quick. As they were caught not too far away, they're both taken to West End Central, questioned and so on, you know the pack drill. Nothing exceptional so far, just another case of a pair of queers going at it in public rather than at home. They were both contrite, profuse apologies given, didn't mean to offend anyone, thought there was no one around, all that kind of stuff."

"What happened to them?"

"Initially given a police caution, told we'd be in touch if

we decided to take the matter further. As it was, there were more important issues going on than a couple of perverts, so the matter's forgotten. They both get sent letters warning them not to do it again or else they'll both get their balls cut off." He smiled as though the prospect amused him.

"So how come you got involved? Commanders don't usually get involved in these matters."

"It was a few months on before I became aware of it. We raided some pawn shop's back room in North London following a tip-off about contraband being stored and fenced on the black market. Caught a few dealers, took a few firearms off the streets. It was a good pull." He was smiling to himself. "But one of the blokes we pulled in was an old lag, one of my occasional informants, Bernie the Buck. I knew him 'cause I'd arrested him twice before. He wasn't part of the gang, just the night watchman at the place it was all stored at and stupid enough to be there when we raided it. He said he had info about some highly placed queen he'd be prepared to share with us in return for charges against him being dropped. He's a toerag, but he'd given a few good tips before, so I went along to speak to him. Incidentally, you know how he got his name? He once tried changing counterfeit dollars in a bank. You wanna know how they knew they were counterfeit? The idiot who'd done the designing and printing had only put the image of the Queen's head on them, the one used on UK paper currency; Bernie hadn't even noticed it." He laughed loudly. "You believe that?"

"What did he mean, *some highly placed queen*?" I asked once we'd stopped laughing.

"Said he regularly sold ecstasy tabs to some posh bloke he knew who's a fairy and claimed to have a boyfriend who's a well-known MP. They used ecstasy when they went to sex parties and also when they engaged in sex in public. Apparently, as homosexuals, the risk of being caught having sex in public heightens their sensual pleasures, so I'm told, something about giving society the middle finger for its intolerance. I'd had a couple of knee tremblers when I was a rookie, but there's no heightened pleasure doing it with a tart down some stinking back alley." He smiled at the memory. "Anyway, he told us he'd name the man concerned if we gave him a deal about not being charged."

"The highly placed man?"

"No. The one he sold the ecstasy to. One would lead to the other. Sounded like a good deal. I knew a couple of tabloid journalists who'd pay good money for a tip-off like this, but anyway my boss talked to your boss, and Smitherman said he'd like to know who this highly placed person was as there could be security implications, depending on who he was and what he did. Bernie names this bloke, Geoffrey Tilling. I check him out. He's a senior civil servant at the Home Office. So we go pay him a visit at his flat in Borough, not too far from the market. He's at home when we arrive. I tell Tilling we know he buys ecstasy and he's got a boyfriend who's an MP and we wanna know his name. Denies it all at first, does the whole outraged bit: *Who told you that rubbish?* and so on. I tell him, if he doesn't cooperate, I'm gonna arrest him there and then. Tilling begins to cry, says he loves this bloke and doesn't wanna drop him in it. He's upset but I don't give a shit, so I wait. He stops blubbing, tells us his boyfriend's name."

"Paul Sampson," I said firmly.

"In one." Thornwyn beamed broadly. I formed the impression he was rather delighted at knowing who this MP was.

"So what then?"

"I tell Tilling, next time he meets Sampson, we'll be nearby and, when they meet, we'll step in. Long story short? They meet in the same flat, would you believe, the very next evening, in fact. Sampson casually strolls in, drops his briefcase and gives the bloke a full-on kiss on the lips, a real smacker, like a bloke greeting a woman. I then step into the room and identify myself. Sampson looks like he's gonna shit a brick at that very moment."

The pleasure Thornwyn was getting recalling this event was obvious. His eyes had lit up.

"You saw them kiss?"

"Took a picture of it on my mobile for posterity." He smiled broadly. "And also to sell to the tabloid press if it came to it."

"What was Sampson's response?"

"Dischuffed, to say the least. Before doing this, I'd also checked him out. Found out he was a prominent Tory MP, in line for great things in the party. He was already a parliamentary under-secretary and on his way to the top. But there was nothing on file about him being a queer."

"I think the word is *gay*," I ventured.

"Yeah, that's the vogue term, I suppose. Me? I think they're perverts. I'm a Tory voter as well and it disgusted me to think I was voting for someone like him." He sounded angry. "Tories used to be the party of the family, now look at them. A bloody poof being tipped to get to the top of the party. Sampson's got a wife and a kid, and he's out there pretending to be normal when it's obvious he's not? What a bloody world."

I'd seen some unpleasant aspects to Thornwyn's character previously but I'd not realised until just now he was also a rampant homophobe. I briefly wondered whether this trait had been on display when I'd been in his team and I'd not noticed it.

"I can guess the next bit, can't I?" I asked. "You blackmail him; you tell him his sordid little secret'll be safe with you and you'll play deaf, dumb and blind so long as he's a good boy and pays up regularly. Am I right?"

"Close enough," he agreed. "He was like a pigeon with a broken wing. Couldn't fly away, could he? He wanted to continue to be an under-secretary, he had to pay up. Told him, if he didn't, the picture of him kissing his boyfriend would be all over the press. So, yeah, I leveraged him."

"How much?"

"Oh, I don't think we need be concerned about that, do we? Suffice to say his filthy secret never made it on the front pages. Tilling certainly won't say anything; he's still working at the Home Office, and his chances of any further promotion would be buggered if this came out about him." He paused for a moment. "Buggered." He laughed at his own joke. "Didn't mean it like that. Nice pun, eh?"

"Hilarious. What was Sampson's reaction to being blackmailed?"

"What do you think?" He said this as though I was an idiot. "He was outraged, but as I told him, do you want the press and the great British public knowing a family man like you also sucks cocks in car parks at night? That shut him up."

I must have looked surprised.

"You see," Thornwyn said, "I'd also found out these were the two who'd been found in the car park the night I mentioned earlier. It was Sampson and this other bloke whom the woman'd seen."

I thought about this. An MP caught in a potentially compromising position but no mention in the press? In the current political climate any MP found in any compromising situation, especially where homosexuality was an issue, would be a target for the tabloid media. Sampson especially would have been fair game because of his position in Government and he'd probably have had to resign immediately, with his political career in ruins. I briefly wondered what Richard Clements would give to be in possession of these facts.

"So how come Sampson wasn't recognised when taken into custody?" I asked. "Didn't his name ring any bells?"

"He was in disguise, nobody recognised him. He had glasses and a wig with different coloured hair. He'd a false driving license with a different name and address; they both had. We got done over. The letters we sent never reached them. They thought they'd got away with it. But I'd looked at Sampson's file and saw a picture of him. I compared it with the one taken before he and Tilling were questioned that evening. Even with the disguise I recognised him. *That's* how I was able to sting him financially, because of this duplicity and also because he was alibied up for the night in question. I found he had two other MPs prepared to swear he was with them on the night in question should his being taken into custody ever come to light."

I thought for a few moments. "So, was this just for money or was there some ulterior motive behind it?"

"Oh, initially, just monetary. I didn't like the idea of some queer at the top of the party I vote for, so I told him, either be honest and come out the closet, or pay up. He said he had too much to lose if he came out, his wife would take his kid and leave, so he paid up." He said this as though he was explaining something perfectly obvious to someone slow on the uptake and it was the natural order of things in his world.

"So when did your priorities change?"

"What do you mean?"

"Sampson resigned from the Government and stood down as an MP earlier this year because you were leaning on him. That's a bit of a step up from putting your hand in his back pocket, don't you think? This has security as well as political implications, and it suggests to me there was something other than money involved. Was being black-mailed the *only* reason he resigned or was there something else?"

He looked at me with a puzzled expression, as though deciding what to say in response. In his own mind I didn't doubt he was still perceiving me as the just-turned-twenty-six-year-old who'd joined his squad as a newly promoted junior DC, the one who'd initially sat back in squad meetings and offered few opinions or suggestions until he knew his way around and knew how things were done. Thornwyn was quite likely thinking it was a damned impertinence for some

————◁◦▷————

junior to be questioning him about his actions and his motives. He was radiating an aura of smugness, as though anything he'd done couldn't possibly be wrong and, despite his current surroundings, he was still making the rules and calling the tune for others to dance to.

"I detest the way this country's going, Rob, I really do." He sighed, shaking his head. "It was fair enough when they were in the closet, but now they're out in public, quite open about their perversions. It's even the case they're allowed to adopt kids! Two bloody fairies raising kids. You want that? I don't. I certainly don't want them in Government either, passing laws on my behalf. So, yeah, I wanted Sampson out of it." He loosened his tie slightly further and sat back in his chair.

Looking at Thornwyn, I was thinking I ought to contact Richard Clements afterwards. As a political journalist, possibly he might know someone who could give me a few off-the-record details about Sampson. I decided I would.

"And that's the only reason you blackmailed him, because he was gay?" I asked.

"Bad enough on its own, but he had a wife," Thornwyn said. "He had a *kid*."

He poured me another coffee. I took two more biscuits.

"So I confront Sampson. I tell him: tell the truth, come out and admit the truth about this guy at the Home Office, or I'll talk to some journalists I know and your name and picture see daylight in the press. He refuses."

"Did you mention this to the press?"

"I held off initially, thought I'd give him a couple of days to chew his options over. He then does the unexpected thing and resigns from Government." He sounded surprised. "Cites pressure of work, health reasons, the usual spiel. 'Course, you know what happened to me not too long after this." He waved his arm around to indicate his surroundings. "I was careless and, well ..." He didn't finish the sentence.

"So the rumours are true. He resigned because of you.

You forced a member of the Government to leave office because you didn't like the fact he was gay."

He thought about it for a moment. "I didn't *force* him; I simply gave him a choice. But, when you put it like that, I suppose I did, yeah," he said casually, sipping his coffee.

"And you kept on blackmailing him," I challenged my ex-boss.

"Oh, no, not after that. It was a kind of victory getting him out of public life, so that was something." He paused for a moment. "If you're expecting me to apologise, Rob, you'll be waiting for quite some time. I won't be doing that."

I looked at Thornwyn with some degree of disgust. Blackmail is a particularly revolting offence, usually targeted against the weak and defenceless, and for it to be employed by a decorated police officer against a member of Parliament, a man also in Government, albeit a few rungs down from the top, for no other reason than distaste at his sexual persuasion, was venal in the extreme. He'd not even been charged with blackmail at his recent trial, so any liability for this would be evaded, assuming it was ever made known: unlikely now Sampson was dead. My admiration for the man I'd looked up to when I'd served in his team was dissolving before my eyes. Any respect for Thornwyn had dropped rapidly whilst talking to him and, if it got any lower, I'd soon be standing on it.

I then remembered something else Smitherman had said earlier. "The press mentioned something about the House of Commons' Intelligence and Security Committee looking into allegations of misconduct amongst Government personnel. It was you who leaked it to the press, wasn't it? That's how they knew: you told them." I said this as an accusation. Any potential security issues relating to MPs would be considered by the Intelligence and Security Committee and also investigated covertly, so any publicising of its considerations could only come from the inside.

He said nothing in response, sipping his coffee calmly and

looking benign, as though he were waiting for an opponent to make the next move on the chess board. We sat silently for a few more moments.

"Possibly." He winked at me and sat back in his chair, looking very relaxed. "Let's just say I had a few fruitful conversations with a tabloid hack I know and told him a few things."

"You knew about investigations by the Intelligence and Security Committee? How did you get to hear about them? Was Sampson part of this?"

He didn't respond. He picked up his cup and finished his coffee. He sat back.

"So, you happy now, Rob? You got what you came for. You now know why Sampson resigned," he said formally. "That'll make Smitherman happy."

"He took his own life a few months ago, you pompous prick." I said this calmly but with slightly more aggression in my voice than I'd intended. "Sampson took his own life because you threatened to *out* him."

Thornwyn looked indifferent for a moment, then he smiled. "Smitherman hasn't told you what the bigger picture is, has he? That's why I wanted to talk to you, but Smitherman hasn't clued you in, has he? He's left you thinking it's all about hidden sexuality. Tsch tsch, naughty Jack." He shook his head.

"Meaning what?"

"Not for me to tell you, Rob. Suffice to say there's much more to this than you might think." He stood up and prepared to leave.

I had another thing to put to him. Smitherman hadn't answered this; maybe he would.

"Something else I'd like to know. Given what you've just been sentenced for, you had to have some help doing all those things you were convicted of." I was curious. "What about the others? Who else was involved?"

He looked almost benign and sat down again. "Not for me

to say, Rob. I'll just say this. When you were in my team, you were the only one I'd have trusted completely. What does that tell you?"

Almost on cue, the door opened and the same senior prison official entered. Thornwyn nodded to him and picked up his jacket.

"You should talk to Smitherman. Thanks for coming, Rob. Appreciate it." He offered his hand again. I didn't accept. He smiled and left.

I walked out the same way I'd come. The same prison officer escorted me to the exit and the atmosphere was somewhat frosty. He was not impressed with what he'd seen.

"Nice cosy little chat, eh? Hope the chairs weren't too uncomfortable for you. Did you like the coffee?" he said, sourly. "I just really love it when my working day revolves around pampering some corrupt cop and one of his cronies. If there was any justice, we'd—"

I turned. My face was about twelve inches from his.

"*Fuck you,*" I said with controlled aggression. He recoiled. He stared at me for a moment, then turned and walked away. I was surprised at my response.

Driving back, I wondered why I'd taken umbrage with the aspersions cast by the prison officer. I realised that, despite everything I'd just heard, despite what Thornwyn had been found guilty of and his homophobia and his blackmailing, which had contributed to destroying the life of someone whose only offence was a sexual tendency Thornwyn either couldn't or wouldn't attempt to understand, and despite my antipathy to everything he'd done, I couldn't quite shake off some warm feelings towards my old boss.

I thought back to joining his team when I'd first become a DC. I'd been part of a new wave of promotions as it was believed several squads needed freshening up and *new blood* introduced to shake things up. Whilst arrest averages were being kept up and there was no political pressure being brought to bear, it was felt some officers were now past their prime and either they were better suited for a desk role or else they should consider their options, turn in their papers and maybe take that position as Head of Security being offered at a large factory somewhere after all.

Thornwyn had introduced me as the FNG, the bright spark with the university degree who'd probably use phrases they wouldn't understand but who could help them spell all the big words they might have to use at some point. However, despite this, I was soon accepted into the team and we all gelled nicely. I later discovered FNG meant *fucking new guy*.

Thornwyn's squad was seen in CID as part of the elite who, along with the Sweeney, went after the hardened villains: the lorry hijackers, the armed robbers and the violent offenders. It was exhilarating work, though occasionally scary, having to tackle criminals armed with guns, knives and other weapons. I remember, soon after joining, someone swinging a lead pipe at me and, had I not ducked instantly, my head would have come off.

Thornwyn's arrest record was impressive and the team managed to secure some outstanding convictions of major villains, though doubt had now been poured over the methods used in a few cases. His command style was a kind of charismatic leadership, in that he was able to convince someone of something needing to be done without using the authority of rank. He'd never had to lean on someone to do something unpleasant. He always exuded an aura of benevolent dictatorship, meaning that, despite his banter, his bonhomie and his ability to appear to be just one of the chaps when we went out on one of the squad's regular piss-ups, he *wasn't* one of the chaps. *He* knew it and, more importantly, *we* knew it as well.

One night in an Indian restaurant in South Kensington, the total bill for the evening, for a group of around twenty people, had been somewhere in the region of a thousand pounds. Thornwyn had startled me when not only did he insist it was his treat, but he produced a wad of £50 notes from his pocket that could choke a horse and paid in cash. Leaving the restaurant I'd asked one of the squad how Thornwyn was able to pay a bill of that size in cash. His reply was along the lines of a jovial, "Come on, mate, it's not like he's spending his own money, is he?" To my bemused expression, as I was a new boy, he'd replied in a light-hearted manner with something like, "It'll all become clear to you soon."

Except it never did. Nobody ever took me to one side and explained just how and why Thornwyn was able to pay restaurant bills running into many hundreds of pounds with equanimity. Now, in hindsight, it's obvious what was being spent was from the proceeds of crime, money extorted from criminals who were financing a squad night out on the razzle. For a while, Thornwyn had found a way to make crime pay.

It was now nearly five o'clock and, unusually, Smitherman had left early as he was off to a black-tie senior police officers' gathering later that evening. I sat at my desk and typed an account of my conversation with Thornwyn, concluding with my now knowing he'd used undue influence to compel Sampson to resign from the Government, and requesting to talk to Smitherman about this matter as Thornwyn had alluded to there being more to the issue than was apparent to me.

I then phoned Richard Clements on my mobile. He was still at his desk. I told him I wanted to pick his brains about a sensitive political issue and asked when he would be available.

He arrived just before seven. I was about a hundred yards away from the pub when I saw him approaching it from the Trafalgar Square direction. Walking north along Whitehall, however, I'd become acutely aware of a woman the other side of the road walking in the same direction and, despite the crowds, staying slightly behind and on the outer edge of the kerb; she appeared to be keeping me in sight. I'd looked over at her a few times and each time she had looked away. I was sure she'd also been behind me when I'd walked along Great George Street just now. But then, it was busy, lots of people walking along Whitehall, so perhaps it was my imagination. Why would anyone be following me?

The Clarence, at the north end of Whitehall, was our usual rendezvous point if I needed to talk to Richard Clements. In the past two years we'd met here a few times and a kind of friendship was evolving between Clements and me. We'd been undergrads together at King's and I'd thought he was just a left-wing jerk-off mouthing the stock phrases and trite clichés such persons usually voiced, like members of a car club. But since becoming reacquainted with him now that he was a journalist on the left-wing fortnightly magazine *New Focus*, I'd found him no longer to be the hothead he'd been as a student. He'd matured somewhat, had married Smitherman's daughter and was now making his name as a political writer. It was this I wanted to tap into because he was active in politics and political reporting circles. He had contacts at all levels of the political sphere and in all parties, and he also knew people who knew people, which I was hoping to benefit from. I could have looked up information about Sampson in the files we maintained, but I wanted the views of someone on the ground, someone in touch with daily events. Clements mingled with journalists and politicians all the time and I was hoping he could help me out.

That he was also Smitherman's son-in-law was a source of considerable amusement for me, though Smitherman's blood pressure wouldn't thank me for that.

I timed my arrival so I got to the bar just as Clements was ordering and I let him buy me a pint as I was now off duty. I noticed his hair was even longer and tonight he wore it in a ponytail. I could just imagine Smitherman's reaction if he saw it.

The quick-drink-after-work crowd was thinning out, so there were tables available. We sat by the window. I looked out the window and could see the same woman standing at a bus stop, looking up and down the road.

"My father-in-law's only just down the road from here," Clements said.

"Where? Having tea in Number 10?" I was curious.

"At the Banqueting Rooms. There's some gathering of top cops for whatever reason, so he's down there schmoozing with the cream of law enforcement. My guess? They're gonna talk about Thornwyn and how they can minimise any damage from the fallout."

The idea of Smitherman schmoozing with anyone was too much to grasp. Smitherman didn't schmooze. He'd probably stand around, making one glass of something last a while, feeling extremely uncomfortable and itching to call a taxi.

"What about Thornwyn, then?" Clements sounded excited. "I was in court for a few days 'cause we're gonna do a piece about the downfall of a top cop, and I couldn't believe some of what I heard. No cop's faced charges like that since the seventies. Did you know him?"

"Yeah, I was part of his team. I was in CID before joining the Branch."

"*Yowzah*," he exclaimed. "Did you know about him then?"

I knew what he meant. "No, I wasn't with his team very long. I had no idea about any of this."

"Can you imagine my father-in-law being as bent as that? He's a boring old sod but at least he's honest. He's so straight, he's probably got a broom handle stuck up his arse." He laughed at his own comment. "Anyway, I'm guessing you wanna pick my brain about something."

"Very prescient." I leaned forward slightly. "You've got your ear to the ground, so I'm hoping you can help me with a few things. You okay with that?"

"Yeah." He was draining his first pint. "Shoot."

"What do you know about Paul Sampson?"

"The MP who took his own life earlier this year?"

I nodded. "Yeah, that one."

"I don't know too much about him. I interviewed him once for an article the *Focus* ran about up-and-coming Tory MPs and which ones we predicted to have a bright political future in the party. We didn't use his contribution, but I've still got it on file if you wanna read it. Seemed a perfectly decent guy to me, though I disagreed with just about everything he said."

"Do you know anything *else* about him?" I looked straight at him, hoping he was reading between the lines.

"Like what? You mean personal stuff?" He'd caught on.

"Something like that. You ever pick up on any rumours about his private life or his sexuality, stuff like that, the usual political gossip?"

"You know something, don't you?" He smiled knowingly. "You've heard something about him and you're hoping to use me as a sounding board to verify whatever you've picked up on, aren't you?"

"Am I that transparent?" We both laughed. It felt easy laughing with him. Were we in danger of becoming real friends? There was no denying I was feeling more and more comfortable talking to him, though we both went out of our way not to let on to Smitherman that this was the situation as his reaction would not exactly be hard to ascertain. Clements would be perceived as an undesirable left-wing influence and I suspected Smitherman would not be pleased knowing one of his team was associating with such a person.

Clements didn't initially reply. He went to the bar and bought two more pints, though I'd not even finished my first. I'd asked him for this meet and yet he was buying the drinks; fine with me. He sat back at the table and opened a packet of scampi crisps.

"Okay. Strictly between you and me, off the record?"

I nodded my agreement. "Scout's honour."

"I did hear it said he might be gay. Someone at the *Focus* saw Sampson out with another guy one time, and he recognised the other guy: some top official at the Home Office. My friend knew him from university and knew he was gay. Sampson was a parliamentary under-secretary in the same department. This official's as gay as a summer fruit basket, so the speculation was whether Sampson was as well."

"He's sure it was Sampson?"

"Oh, yeah, no doubt."

"Where'd he see them?"

"At the gay pride march last year." Clements smiled broadly. "My friend was taking part in it. They weren't, they were just walking along the pavement watching. My friend was sure it was this Home Office guy. He checked it out, it was definitely him. Sampson, of course, he recognised immediately 'cause he's in Government."

"Was it Geoffrey Tilling Sampson was seen with?"

"Yeah, it was." Clements looked surprised at hearing this. "I was right; you *do* know something, don't you?"

"I'm not sure." I was hesitant.

I decided to take Clements into my confidence. I lowered my voice.

"Your friend's right. Sampson *was* gay, but he wasn't out. He was still in the closet, and I did hear he'd resigned from Government because of being blackmailed about his sexuality."

Clements' eyes opened wide in surprise. "*What*?" He almost spat his beer back into the glass. "You're kidding, right?"

I shook my head slowly.

"Who told you this?"

"Someone who knows him; a well-connected, *very* authoritative source." I didn't mention the source was the actual blackmailer himself. "You know much else about him?"

He looked deep in thought for a few seconds. "No, I don't think so. His resigning from Government made headline news, of course, especially when he stood down as an MP soon after. All the hacks I'm in contact with were sure he'd be promoted if the Tories won the next election, probably get something near the top of one of the major departments of state, Foreign Office or Defence, something like that. Makes you wonder why he resigned when he had so much going for him and could have toughed it out." He sipped some beer. "I mean, it's no big deal being gay nowadays, even in the Tory party, so why didn't he just come out and declare himself? It wouldn't be the first time an MP's done that and survived. Even top-class rugby players have come out as gay and played on with no problems."

Clements shook his head, looking bewildered. "I don't buy it, Rob. There's gotta be something more than being gay making him resign as an MP. He must have stood down because whoever was blackmailing him knew something else. I know a few MPs from both sides of the House who've done much worse things than being gay, and it wasn't always consensual either, but they've still got their seats in the palace of varieties down the road." He laughed knowingly. "But I'm keeping those secret until my autobiography comes out."

What Clements said made some sense. Why hadn't Sampson just called Thornwyn's bluff and come out? It would probably have caused a small political earthquake for a day or two but, once settled, would have removed Thornwyn's hold over him and allowed him to continue serving as an MP. Life would have progressed and he'd have continued his climb up to the political summit. Was it *really* as he'd supposedly said, that his wife and child would have been lost to him? Or was Clements correct in his assumption about there being something else in the background preventing him? I remembered Thornwyn saying a few hours earlier I didn't know the bigger picture.

<hr>

Clements had more to say. "I was told he'd assured the party Chief Whip he wasn't gay when the rumours first started, and what was being said was just scurrilous gossip spread around by his political opponents. I heard this from my contact at the *Guardian*, who'd heard it from an MP he's friends with, so that could be one reason why he kept the closet doors closed. I mean, lying to the Chief Whip in private's no biggie, is it? MPs do it all the time. Profumo lied to the whole House from the floor of the Commons, but Sampson didn't do anything like that." He drained his second beer. I wasn't even halfway through mine.

"What else do you know?" I asked.

"That's it, really. There's probably more gossip out there somewhere, though." He had an evil grin. "You wouldn't believe how incestuously gossipy reporters are, particularly the political hacks in the lobby. Sampson had a few friends in the lobby. I can ask around, see what else is known, if you want."

I took him up on the offer. I told him to be discreet, make out it was for a story his magazine was preparing and certainly not let on it was for someone in Special Branch. He said he'd do it after the weekend because tomorrow he was going on a demonstration against selling arms to despotic Middle East regimes and probably wouldn't see too many of his journalist friends there.

"Oh, yeah, when Special Branch photographs me, can you ask them to get me in left side profile? That's my photogenic side." He laughed again.

I thanked him and left.

Walking back along Whitehall toward Westminster tube station I had the same feeling I was being followed. Nothing I could pinpoint, but then I saw the same woman from earlier on the other side of the road also walking towards Parliament Square, making sure she stayed slightly behind me. I couldn't be absolutely sure, but something inside me said I was being tailed. There was something in her mannerisms making me think she wasn't just taking a mid-evening stroll in central London.

I stopped outside the Red Lion, a popular Westminster watering hole for politicos and journalists, pretending to be looking at the tariff listed on the door. In the reflection of the glass, I saw the woman across the street also stop and wait by the bus stop. I entered the pub, went into the bar and looked across at her. I didn't recognise her. I waited a few more moments, then went back outside.

I walked fast to the corner of the road, then sprinted a few yards and, at the nearby Tesco Express, ducked into the shop and waited inside by the door. Ten seconds later the same woman came past, walking quickly and looking anxiously towards the tube station. She quickened her pace. I stepped outside and followed her into the foyer of the station. She was looking around when I walked past, gently nudging her as I did.

"Sorry, sweetheart," I said jovially. "You got the right time?" I looked at my watch, then at her. For a split second our eyes locked. I'd clocked her and she knew it. Without a word she turned around and walked away, and without telling me the time.

I was being followed. Why?

TWO

Saturday

I WAS READING THE POST-MORTEM REPORT concerning the suicide of Paul Sampson. As he'd been an MP it was easily accessible from his file.

The facts of the case were straightforward and not in dispute. His wife, Martha, had gone into the bedroom around 11 pm and found her husband lying in bed. She'd thought initially he was asleep but, as she had gone to turn off the bedside lamp, she'd noticed his eyes were open and his pupils were dilated. She'd also noticed his chest was barely moving and his breathing was erratic. She'd felt for his pulse but had struggled to locate one and, when she had managed to, it had been very weak. She'd immediately dialled for an ambulance and one had arrived inside six minutes. He'd been taken to a nearby hospital. The medical team had recognised the signs, his stomach had been pumped and a considerable number of very strong prescription-only sleeping pills had been extracted, mixed in with a quantity of a rather good cognac. The mixture of alcohol and strong sleeping pills, coupled with the time elapsing between the estimated ingestion of the pills and alcohol and his wife finding him, had meant Paul Sampson had lapsed into a coma and, according to his doctor, Radeep Singh, there was the very real possibility of permanent and irreparable brain damage. He'd died the next day without ever regaining consciousness.

The only fingerprints on the pill tub and cognac bottle belonged to Sampson and there was no suspicion of any foul play. The coroner had recorded the cause of death as a suicide. No note had been found. It was noted there was no history of suicide in his family, nor any history of mental illness. The family GP had confirmed the issuing of the prescription for the sleeping pills and this wasn't considered to be suspicious.

Questioned by police, Martha Sampson had said her husband had been suffering from a very deep depression since standing down as an MP and was often morose and seemingly devoid of any real purpose in his life any longer. Asked what he'd been doing since leaving the House of Commons, she'd replied he'd largely spent his time just sitting in his study and looking out the window at the garden. He'd made no contact with any of his parliamentary colleagues and had refused all requests for interviews from the media, even from friendly journalists he'd known for years, though he'd maintained contact with a couple he'd regarded as personal friends rather than just writers.

The report did not make for happy reading. Paul Sampson had been only forty-three when he'd taken his own life. But for his being pressured by Thornwyn to come out or be named in the media, he would have been justifiably confident of many more years as a top Tory MP and, if Clements was to be believed, securing a top Government position and possibly a seat in the Cabinet. The file didn't mention anything about blackmail or any speculation as to his sudden resignation as an MP.

There was no mention of any suspicions about his sexuality either. Sampson was listed as being married with a seven-year-old daughter, Jade. Tilling's name wasn't mentioned anywhere. As a parliamentary under-secretary Sampson would have had to undergo positive vetting before entry into ministerial life, which made me wonder how thorough the vetting had been. Either Sampson and Tilling had been very careful indeed – and, according to Thornwyn, they had false driving licenses for ID purposes – or the vetting had been poorly conducted.

Could Clements have been right in suggesting Sampson was under other pressures than just to come out? There was no doubt he'd left a glittering career behind when he'd resigned and now he'd left everything behind. I was unsure whether the coroner's report had included everything.

I needed to talk to someone who knew him well, and the obvious candidate was Geoffrey Tilling. He would know more about Sampson's state of mind in the months leading up to his resignation and his premature death, and there was nothing indicating he'd been interviewed concerning Sampson's suicide.

There was no answer from the phone in Tilling's flat. I checked with the duty officer at the Home Office and found Tilling was in his office. I decided to try him there.

The Home Office no longer has its grand Whitehall base. After being relocated around the corner in Petty France for a while, it's now to be found in Marsham Street, in the very heart of political Westminster, near to Parliament and the main parties' headquarters. I walked there from the Yard and, inside at reception, showed my ID and asked for Geoffrey Tilling. A call was placed to his office.

He appeared a minute later. He was about five foot eight and had dark layered curly hair on top but cut very short around the sides in the modern style, and he wore earrings and wire-rimmed glasses. I guessed his age at around forty to forty-five. He was dressed casually as it was the weekend, beige chinos and a dark open-collared floral shirt with no tie. He was also wearing sandals with no socks. If I'd not known better I'd have assumed he taught drama or art. The woman behind the reception desk nodded towards me. He looked at me with seeming curiosity, as though I were an abstract work of art he couldn't begin to understand.

"You wanted to see me?" He sounded very upper-middle-class, his enunciation definitely the product of an expensive education.

"DS McGraw, Special Branch," I identified myself. "Where can we talk?"

———◄○►———

"Why do you need to talk to me?" His eyes narrowed.

I didn't reply. No one spoke for four seconds.

"Not here." He sounded nervous. "Let's go for a walk. Do you like St James's Park?"

We left the building and turned right. We walked in silence to the park. I noticed his eyes were firmly fixed ahead and at no time did he even look in my direction. He had an intense expression, like he was focusing on only one thing and was walking with a purpose in mind.

At the tea stall where I occasionally came to buy lunch I bought teas for both of us and a cake for him. We found a park bench.

I was taking in the surroundings. I loved this park. The Whitehall buildings in view were almost magisterial in design and it was always something to hear Big Ben chiming. Small wonder tourists from everywhere flocked here to photograph history. The park itself was beautiful and when the sun was shining and there was very little breeze on a Saturday, like today, there were plenty of people around: dog walkers, joggers, tourists, families on a day out in town, plus a group of schoolkids sitting excitedly on the grass whilst two teachers looked at a map and pointed towards Buckingham Palace.

Tilling was just staring at his cake. I was wishing I'd bought something to eat, as seeing him look at the cake was making me hungry. We sat quietly for several seconds.

"Actually, I can guess why you want to see me, can't I?" he finally said. He looked determined as he spoke.

"Can you?"

"I think so. You want to talk about Paul, don't you?" He turned to face me. His face had hardened and he had a firm steely glint in his eyes.

"Yeah," I agreed.

"I suppose you're like that other cop, the one extorting money from Paul. Now he's dead, you're going to blackmail *me*, aren't you? That other cop said this wasn't finished, so I've been waiting for someone to approach me and tell me how much their silence is going to cost. Well, I've got news for you, sunbeam: I'm not paying you a fucking penny and I'll take whatever consequences come, so you can just fuck off, alright?" He looked and sounded defiant. "You're getting nothing from me."

I'd not heard an expletive pronounced so well for a long while. I hadn't been called *sunbeam* often, either. "Good for you, Geoffrey, but that's not why I wanna talk to you."

His eyes opened wide in surprise. For a couple of seconds I think he stopped breathing.

"I already get paid. I just wanna hear your side: what you know about Paul Sampson being blackmailed, why he stood down from Parliament, things like that. I'm not here to blackmail you." I hoped I sounded reassuring. "Though I might make you pay for the tea and cake if I don't like your answers." I smiled, trying to lighten the mood.

His defiant expression changed. He exhaled and looked relieved. He sat back against the bench, produced a handkerchief and wiped his eyes. Was he crying? He blew his nose.

"Sorry," he eventually said, his voice choking with emotion. "I've been expecting someone in authority to get in touch with a blackmail demand ever since Paul died, because that other policeman said it was gonna happen."

He did some yoga-style deep breathing exercises for a few moments.

"It's alright, I'm okay now. What did you want to ask me?"

For the next fifteen minutes, he told me about his relationship with Paul Sampson. They'd met six years ago when Sampson, an MP since 2001, was introduced to him at a meeting they were both present at. Tilling was a Grade 8 rank, so he was there as a junior ministerial advisor. They'd become friends and gradually Sampson had become more comfortable in his presence. How they had discovered each other's sexuality wasn't mentioned, and I didn't ask, but they'd become lovers soon afterwards and had been together, albeit covertly, until Sampson's relatively recent death.

They'd kept their relationship clandestine because Sampson came from a very devoutly religious family who saw homosexuality as a sin against God; they would not have understood his desire to be with a man, rather than the woman he'd married, and would have cut him off. His wife, Martha, was the daughter of a leading industrialist: the production director at Bartolome Systems, manufacturers of weapons guidance systems which were sold to the UK Government as well as governments abroad. Her father would have taken Sampson for everything if he'd left Martha for another man, and he would have ensured Sampson would never have seen his own daughter again.

"Paul had too much to lose if he came out," Tilling said, sorrowfully. "He wanted to, his secret life was killing him, he was under so much pressure, but it would have cost him everything if he had. That cop Thornwyn, he'd found out about Paul's background, and he used it to extort money from him. He'd asked Paul how much it was worth not to tell his family. I told Paul, I'm not worth this sacrifice, I'm really not, but he wouldn't hear it. He paid up so we could be together," – he sounded choked and was swallowing hard – "and the pressure finally became too much for him."

"Who else knew about you and Paul?"

"Just a few trusted members of our community; that's it, really. You can understand why we didn't exactly shout it from the rooftops," he commented ironically. "Despite all the legislation and what the courts say, sadly we still live in a world of small minds, people like Paul's family. Laws will never change their righteous brand of bigotry. You ever read *The Crucible*? His family regards homosexuality in the same way the puritans regarded witchcraft. *Inclusion* was a term they refused to acknowledge. Be straight or be cast out." He almost smiled as he spoke, staring into the far distance, as though addressing a much larger audience than just me.

"What was going on in Paul's life at the time he resigned?" I asked. "Did he really just resign from politics because of being blackmailed? Surely he'd not have to endure that much if he came out. Some publicity in the press and then it'd all be over. I think there's more to this than you're telling me, much more. If there is, you should tell me. That's why I've come to see you. His suicide's being investigated."

I was hoping Tilling wasn't offended by my challenging his account of the situation. I could understand Sampson's desire to avoid losing his family and that he'd hoped to maintain his position in the machinery of Government. But I was finding it difficult to believe, in today's inclusive Conservative Party, that being faced with coming out in public to extricate yourself from being blackmailed would be a reason to commit suicide.

Tilling sat silently for some time, still staring into the far distance. After a while he took out a tissue and dabbed his eyes. Then he started crying quietly. He wiped tears from his cheek.

"Sorry about this." He sniffed. "It still hurts."

"I imagine it does. Take whatever time you need."

He sobbed quietly for about a minute, occasionally dabbing his eyes with the tissue. People were walking past and a few cast furtive glances. I wondered what they thought about what they saw: two men sitting together on a park bench, one crying. Would they think we were a couple in the process of breaking up?

"He loved working over there." He nodded towards Whitehall. "He loved being at the centre of the political machine, being involved with the big decisions of state. He liked being sounded out by journalists and enjoyed being interviewed on politics programmes and, when he stood down, the hole in his life was immense and obviously nothing filled it."

He sipped his tea but didn't touch the cake.

"Paul was the love of my life," he said sorrowfully, more to someone else than to me, in a low voice suggesting he was choking up. "I'd never met anyone like him before and I wanted to spend the rest of my life with him. That bastard Thornwyn." He started crying again, this time more forcefully.

I'd never sat next to a man crying about lost homosexual love before and was unsure what to do. I sat and waited. I wondered briefly whether he'd yet to fully grieve for his lost partner. He stopped crying.

"I don't think he committed suicide," he eventually said. "I think he was murdered but, of course, I can't prove it."

"Huh? Why do you think that?" I was startled by his comment.

"I know Paul. He'd never contemplate suicide. He enjoyed his life too much to even think about taking his own life." He still sounded choked up. He was uncorking the lid on emotions he'd kept buried. "Oh, it's too complicated to go into. I don't wanna talk about it anymore. I don't wanna be the next one."

He blew his nose, then quickly got up and began walking back towards Birdcage Walk. I left the seat to catch him up but, as I did, I spotted the same woman who'd been following me in Whitehall the previous evening. She was standing by the junction of Birdcage Walk and Horse Guards Road, pretending to be glancing at a newspaper. Had she been following me since I'd left Marsham Street? Had she been there all the time and I'd not noticed her? Tilling could wait. I wanted to know who this woman was. Her presence was now an irritation.

I watched Tilling cross over Birdcage Walk and then I started walking away in the opposite direction. I walked north in the direction of The Mall, certain she'd follow me. She did. By the north side of the park I abruptly doubled back on myself. The same woman was walking about 150 yards behind me. When she saw me coming towards her, she quickly turned right and walked fast towards Horse Guards

Road, looking over her shoulder to see how near I was. This proved beyond doubt I was being followed.

I increased my pace to narrow the distance between us, but then, at the kerb, she suddenly sprinted diagonally across the road, narrowly dodging an oncoming taxi which screeched to a halt, and she turned left. I did the same and chased her along The Mall. She was fast and she'd opened a bigger gap between us. I saw her running under Admiralty Arch and towards Trafalgar Square. I crossed the road, passed under Admiralty Arch and into the square. I looked around but couldn't see the woman I was looking for because there was a sizeable crowd gathering for a march. This was the one Clements had alluded to last night. The numbers present made it impossible to pick out any one person. After a couple of minutes looking I gave up. I'd lost her.

Who was this woman and why was she following me?

I also realised I'd left the cake on the park seat. Sod it.

Back in the office I requested and played the CCTV footage of the area for that time. I spotted her running towards Admiralty Arch with me running across the road. It was almost bizarre watching myself pursuing someone, knowing she was somewhere in front of me but not being able to see her, though I was impressed with how fluidly I was running. I zeroed in on her to ensure she was kept in the picture. She was wearing a loose sweater and tight jeans and I noticed she had great legs, though this wasn't the time to admire them.

At the Arch, however, she'd turned left and, instead of going into the square to lose me amongst the crowd, as I'd assumed she would, she'd turned into Cockspur Street and then left along Pall Mall. I saw myself looking around, wondering where she'd gone, whilst she walked away in the opposite direction. I didn't see Richard Clements in the crowd.

Through switching cameras and adjusting angles, I

———◄◦►———

tracked her going west from Pall Mall, through St James's Square, across Piccadilly and into Mayfair, looking furtively over her shoulder occasionally to ensure I wasn't still following. Tracking her had involved a little luck as two cameras weren't recording, so I'd guessed which direction she might be going in. She finally stopped outside a building in a street just south of Grosvenor Square and entered. It was a place I knew well. It was the headquarters of Prevental.

Prevental was ostensibly a security firm, providing night watchmen and security guards for office and factory premises, plus advice on how to protect and secure your property. At least, that was what their somewhat anodyne website and corporate literature said. But for those of us who knew the truth, the firm offered *so* much more. It was actually a brokerage house for mercenary soldiers and others offering their services in theatres of war anywhere on Earth. You were looking for trained ex-soldiers who still wanted to fight? Contact Prevental and chances were they'd have access to people matching your requirements. It also hired out ex-Special Forces personnel to act as bodyguards to leading industrialists and anyone who felt they were in danger of attack whilst in the UK. It had, to my certain knowledge, at least one professional American assassin on its books. It survived, I was certain, because of its close ties with MI5, who occasionally outsourced work to the firm. This was no coincidence; the two men who'd founded Prevental were both former long-time senior MI5 officers.

I knew someone who worked there. He was ex-police and had been my training officer when I'd left Hendon and been based at West End Central. He had left to go into the private sector, initially training and working as an inquiry agent, but was now a Prevental operative. We'd fallen out over a case a little while back and I'd assaulted him, though not seriously, but he'd forgiven me when I had next met up with him. Time to visit him again.

I expanded the CCTV display further, froze the image and

took a good facsimile of the woman who'd been following me. She was a good-looking woman and I briefly speculated, with legs like hers, whether she was following me because she wanted to ask me out on a date, but I suspected this was unlikely. I printed off a copy, then entered the picture into the Branch database, the *family album* as we flippantly referred to it, and requested details but was informed there was nothing on file about her, which was very suspicious. Smitherman was in his office but I decided to go to Prevental first.

Prevental occupied the top two floors over a very chic and pricey boutique in Mayfair. I wondered what the rental would be for such a location as this. I glanced through the boutique window at what appeared to be just a piece of coloured oriental silk dangling from a mannequin's shoulder, saw a £4,000 price tag and winced.

Outside Prevental's entrance I looked up into the camera monitoring the double doors. I blew a kiss at it as I was buzzed into the building.

I went up the stairs and into their foyer, which was decorated with tasteful and very expensive furniture. There was soft lighting giving a warm glow and pictures of various dignitaries such as the Queen and Barack Obama on the walls. There was also a deep blue carpet bearing the emblem of Prevental, a shield with various firearms protruding from it, facing the entrance to the foyer, and a table by the armchairs with a pile of glossy magazines. I could see a magazine entitled *Guns and Freedom* and I briefly wondered who published such a title, though I was sure it was an American publication.

The foyer radiated calm and efficiency. There was a secretary sitting behind a mahogany desk who was typing fast but also looking over her glasses at me as I approached her desk. I didn't doubt she'd have a gun close to hand.

I'd phoned ahead so I was expected. Nobody just drops into Prevental unannounced for a quick chat.

———◆———

"DS McGraw." She told me rather than asked me. She handed me a visitor's lanyard and told me the person I wanted to see was in a meeting which would finish soon, so I was directed to a seat against the far wall, underneath a large reproduction of Constable's *Dedham from Langham*.

I was reading the weekend's football news in the *Times*, having decided a magazine called *Guns and Freedom* sounded a little too intense for me, when my name was called. The secretary led me along a corridor and into an office.

Gavin Dennison was sitting behind his desk. He was casually dressed, T-shirt and jeans, and smiling as I entered. He looked like he'd been hitting the iron recently as his pectoral muscles were pushing against his tight shirt. He stood up as the secretary left the room.

"Rob, how's it going, mate?" he asked amiably as he came around from behind his desk and patted my shoulder.

"Yeah, okay. You?"

We engaged in court gossip for a few moments about someone we both knew who'd been appointed to the rank of Superintendent and about how undeserved this was, remarking that *Private Eye*'s 'Order of the Brown Nose' would be a more appropriate reward for his obsequiousness.

"So, what's up, mate? Why're you disturbing me on a Saturday?" He grinned and sat on the corner of his desk rather than behind it. "It's the only day I get anything done."

I took a picture from my pocket. "You can tell me who this woman is," I said pleasantly as I handed it to him.

He looked at it for a few seconds. From his expression I could see he recognised her.

"Why d'you need to know that?" he said in a neutral tone.

"She was following me last night in Whitehall and, this morning, she was watching me in St James's Park when I was talking to someone about a case. She ran off when I approached her and I've tracked her to here. That suggests to me you know who this *femme fatale* is. I wanna know why she's on my tail."

---◆---

Dennison looked at me for a moment, nodding slightly. There was an awkward silence.

"I know who she is." He handed the picture back to me. "Her name's Gillian Redmond, and she works for the same inquiry agency I worked for after leaving the police. She does the occasional job for us if we have something she can be useful for."

"So following me's now a Prevental job?"

"Is that what she was doing?"

"Yeah, and not particularly well either. I clocked her instantly last night and again earlier today," I gloated. "I think this chick couldn't trail a bull through a china shop."

He looked at me for a few moments, then spoke. "We were contacted recently by quite a large, important firm who wanted someone to do some legwork for them, look into a few things. They've got their own security people but they wanted someone from outside, and it was the kind of thing Gill's good at. We offered it to her, she took it. I don't know what exactly they wanted her for, but I honestly didn't know it meant following a police officer."

"Which firm? I'll ask them."

"That's confidential, mate, can't tell you that."

"Why's it confidential? Why would this firm want a Special Branch officer followed? What have I done to get onto their radar? Are they planning on offering me a job? They could just come straight out and ask me."

"As I said, it's confidential. Look, Rob, I'll be honest. I'm not certain I know why they wanted someone to do whatever Gill's doing, but even if I was, you know I couldn't tell you. A client's business is always a matter of trust between us and them. You know that. If I asked why you're asking about Gill, would you tell me?"

"Yeah, I'll tell you. I went to meet a friend for a drink last night and this woman" – I nodded at the picture – "followed me there. I clock her, she leaves. This morning, I go to talk to someone in connection with an investigation about something the Branch has an interest in and she's on my tail again. I approach her, she runs. I wanna know why she's following me. If she's trying to interfere with a police investigation, that's obstruction. I don't have to tell *you* that, do I?" The question was rhetorical.

There was silence for a few moments. I was waiting for Gavin to reply. He then stood up.

"I'm sorry, Rob, I really can't help you with this. All I know is she's doing work for a firm who asked us for someone good to do something for them. As long as it's not unlawful, we don't keep tabs on what people working for us do."

"You mean so it's legally deniable if they get caught."

"Ever the cynic, eh, Rob?" He grinned. "You really should think about coming to work here. There's always room for a good freelancer. You know how much freelancers can earn? You know how much some of our clients'll pay for our services?"

"I'll keep it in mind." I stood up. "Tell her, if she's gonna follow me, she'd better up her game because I'm looking out for her. I've sussed her twice, next time I'll grab her. If I don't like her answers I'm gonna take her in. Tell her, also, with legs like hers, if it's a date she wants, not to be so coy, just ask me," I said, somewhat cheekily.

Dennison looked as though he was about to speak, then sat down behind his desk. "I'm sorry, Rob, I can't help you. I've helped you out before but I can't do so now because I don't know why Gill's doing what she is." He shrugged. I didn't believe him but didn't call him out about it. "Keep in touch, mate. Let's have a beer soon."

"Yeah, alright. Take care, Gavin."

I left, somewhat frustrated at not learning anything other than the identity of the person who'd been following me. I was also certain Gavin hadn't been completely honest with me.

*

There'd been nothing on our database about Gillian Redmond, which was somewhat surprising, but I'd found details about her by calling in a favour from one of the Branch's IT specialists. The specialist had logged onto whatever site it was giving her access to a wide range of persons held on file by the security services, and sent over what details she could find, including a picture, which wasn't as grainy as the one from CCTV.

Redmond was thirty-one and had obtained a history degree from Oxford before being recruited into MI6. *MI6?* She'd been a spook for nearly six years but left to join the inquiry agency DeeCee Inc. All inquiry agents have to be licensed, so I checked with their central registry to ascertain what this agency did and was told she'd done the requisite training and was qualified to operate as a licensed private inquiry agent. I wondered how much training she'd had as I'd clocked her twice already but, walking back from Prevental, I'd not spotted her.

DeeCee Inc. had its offices on the top floor of a building in Chancery Lane, just east from Lincoln's Inn. The business advertised itself as specialising in all manner of inquiries ranging from industrial to international to personal and it guaranteed total discretion in every investigation undertaken. I was amused at the idea of a firm like this employing ex-MI6 operatives and involved in a messy divorce case. With Redmond's background, it was easy to see why Prevental would offer her work occasionally. She'd have the training and the skills they'd want. Her intelligence background would explain why we had no details about her.

I was thinking about this and wondering which firm it was that had hired her, and why did this involve following me? What was I doing, or had I been doing, likely to merit someone being put on my tail?

Early evening; I'd decided to see if I could catch Geoffrey Tilling at home. Tilling's flat was on a side road just off

Borough High Street. I parked nearby and saw a light on in the front window, so I rang the bell and, when asked, identified myself over the intercom. A buzzing sound and the latch on the outer door clicked, the door opened and I entered.

He lived on the top floor of a four-storey building and I took the stairs two at a time. He was at the door of the flat and nodded as I entered. He was dressed as he'd been earlier.

The flat was well lit, spatially well appointed and mini-malist in content. A few large Habitat pine scatter cushions were placed strategically on the floor around a coffee table; there were only a few other small items of furniture in what I assumed was the main lounge and there was the pungent smell of jasmine joss sticks burning. There were three shelves filled with books and plenty of arty-type pictures and posters of abstract images on the wall, none of which meant much to me, as my glazed expression probably suggested to him.

He offered me a glass of wine but I refused. I don't drink wine. He sat down on a cushion. I remained standing.

"Why do you wanna see me again? Why are you here?" he began.

I resisted the temptation to say *everyone has to be somewhere.*

"We didn't finish our chat earlier. You went off and I saw someone in the park I had an interest in." I didn't explain further.

He slumped down against his cushion, looking morose and with an expression suggesting his mood hadn't improved since he'd left me in St James's Park earlier.

"I'm sorry I broke down in front of you in the park," he began. "I'd been waiting for someone to get back to me and tell me how much he was going to take from me to keep quiet. It took me by surprise when you said you weren't there for that."

He drained the rest of his wine in one gulp. It wasn't his

first glass either as there was an empty bottle on the coffee table. He poured himself another from an open bottle.

"What I don't understand is" – he paused for a moment – "how did that cop Thornwyn even *know* about Paul and me? We'd been so discreet, so careful. Paul said his sexuality didn't even come up when he was vetted before he became a minister." He shook his head. "I just don't get how he would know about us."

"You really wanna know?"

"Indeed I do." He looked interested.

"The guy you get your ecstasy from? He's one of Thornwyn's informants. That's how Thornwyn found out. He told Thornwyn about you two to save his own neck after he'd been arrested. He offered you and Paul up on a plate."

"Oh, the bastard." His voice rose an octave at what he'd heard. "We were good customers. How could he do that to us?" He sounded indignant.

How naïve *was* Geoffrey Tilling? Did he really think drugs like ecstasy were distributed and sold by Benedictine monks?

"Scum like that'd sell their own mothers into slavery for drugs," I said. "This guy's name, it's Bernie, isn't it?"

"Yes, but I don't know if that's his real name."

This was the name Thornwyn had told me when I'd spoken to him in Belmarsh yesterday.

"Where do you go to buy ecstasy from him?"

"Usually met him someplace. I've a number for him. I'd call when Paul and I wanted to get high. We'd meet someplace, usually the pub he drank in, I'd buy off him." He shrugged.

"Give me the number."

Tilling recited the number to me, and I noted it.

"Earlier today, you said you thought Paul Sampson was murdered," I said. "Is that just a guess on your part or do you know this for a fact?"

"Who knows?" He sighed resignedly. "I know how it's all supposed to have occurred. Paul was supposed to have drunk a whole bottle of some kind of cognac, but he *never* drank spirits, he only ever drank wine. He couldn't handle anything as strong as cognac." He looked bemused, shaking his head. "He took the occasional sleeping pill but nothing like as strong as the ones he was supposed to have taken. It just doesn't make sense."

I didn't say anything.

"Living a double life, having to hide in the shadows all the time, it really got him down. That's partly why he liked ecstasy. It took him out of himself, took him to another place, it helped energise him. He was always happy whenever we did ecstasy." He smiled as he reminisced about Paul Sampson. "It lifted his spirits and he enjoyed life a lot more. You ever had sex using ecstasy?"

I had to admit I hadn't.

"It's wonderful, especially if it's with someone you love. There's nothing quite like it on this earth."

Tilling was looking around as he spoke. He was smiling, probably thinking of happier times under the influence of a mind-altering stimulant with his lover.

"But all the thrill went when that swine Thornwyn began squeezing Paul for money. The feeling he could blow the whistle at any time played on Paul's mind constantly and he couldn't focus on anything. He began to lose interest in everything. Things between us were not good at that time, but I stood by Paul. He was worth it."

His voice choked up. I wondered if he'd been bottling up his feelings and hadn't opened up to anyone yet. He clearly had unresolved issues to deal with.

Time to ask a direct question.

"What I don't get is, why didn't Paul either go to the authorities, tell them about the blackmail, get Thornwyn off his back, or just come out and admit his sexuality in public? Surely this would have defused the whole situation. He'd not have had to resign, he'd still be alive. You guys'd still be together."

Tilling pursed his lips and nodded a few times. He smiled enigmatically.

"Easy for you to say, a white hetero male." His voice hardened as he looked at me. I got the impression he didn't like what he was seeing. "Relationships are simple for people like you. Never having to bottle up your emotions and your love for someone. Everything's out in the open for you. Paul's life would have been ruined had he done that. I told you earlier, he'd have lost his family, his career, everything he'd worked hard to achieve, and he didn't want to lose it. I told him I'd walk away if that's what it'd take to put his life back in balance, but he broke down when I said that, begged me not to leave him as I gave him the only real happiness in his life, apart from his daughter, little Jade. The thought of losing access to her was too much for him."

He began crying again. I wasn't sure what to do, so I remained standing. He sobbed for a few minutes, then drained his wine glass. He refilled it again. I wasn't sure alcohol was the answer to his grief, but then neither was milk.

"If he'd thought he could've counted on his wife's support, that would've at least been a help, and he'd have seriously considered it. But Martha's as homophobic as they come, probably as much as Thornwyn. I met her once at a BBQ at their house, the only time I ever went there. God, she's a ghastly woman, a social-climbing status-seeking upper-middle-class bitch of the worst kind." His words were drenched in acid. "I'll tell you the kind of woman she is. She used to tell people one of her uncles was a colonel in the army. You wanna know where? The bloody Sally army, that's where." He laughed at the memory for a moment.

"Do you know the play *Abigail's Party*?" he continued.

I said I'd heard of it but hadn't seen it. This, along with not drinking wine plus the bewildered way I'd looked at the artwork on his walls, probably marked me down as an uncultured pleb in his eyes.

"The lead character, the repulsive Beverly Moss, is her role model." He stated this with quiet satisfaction. "If he'd come out, she'd have ruined him in every way possible. I couldn't even go to his funeral, you know that?" He sounded sorrowful.

"Did she *know* he was gay?"

"I don't think so." He paused and looked upwards. I followed his eyes and noticed someone had painted a religious image of a deity on the ceiling. "No, Paul would have told me if she knew about him! I suppose if there are any positives about his death, at least he's free from her claws. God forgive me for saying that." He crossed himself.

"What about his work in Government? What do you know about that?"

"Not much, really. He didn't talk much about it. It was just something he did. I'm not much interested in politics, so we didn't talk about it."

"What, never?" I was surprised.

"Occasionally, we'd talk about some meeting he'd gone to and who was there, or perhaps about something he'd got to do next day, but, no, we didn't really talk that much about it."

"You're a Grade 8 civil servant. You'd come into contact with junior ministers and the like a lot of the time, yet you're saying you and Paul never discussed politics or his work?"

"No." He shook his head carefully. "Very seldom. We attended the same meetings occasionally but not that often. We had other things to talk about. We had a life we wanted to build. That was much more important."

"Standing down as an MP and resigning was quite a dramatic step. Had he given you any indication he was thinking about this?"

"Not to me, no. I was as surprised as anyone when he told me." He shuffled about on his cushion for a moment. "He withdrew into himself. Wouldn't talk about anything. I didn't even see him the last few weeks of his life because he was at home all the time. The last time I spoke to him, he said he had things he needed to think about and he'd be in touch soon. I thought about visiting but his unspeakable wife probably wouldn't have let me into the house. Then, when I heard about what he'd done ..."

His voice tailed off. I knew what he meant, though not how he must be feeling; that I had no idea about. I'd never had and lost any clandestine relationship.

"And I've just been waiting for someone to come along and tell me I was to be tapped for money," he said resignedly, "which is why I was so hostile towards you this morning. I thought it was you, you see." His voice was now beginning to sound slurred and he mispronounced a couple of words as he spoke, with *hostile* sounding like *hoshstile*.

From his loud sighing and shaking his head, I could see he was shutting down. He put his glass on the coffee table and closed his eyes. He wasn't focused. I wouldn't get any more from him in this state. I told him I'd probably be in touch again and left him to his Saturday night misery. I wondered if he'd even heard me leave.

Paul Sampson had ostensibly committed suicide because the pressure of keeping his sexuality secret and the blackmailing from Thornwyn had become too much for him; he'd taken his own life whilst the balance of his mind was disturbed. I was convinced this was the situation and I was also convinced Thornwyn was directly responsible.

There was something else, however. I was finding it difficult to grasp why keeping his homosexuality secret could have led to suicide. Even professional rugby players, in that most macho of sports, had come out, declared their homosexuality and continued to play the game exactly like before. In the USA, baseball players and American foot-ballers had come out to hardly any adverse reaction.

No, there had to be something else and I was convinced Thornwyn was either directly implicated or else a main player behind the scenes. I was no psychologist but I was finding it hard to accept a life and career as promising as Paul Sampson's could be thrown away because of blackmail, given the times we now lived in.

I thought about whom I'd known when I'd served in Thornwyn's team and who I thought could be trusted. I'd heard a couple were under suspicion of having helped him in his endeavours.

Driving back home I went through the team in my mind and decided my safest bet was probably Larry Jasper, who'd been a DS in the team when I'd joined. He was reliable and honest and I couldn't imagine him with his hands in anyone's pocket.

At home I obtained details for him from Special Branch files. He was now a DI in Surrey, based in Egham. I called his mobile phone.

"Rob, fucking hell, mate, how are you?" he exclaimed after I told him who was calling. He sounded surprised to hear me. We chatted briefly for a moment about what we were doing and where we were based.

"What about ol' Thornwyn, eh?" he began. "Christ, he'll go down for the big one, no question. Did *you* know about all this?"

"No, I didn't. You?"

"Same, though I had some strong suspicions."

Interesting he'd had suspicions things were not right in the team. Had I really been that naïve when operating in Thornwyn's team? Had things been happening under my nose and I'd not spotted them?

"I wanna ask you something," I said. "I'm looking into something where Thornwyn's name has come up. I can't go into details but it's likely he didn't do all this on his own. I've been told there's two others in the squad we were in who helped Thornwyn and I might need to talk to them. You have any idea who they might be?" I assured him of my total discretion regarding what he could tell me.

———◄○►———

73

"I'm not gonna speculate on that one, Rob. I'll just tell you one thing. Paine and Turley, remember them? I've heard on the grapevine they've both been suspended from duty. Did you know that?"

"No. No, I didn't."

John Paine and Brian Turley were the two officers in the team who worked the closest with Thornwyn and had served the longest with him. Now I thought about it, I should have realised who they were when Smitherman told me two others were being investigated alongside Thornwyn. In fact, it'd been Turley who'd informed the rookie DC McGraw about Thornwyn not using his own money to settle a restaurant bill and how it'd all soon be made clear to me. I should have seen this one coming; further evidence of my naivety.

"So, what about you? Any of this crap flying about hit you yet?" he asked.

"Not so far. I'm good at ducking," I said with a laugh. I didn't mention I'd been given a clean bill of health by the IPCC. "You?"

"I transferred out to Surrey when I got promoted, just before you did. I knew there was something going on and I wanted out before the shit really hit the fan."

"Such as what?"

"This is in confidence, right? I got your word?"

I agreed he had it.

"Turley once offered me a share of what they'd taken from some dealer somewhere. There was a major bust and, as well as drugs, they found a lot of money, fucking thousands it was. They turned the drugs in but the money was never reported. I can only assume they split it up. I didn't take their money and, soon after that, I put in for a transfer. They were getting brazen about how much they were raking in. I didn't want anything to do with it. I've heard from my boss IPCC wanna talk to me about it, so I'm keeping my head down for the moment till all this passes over. Anyway, what's up? Why are you asking these questions?"

"I'm calling 'cause I wanna know if you know someone named Bernie. He was one of Thornwyn's informers."

"Bernie the Buck? Yeah, I know the scrote. Horrible little bastard. We pulled him in once when we raided some shop looking for illegal firearms but Thornwyn let him go, said he was an informant and it'd been his tip we'd acted on. Why d'you need to know about him?"

"His name's come up in something the Branch is investigating, and Thornwyn's in Belmarsh, so I can't exactly ask him, can I?" I tried to sound light-hearted.

"Thornwyn used to meet him in a pub up by Chalk Farm," Jasper said. "Local boys know him and what he does but he gets left alone. He lives round that way. I don't know where, though."

"Which pub?"

He told me. I knew the pub and where it was. I also had an informer in the area I decided I was going to put to good use.

THREE

Sunday

IT WAS JUST AFTER NINE and I was driving through sunny
Hertfordshire. It had been an easy ride as there'd been next
to no traffic leaving London and I was making good time. I
wanted to know more about Paul Sampson, so I was going to
Berkhamsted to talk to Sampson's wife. I was hoping to hear
from her what she knew about Sampson's last months alive
and what her thoughts were concerning his taking his own
life. I was also curious to see if she really was the middle-class
harridan Geoffrey Tilling had made her out to be.

The Sampson residence, just off the A41, south of the
town, was a testament to serious money: a large, detached
five-bedroomed property with a substantial garden front
and back. There was a large garage to the side of the house,
capable of accommodating two vehicles side by side quite
comfortably, and one of the cars in the garage was a top-of-
the-range Land Rover. There was an ornamental pond in the
front garden with a statue of someone or something I didn't
recognise in the centre. I parked on the road, walked down
the garden path to the front door and rang the bell.

The door opened and I was greeted by Martha Sampson. I
introduced myself, showed ID to her and she admitted me
into her home. She took me into the lounge to which was
attached a conservatory which, at first glance, was probably
bigger than my flat and, with the large patio doors opened,
was bathed in bright sunshine. The room smelled of
gardenia and was very tastefully furnished.

She invited me to sit. I did. She sat opposite, knees
bunched tightly together and looking very prim and proper.
I guessed she was around forty. Wearing jodhpurs and a
beige waistcoat over a white shirt, she was dressed as though

she was about to go horse riding and she looked like she'd be part of the local twinset and pearls country clique, assuming Hertfordshire had one. She had shoulder-length brown hair, tucked behind her ears, and, even though she was smiling, I formed the impression she was really thinking, *What the bloody hell do you want?* She began by asking me that very question, though worded more politely.

"Special Branch's investigating something where your late husband's name arose. I can't explain exactly what, you understand, but it concerns his work at the Home Office. Did he ever talk to you about his work when he was still a parliamentary under-secretary?"

"No. He couldn't, you see. Bound by the ministerial oath as well as the Official Secrets Act. I'm afraid I've no idea what he did in office." She spoke in well-modulated tones which made me think of Cheltenham Ladies' College.

"What about after he stood down? Did he talk about it then?"

"No." She shook her head. "He never shared that part of his life with me. He didn't talk much at all, actually, particularly in the last few years. Afterwards, when he'd resigned, he just sat in his study and moped."

"Were you surprised when he stood down as an MP? Had he talked to you before he made his announcement about it?"

She paused for a moment. "It came as a complete shock when he told me what he'd done. He left his London flat in the morning a minister of the Crown, went to his office and wrote a letter to the PM resigning his office and, just after that, stood down as an MP, and not long after ..." She shrugged her shoulders and looked straight at me and didn't finish the sentence. I knew what she meant. "I couldn't understand his decision to throw it all away. I still can't. It came as quite a shock, I can tell you."

"Apologies if this sounds insensitive, but do you have any idea at all *why* he stood down and soon afterwards took his own life? I've heard he was an effective minister and highly rated in his party."

"None whatever," she replied instantly. "He *was* an effective minister and, so far as I knew, he loved his life as a politician, and all the perks that went with it. He loved being interviewed on TV and talking to journalists. It was a big deal for him when he got to go on Radio 4's *Today* programme, answering questions on behalf of the Government, because it's the flagship politics show. Anyone who's anyone listens to it. He loved travelling and representing the Government and being thought of as a Government spokesman, especially when he took questions in the House." She briefly smiled at a happy memory. "But he threw it all away and I'm afraid I don't know why."

"And it was you who found him, wasn't it?"

"Yes." She looked solemn. "I went in to say goodnight and found him in an almost comatose state. I called the ambulance to get him to hospital, but ..." She didn't finish the sentence.

"Had you ever suspected he was suicidal?"

"No, never." She was adamant.

"Had he given any indication this was what he was thinking?"

"Not to me, and from the conversations I've had with a couple of his colleagues, he'd not spoken to them either about what he was planning. They were as shocked as I was when they heard what he'd done."

"The coroner's report said something about how, when his stomach was pumped, they found he'd been drinking cognac."

"Yes, he had."

"I've been given to believe he never drank spirits, only wine. Why would he suddenly develop a taste for expensive cognac? Did he go out and buy it?"

"I don't know." She shook her head.

"I've also been told the pills he took were much stronger

---◦---

than the ones he normally took for sleeping. Where would he have got those from?"

"Again, I don't know. Why are you asking me these questions?" She stared directly at me, looking concerned. "I've already spoken to the security people."

"As I mentioned earlier, the Branch is looking into something relating to what he was doing prior to resigning his position and standing down. Anything pertaining to his state of mind is of interest to our investigations."

"Well, I'm afraid I can't help you on that." She looked out of the window at her back garden for a few moments. The well-manicured lawn was probably the size of a football pitch and there were lots of brightly coloured flowers along the edges, though I couldn't put names to any of them. I could see a border collie sitting against the garage wall, taking in the sunshine.

"Did he ever give you the impression he was disturbed about anything at all before he took his own life? You know, was he worried about anything in particular? We're led to believe he was concerned about something." I was trying to open her up.

"I do know something was bothering him," she said after a few seconds' pause. "But I don't know what. He was absorbed by something that was eating him up and it was really distracting him. I think it was related to work. You could see something was on his mind just by looking at him. At first I got upset; I thought it might have been he was having an affair, but I disabused myself of that notion. I'd *know* if he was seeing another woman. But, as I said, he just withdrew into himself, became even more non-communicative. So I'm afraid I can't help there."

"Did he ever talk about anyone called Neville Thornwyn?" Time for the big one.

"Thornwyn?" She thought for a moment. "What, the policeman in Friday's papers who's just been found guilty of all those crimes?" She sounded surprised.

"Yeah, that one."

"What would Paul have to do with him? How would Paul's Government duties bring him into contact with this Thornwyn person?"

"What's this about Neville Thornwyn?" a voice behind me asked. I turned.

A man had entered the room from the hallway. He was about six foot tall with steel-grey hair which looked like a wire brush and the type of moustache which gave him the look of being distinguished. He was probably early sixties and looking dapper in a smart shirt and tie, as though off to church.

"This man's from the police, Daddy. He's asking some questions about Paul."

I stood up. "And you are?"

"I'm Martha's father. Why are you asking about him now?"

"Paul Sampson's name's been mentioned in one of our investigations. I'm making a few general inquiries about him, and his wife seemed a good place to start."

"Ask his boyfriend, he'll have a better idea," he said light-heartedly, though I suspected not quite as jovially as he intended.

"Huh?" I played ignorance on this point. One of my better qualities.

"You're obviously not talking to the right people." He laughed.

I looked at Martha Sampson as if to say *what?*

"Daddy thinks Paul was a homosexual, which is nonsense. Don't you think I'd know if my own husband was homosexual?" she said, giving her father a look I found hard to read. "I'd have thrown him out on his ear if he was. Anyway, as I said, I can't really tell you anything about Paul's state of mind leading up to what he did because I just don't know." She shook her head. "One minute my husband's in the Government, the next he's a

recluse and kills himself. This is all so bloody unnecessary."
She sounded bitter.

I looked at her father. He was staring at me in a way that made me think he doubted what I'd said about why I was in the house.

"Is there anything *you* can tell me about Paul Sampson's state of mind before he took his own life?" I asked him.

"Not really. I'd not seen him for a little while before he did it." His body language made me think he wasn't entirely unhappy at the fact.

I sensed a tension in the room between father and daughter. I couldn't read what it was, but the atmosphere had changed. I didn't think I'd get any more from either at this time. I thanked Martha for agreeing to see me at short notice and got up to leave.

The father escorted me to the front door and then followed me outside. "Well, good luck and all that with your inquiries. Oh, yeah, what was that about Thornwyn? You were asking if Paul knew him."

"I was. His name came up in a related matter and I was just wondering if Paul had ever had any contact with him."

"I see. Well, anyway, goodbye, DS McGraw. Drive carefully."

Driving away, it dawned on me he'd not been in the room when I'd introduced myself to Martha Sampson. How did he know who I was?

Heading south-east towards London on the A41 I noticed a car behind me, about three vehicles back. It was a dark-coloured Volvo and was cruising along, maintaining the same speed as my car. I could see there was a woman driving but at this distance I couldn't make out who it was or the registration number. There was more traffic on the road now, but it was moving freely, so I sped up slightly and the vehicle behind followed suit. I pulled out to the outside lane and overtook two cars and an HGV, then moved back to the inside lane; the vehicle behind did likewise. I was doing sixty-five so I slowed down to fifty and the Volvo also reduced its speed correspondingly. I sped up, it did the same. This confirmed my suspicion; I was being followed again.

Was this Gillian Redmond? If it was, she was really inept at following, because this was the third time I'd sussed her. Either that or she didn't care I knew she was behind me. What was her connection to this case? Had she followed me to Berkhamsted and been waiting to pick up my tail again when I left? How would she even have known I was going there? I resisted the urge to pull over and see if she did the same.

I continued my drive along the A41 into central London and, by Swiss Cottage, I noticed the Volvo was no longer behind me. I'd been glancing in the rear-view mirror but hadn't noticed at what point I'd lost my tail. Had she realised I was just going back to the Yard and decided not to follow or, inadvertently, had I lost her?

Whatever the case, Gillian Redmond and I were going to meet face-to-face and very soon, whether she liked it or not. I was starting to resent seeing this bitch behind me every time I turned around. Before that, though, I had some fact-finding to do.

Martha Sampson's father had alluded to Paul being gay but she'd denied it. Had Paul managed to keep the fact of his sexuality from the woman he was married to and had conceived a child with? It wasn't an impossible feat but it would require the consummate thespian skills of a Gielgud or Olivier, as well as the psychological ability to compart-mentalise life into separate and unconnected boxes, in order to maintain the charade successfully for any sustained period of time. On top of that, he had been a government minister, with all the attendant pressures and public prurience, not to mention the relentless media scrutiny. But evidently he'd not fooled his father-in-law. How did *he* know this?

The pressure Paul Sampson must have been under at times was quite something to consider. Successful spies like Kim Philby must have been living the same kind of life, with all the same stresses attached. The thrill of pulling the wool over people's eyes was counterbalanced by the terror of being uncovered and possibly losing everything. The moments of bliss Sampson managed to snatch with Geoffrey Tilling must have been the purest joy, especially if under the influence of ecstasy. Tilling's flat probably felt like the Garden of Eden when escaping from the pressures of his life.

I remembered Geoffrey Tilling telling me Paul had said he'd be taken for everything he had by Martha's father if he left her for Tilling. The man himself had said he knew Paul was gay, but it didn't seem he'd taken any action.

I looked in the family album to check details about Sampson's father-in-law. Jeremy Godfrey was sixty-four and the production director of Bartolome Systems Ltd, based just outside Berkhamsted; he'd been with the firm since joining it from the army. It was a company valued at several billion pounds, based on its current market capitalisation. Bartolome's core business was developing the sophisticated weapons guidance systems for missiles like torpedoes and it was well regarded in military circles, enjoying *most favoured* status with the Ministry of Defence, meaning it was the company of choice when weapons updates or technological changes were required. It provided some of the navigational systems included in nuclear submarines and other similar war crafts. It also had an interest in making small-calibre handguns under licence from various American manufacturers.

From the impressive array of contracts and supply deals Bartolome Systems Ltd had with the British military establishment, it was evident this company was at the heart of the

———◄○►———

UK's defence efforts. It was also a major supplier of weaponry to countries like Sweden and Belgium, so its influence within the NATO alliance was quite pervasive. I remembered Smitherman telling me about weapons being supplied to countries the UK officially blacklisted and wondered whether Bartolome was one of the firms involved. As production director, Jeremy Godfrey would be at its epicentre.

Details about Godfrey were mostly uninspiring: education, military service, current occupation, place of residence and so on, nothing of which was remotely contentious. He had no criminal record apart from a couple of fines for speeding, and he'd served one stint as a juror. It was noted he was the father-in-law of a Conservative MP, Paul Sampson, now deceased. The file told me little I couldn't have made an educated guess at.

I was surprised to learn Paul Sampson had been a non-executive director at Bartolome Systems Ltd right up to the time he'd died. I remembered he used to work for the firm but I'd not known of the directorship. I recalled, last Friday, Smitherman alluding to Sampson being involved in lobbying on behalf of his firm to secure contracts. If this had been done whilst he was still in office, this would certainly breach the ministerial code of conduct. Was this what he was worried about prior to his suicide?

Sunday lunchtime, I was on my way to the pub near Chalk Farm tube station, just along from the market, where Bernie the Buck did his drinking and pursued his ecstasy-selling enterprise. I'd looked up his file and seen his picture so I knew whom I was looking out for. I had his mobile number and dialled it. I was going to pretend I was Tilling and arrange a meet to score some ecstasy, but it went straight to voicemail.

Bernard Rayes was a small-time criminal with two spells inside to his name, of eight months and two years respec-

———◦———

tively. He was known to operate on the fringes of criminality, mainly handling stolen goods and arranging for their dispersal to wherever. I didn't doubt the criminal enterprise he worked for was the Chackarti family, who were the biggest and most successful criminal enterprise you've probably never heard of, with their fingers in just about everything you'd care to name. Nobody in this part of London would be selling drugs unless it was for the Chackartis, as it was common knowledge they had the market sewn up tight. Anyone selling any sizeable quantities without their fiat was unsubtly persuaded this was not a good business plan if they wanted to keep breathing.

Before going to the pub I'd contacted my informant in the area. Andy Harris was a repulsively unhygienic specimen but, for reasons I couldn't begin to fathom, I was curiously fond of him. He was about as much use to society as plywood tissues and he earned his living stealing from tourists in nearby Camden Market where, for someone so inept, he was a master pickpocket. He could have a wallet out of a bag or the purse from around the neck of a foreign student before the victim even realised it was gone, and in the busy summer tourist season his weekly illicit earnings ran into several hundreds.

I used him because he was a well-known local character, always seen around the market and in the local pubs, and because he was known to be an associate of the local tea leaves and drank with them, meaning he often heard snippets of information useful to police. I'd previously benefited from his ability to merge into the background and hear things, and I was hoping to do so now.

Harris's flat was just off Camden High Street at the top of a dilapidated three-storey building. It was as dishevelled as he was and it looked like the Monday after the Glastonbury festival, with all manner of dirty crockery, partly eaten fast-food leftovers and clothing strewn everywhere. Next time I met with him, I decided, it would be in a café somewhere.

————◄○►————

It was just past twelve twenty and I'd woken him up. He looked like he'd just been resurrected from the dead and had eyes so bleary I wasn't sure he could even see me. I refused his offer of a tea and leapt straight in, as I didn't want to be here any longer than necessary.

"Andy," I began jovially, looking around. "You've tidied up your flat. I'm sure it wasn't this tidy last time I was here. You got a cleaning lady coming in?"

"Leave it out, Mr Jack." He slumped into an armchair. *Mr Jack* was what he called me when we spoke on the phone. "What you want from me?"

I couldn't find an uncluttered surface to sit on, so I stood. Just as well. I'd probably have stuck to whatever surface I sat on. "You know a character round this way called Bernie?"

"What, Bernie the Buck?" He laughed. "Yeah, I know him. What about him?"

"What do you know about him?"

"Pushes drugs for the Chackartis, don't he? He sells in the pub up the road. Everyone round here knows that. You want some gear, go see Bernie. He's usually got something."

"You buy from him?"

He looked horrified. "God, no, Mr Jack. I don't touch drugs, you know that. Them's bad things. I don't go near them. They don't do you no good," he said, earnestly.

"You know what, Andy? That's the first sensible thing I've ever heard you say in all the time I've known you." I smiled at him. He frowned. "So, what else do you know about dear ol' Bernie?"

"Only what I hears from me mates."

"Such as?"

"I did hear someone say," he said, sitting forward almost conspiratorially, "he had something going on with some top copper."

"Like what?" I was curious.

"They said him and this copper was putting the squeeze on someone," he said casually.

———◆———

"You know who?"

"I don't. How would I know that?" He looked puzzled. "I just know what I hears from me mates in the pub."

"And your friend's certain about this?"

"Yeah, yeah, he is. He sees Bernie talking to this smart geezer, who he guessed was a copper. Bernie told him about it. Said he was helping this copper squeeze someone and was getting a few bob for his troubles."

"But he didn't say who this person was."

Harris shook his head. "No."

"Does he still go to the pub?"

Harris looked as though he was thinking. This wasn't one of his usual activities and his face resembled someone in discomfort waiting to use an occupied toilet.

"Now you mention it, I ain't seen him in the pub for the last week or so. He's usually there at least once a day, selling stuff and all that, but" – he paused and looked up at me – "I can't remember seeing him at all last week. I mean, Bernie's always around. Even the landlord there said it's unusual not to see him about." He looked almost contemplative.

"Does he drink elsewhere?"

"Wouldn't have thought so."

I took out my wallet and produced one £20 and three £10 notes. I handed them over to Harris and his eyes lit up.

"I want you to go to that pub over the next few days and have a beer but keep your eyes and ears open. Bernie shows up, or you hear anything at all about him, I wanna know. You got that?"

He beamed as he tucked away the money. "Aw, thanks, Mr Jack. I'm a bit boracic lint, so this'll help me out a lot. Ta very much."

I left the flat after warning Harris against wasting my money buying rounds of drinks for his boon friends. I'd advised him to be very careful when he spotted Bernie and not to let on he was asking about him.

*

Thornwyn had admitted to blackmailing Paul Sampson and, if Harris was to be believed, Bernie the Buck had been in on the scheme as well. Thornwyn had maintained he was extorting money from Sampson because he was refusing to come out, but I was finding this difficult to grasp. There had to be another reason for this. I was also being followed and had only noticed this after my visit to Belmarsh two days ago. Coincidence?

Thornwyn had said Smitherman hadn't told me the *big picture*. Was this connected to anything?

FOUR

Tuesday

YESTERDAY HAD BEEN SPENT at the Central Criminal Court, the Old Bailey. I'd been due to give evidence in a prosecution brought against a highly placed senior executive officer in the Ministry of Defence who'd been charged with leaking classified information about Government plans to modernise and streamline the armed forces, which would involve the disbanding of a few long-established regiments, as well as merging other regiments together.

I'd been one of the team of detectives keeping the civil servant and the journalist concerned under observation and, when the defendant had eventually met with the journalist in a central London hotel to pass on the information, they'd both been arrested. The journalist had been released without charge after the expected firestorm of protest from the media, claiming the writer concerned was simply doing his job and had not actually received the plans as they'd been arrested during the exchange.

The civil servant, though, had been charged under section two of the Official Secrets Act. His defence was initially going to be one of justification. He claimed to be a supporter of the armed forces and thought the Government's plans would lead to regiments with long and distinguished records of service to the country being unjustly disbanded. Because of the uncertainty surrounding Russia and President Putin's attitude towards the West, not to mention the continued political uncertainty in the Middle East, he'd become concerned about such major changes being simply announced as a *fait accompli* with no public discussion whatever, and so he'd considered it his patriotic duty to inform the public of what was being done in its name.

As it was, I'd sat outside court number one all day yesterday, waiting to be called to give my evidence and gradually losing patience as I watched lawyers and witnesses milling around and talking solemnly in hushed tones. Eventually, mid-afternoon, I was informed by an extremely plummy-voiced prosecuting counsel who made Martha Sampson sound like an extra from EastEnders that I wouldn't be required to testify after all as the defendant, at the last minute, had changed his plea to guilty, and speeches in mitigation were to be given by defence counsel after a short recess. It seemed the defendant had been convinced by his learned counsel that courts of law don't deal in absolute concepts like justification when the words of the Official Secrets Act are clear, irrespective of however honourable the motive might have been.

Thanking her kindly through gritted teeth I'd decided the day was wasted, so I went off duty early. I went to the gym instead and took out the frustration of sitting around all day on a punchbag and the treadmill, feeling much better when I got home.

Chancery Lane was busy as I strolled along at nine fifteen in the morning, with several members of the legal profession for company. This was right in the heart of legal London, with three of the Inns of Court close by plus a couple of famous law bookshops, including Wildy's, which specialised in second-hand legal tomes. The Royal Courts of Justice on the Strand were also close by, as well as the bankruptcy court in Carey Street.

I rang the bell for DeeCee Inc. and gave a false name when a sonorous female voice on the intercom asked who was calling. I asked for Gillian Redmond and said it was about an inquiry she was making on my behalf, but I was told she wasn't in the office yet, though she was expected later in the morning. I said I'd return then.

My inner scepticism told me not to believe she wasn't in,

so I wandered along the road, bought a coffee and stood in a nearby doorway to await developments. Fifty minutes later Gillian Redmond herself came out of the building. She crossed the road and walked along Carey Street. I followed. She turned right into Lincoln's Inn and strolled along the south side of the square towards Kingsway, walking along calmly with no reason to believe she was being followed. I stayed about a hundred yards behind. I remembered Richard Clements' magazine, *New Focus*, had its offices the other side of the square.

In Kingsway she turned right, crossed over the road and turned into High Holborn, where she entered a building. I saw the nameplate. Bartolome Systems Ltd had its London offices on the first floor. Was *this* the firm that had hired Gillian Redmond? Why would they want *me* followed?

I phoned Prevental on my mobile and asked for Gavin Dennison.

"Gavin, you know anything about a firm called Bartolome Systems Ltd?"

There was silence for a few seconds. That was my answer.

"Gavin, you didn't really think I wouldn't find out who Gillian Redmond was working for, did you?" I laughed. "I've just followed her to their London office in High Holborn. She's in there now, reporting back on her lack of progress, no doubt. Honestly, mate, tailing her's like following a weasel in a henhouse." I was in a jokey mood.

"I don't know what it's about, Rob. I don't know what she's doing for them."

"She started following me just after I'd been to see my old boss, Neville Thornwyn. What's the connection to Bartolome?"

"That's classified information, mate. Can't tell you."

"Yeah." I snorted derisorily.

"No, seriously, Rob, it is. Bartolome's an important firm in our world. You know what they do and how strategically important they are. You go near them, you'll have MI5 all over you."

"Now, why would that be?"

"Look, Rob, I can't talk about this with you, you know that."

"Yeah, okay, Gav, take care." I rang off. I was unconvinced.

Friday last, Smitherman had asked me to go talk to my ex-boss, Commander Neville Thornwyn, ostensibly about what he knew concerning the resignation of a parliamentary under-secretary. He'd admitted to blackmailing the individual concerned, Paul Sampson. Since then, I'd found I was being followed by Gillian Redmond, an ex-MI6 operative who, I'd been told by Gavin Dennison after I'd traced her movements to Prevental's front door, had been hired by a leading manufacturing company to do some work for them. I now had every reason to suspect that company was Bartolome Systems Ltd, a major supplier of essential and strategically important military hardware to the UK armed forces, plus several others across the globe. I'd also learnt Paul Sampson's father-in-law was the production director at Bartolome and Sampson himself had once been a non-executive director of the company.

I remembered Gillian Redmond following me out of Berkhamsted on Sunday. Martha Sampson's father worked for Bartolome; Redmond had been hired by the same firm. That would explain how she'd known where I'd be; Jeremy Godfrey had told her.

Why would Bartolome Systems Ltd put someone on *my* tail? This had all begun after I'd talked to Thornwyn last Friday afternoon. Was *he* connected to this in some way?

Thornwyn had also alluded to Smitherman not giving me the big picture about the situation. I was confused. But I was also outside Bartolome's London offices, so I waited until I saw Gillian Redmond leaving their premises. I was standing across the road and I resisted the urge to call out and wave at her as she left, hoping she saw me.

*

———◂◦▸———

At the reception desk on the first floor I showed ID to the young woman behind the counter and asked to speak to a manager or whoever was in charge at Bartolome's London office. I stressed the importance of my request. She dialled a number and a moment later, just as I was thinking her shoulder-length thick ginger hair was gorgeous and wondering whether the star-shaped tattoo on her neck and the two small studs either side of her nose were essential adornments for the modern attractive young female, a forty-something woman approached me. She introduced herself as Diane Leander and said she was the manager of the firm's London offices. She was quite short, the top of her head barely up to my shoulder, and she was wearing what would be regarded as a power business trouser suit with a crisp white blouse under the jacket, plus sensible shoes. She invited me to follow her.

I was seated in her comfortable albeit small office. I could see along Southampton Place from here and I could hear traffic noise below because her window was slightly open, negating the effect of the double glazing. On the wall behind her desk was a large picture of a military aircraft but I didn't know enough to identify it. I declined an offer of tea or coffee. She sat forward in her chair.

"We don't get many visitors from Special Branch," she said in a pleasant manner. "So, what can I do for you?"

"The woman who's just left this office, ten minutes back? Her name's Gillian Redmond, and I'm wondering what her connection is to your firm because I know she's not an employee here," I said, equally pleasantly. "She's an inquiry agent and she's also an ex-MI6 operative. She come in here to submit her CV?"

"Whoever she is, she doesn't work for this firm, you're right, so she has no connection to Bartolome Systems." She maintained the pleasant front.

"Oh, really? Redmond's been following me for the past few days, including up to Berkhamsted last Sunday. I was puzzled as to why this lady's on my tail. What was I doing to arouse her curiosity? So I trail her to the firm she was hired through, Prevental – and I'll bet you know who they are, don't you?" I said, only slightly flippantly. "And I learn, through them, a leading company's hired Redmond to do some work for them. The thing is, your production director just happens to live in Berkhamsted. I was there to talk to his daughter and then, out of nowhere, Gillian Redmond appears on my tail once again. Funny, eh? What do you think? How would she know where I'd be going, and why would the investigations of a police officer be her concern? So I follow her again and, guess what, she leads me right to the London offices of Bartolome Systems Ltd. And, even more coincidentally, the father of the woman I went to Berkhamsted to talk to just happens to work for Bartolome, and he was there with her when I arrived. He even knew who I was without being told. I wonder how he'd know that?"

She sat back in her chair and looked directly at me, clearly displeased with my little speech, but didn't reply.

"I should tell you, if you're gonna hire someone to sit on my tail, hire someone who's better at the game than Gillian Redmond. I'm pretty sure I've caught her out every time she's tried following me. I don't think you're getting the quality of service you're paying good money for." I gave her my best evil grin.

She said nothing.

"So, is Bartolome's interest in me or in Paul Sampson?" I asked formally. "He also used to work for this company, didn't he?"

"I don't know what you're implying, Detective, but this company's done nothing wrong," she finally said as she sat forward, "and unless you can show evidence of wrongdoing, it also doesn't have to justify what it does or doesn't do to you."

"Is that right? You should be aware any interference with the actions of an officer of the Crown in pursuance of his or her sworn duty is an obstruction. That's a criminal offence, and putting a tail on a police officer counts as obstruction."

I heard the door behind me open as she stood up.

"I stand by what I've just said, Detective, and I've nothing further to add, so, if you've no objections, this conversation's concluded." She looked at someone behind me. "This man'll show you the way out. Show the detective out, will you, Josh?"

I stood. I then felt someone grabbing hold of my left arm. I turned and saw a man, slightly bigger than I am, standing alongside me, wearing a fawn-coloured shirt and a tie, plus a badge stating *Security* pinned to his shirt pocket. He was around mid-fifties and probably ex-military, working as a security guard to supplement his pension. He had a very stern expression on his face.

"C'mon, pal, this way." He tried to pull me along.

In a flash I grabbed his left wrist firmly and, in a swift movement he wasn't expecting and was wholly unprepared for, I twisted his wrist around, turned him and bent his arm up behind his back, wrenched my arm free from his grip, grabbed his shirt collar and slammed him up against the nearby wall, face first. Neutralising this clown had taken less than three seconds. I maintained my firm grip on the wrist halfway up his back and I kept his face pinned against the wall. I could hear from his moans he was in some discomfort.

"You wanna dance with me, you should ask first 'cause I like to lead. That clear?"

He gasped his agreement. I turned him around, releasing my grip, and pushed him away with some force. He stumbled against Diane Leander's desk, knocking over her desk lamp, spilling her drink and pushing a few folders onto the floor. She had an astonished look on her face, as though she was gawping at one of the Seven Wonders of the World.

"It's okay, I know the way out." I smiled at both of them and left.

*

Larry Jasper had told me a couple of days earlier that Brian Turley was one of the two detectives on Thornwyn's team who'd been suspended from duty pending further investigations concerning his dealings with Thornwyn. I knew Turley quite well as we'd occasionally partnered up.

Towards the end of my time in the team, Turley'd been drinking heavily and he'd become about as reliable as a second-hand watch bought from a boot fair. His absences because of back pain or having a cold were covers for his sleeping off the after-effects of yet another bender. On more than one occasion someone in the team had made excuses for him, either saying he was with us for an arrest when he wasn't even at work that day, or writing a report for him to sign off on. Everyone except the senior brass knew this but somehow he got away with it.

Even though I was unsure how reliable he now was, I decided I'd go see what I could learn from him. He knew Thornwyn better than most, so he would be a good place to start.

I knew he used to live somewhere around Shepherd's Bush, so I checked with the Branch office and obtained an address for him. He had a small place in Loftus Road, and I remembered him always complaining about the increased volume of traffic on the days QPR played at home and his never being able to find a parking space on those days. He'd moved there when his wife had become sick of his habits and had thrown him out because he was rarely at home and, when he was, he was usually drunk or getting drunk. The inevitable divorce had been bitter and he'd been denied access to his children until he dried out. What had happened to him after this I didn't know because I'd been promoted soon after and had lost contact with him. Still wondering if I was doing the right thing, I took a taxi to his address.

He lived on the ground floor of a terraced house. There was an overflowing wheelie bin just inside the front gate and the smell emanating from it was putrid.

I rang the bell and he answered almost immediately. To say he was surprised when he saw me would be to understate the case. He looked like a fish struggling to breathe on dry land. He squinted his eyes a few times, trying to focus on the person at the door.

"McGraw?" he eventually exclaimed after regaining his composure. "What the fuck you doing here?" He laughed. He was holding a small glass of something in his hand. I guessed it was liquor. His fondness for the bottle was the stuff of legend and, from the glazed expression of his eyes, I suspected he was already well into one, despite the early hour.

"Good seeing you as well, Bri." I patted his shoulder. "I need to talk to you about a few things when we were in Thornwyn's team."

He tensed up hearing Thornwyn's name and he looked worried. But after I'd eventually convinced him I was still in Special Branch and not from the IPCC, and I wasn't there to interrogate him about the reasons for his suspension, he invited me into his home.

It was a large bedsit with a single unmade bed in the far corner, a couple of creaky armchairs, a coffee table and a TV. The wallpaper had several bare patches and the ceiling was a delightful shade of nicotine yellow from years of accumulated cigarette smoke. The place was a mess but, compared to Andy Harris's flat, it was a page from a glossy magazine advertising new home furnishings.

Turley offered me a drink and I settled for tea. I assumed the corner where the sink was also functioned as his kitchen because it housed an electric kettle and two cartons of Pot Noodles. There were also a few empty spirits bottles.

He made a cup of tea by putting a teabag into a cup and adding hot water from the tap. There was a film of something floating on top and it looked about as appetising as drinking dirty bath water. I sipped it. It tasted disgusting.

He sat down or, rather, he slumped down as his

movements were uncoordinated due to alcohol. It was sad realising how much he'd really let himself go. In that brief moment I found myself wondering, if he eventually ended up going inside, how he'd cope in his current condition. But that wasn't my problem.

He confirmed he'd been suspended and wasn't able to talk to me about his case as he was waiting to hear from his police union rep before deciding on his next step. I assured him this wasn't an issue and I wanted to talk to him about something else. He looked relieved.

"What about our old skipper, then? How long you think he'll get?" He sounded excited to know my answer.

"No idea. I'm just following up a couple of leads concerning something he was involved in before he was arrested. You might be able to help me. You okay with this?"

"Yeah, I suppose so." He didn't sound too certain.

"Okay. Did Thornwyn ever talk to you about someone called Paul Sampson?" I began. He pursed his lips and briefly looked at the ceiling. "Did he ever mention the name?"

"No." He shook his head. "At least I don't think so. Who's he?"

I briefly described who he was and what had happened to him. "Thornwyn was blackmailing him about something." I didn't say it was for refusing to publically declare his homosexuality. I didn't want to broadcast details about this to anyone who didn't need to know about it. "You worked closely with him; did you know anything about this?"

"Why would he be blackmailing an MP?"

"That's what I was hoping you might be able to tell me. He was into him for something. I can't exactly ask Thornwyn 'cause he's being kept incommunicado at Belmarsh," I said, grinning, "so, given how close you and him worked together, I thought you might know something. Trust me, it'd be a big help to the Branch if you did."

He poured himself another drink. It was vodka and the

———◄◦►———

bottle displayed a brand label I didn't recognise. Was he now so desperate for alcohol he was plumbing the lower, less discerning end of the market? Had he fallen this far?

"No, I don't know anything about him blackmailing anyone." His voice sounded slightly slurred.

"Did you ever hear him mention a firm called Bartolome Systems Ltd?"

He thought for a moment.

"Yeah. Yeah, I did." He suddenly sat up in his chair.

"In what context?"

"I remember him saying once he'd just bought shares in the company. He said he was looking for a decent investment for the future and he'd bought a whole batch of shares in the company. Spent quite a few thousand buying them as well."

"How would *he* know what's a good financial investment?" I was scornful. "Since when did *he* know anything about playing the stock market? He wouldn't know preferred stock from livestock." I smiled at my weak attempt at a witticism. I'd remembered once hearing this said by an accountant friend who'd thought it a highly amusing description of one of his less-than-financially-savvy clients. But it went right over Turley's head. It'd been wasted on him. In his current befuddled state he probably didn't even know what livestock was.

"I don't bloody know," he exclaimed, almost irritably. "He just said he'd got shares in some firm called Bartolome. I don't know how he knew about them."

Paul Sampson had once worked for Bartolome Systems Ltd. Thornwyn had been putting the squeeze on Sampson. Thornwyn now bought shares in the firm. A tenuous connection, but a connection nonetheless. A lead?

"You and Paine buy shares in them as well? Is that what you did with all that extra money you two were raking in from the Fund?" I said wickedly.

"Me? Fuck no. Got better things to waste *my* money on."

He smiled and lifted his glass in a toasting gesture towards me. I could guess what those things were. Interestingly, he didn't refute my suggestion of extra money coming in. Neither did he seem concerned about hearing John Paine's name or mention of the Fund.

He drained his glass and put it down on the heavily stained coffee table. He had a satisfied expression. Cheap liquor was obviously having the desired effect.

On a whim I asked him something else. "Did he ever mention someone named Jeremy Godfrey?" The thought had dawned on me that Thornwyn might know him.

"Jeremy, Jeremy Godfrey." Turley looked thoughtful for a few moments. "Name does sound vaguely familiar. Who's he?"

"Something to do with Bartolome, company you just mentioned."

"Maybe that's where I've heard the name. It definitely rings a bell with me." He sounded certain.

"He also has a connection to the guy I was asking about earlier, Paul Sampson. It'd be logical to assume Thornwyn knew Godfrey as well."

"I never heard him mention anyone called Sampson." He got up and went to the toilet.

I looked around the bedsit. It was possibly the untidiest I'd seen in a long while, though it wasn't as filthy as Harris's flat. The curtains were partly pulled and, despite it being midday, you'd be forgiven for thinking dusk was falling as the room was quite dark.

The thought struck me that Brian Turley was probably a very lonely man and quite likely spent most of his days engaging in solitary drinking here in this flat, watching daytime television and sleeping one off. Maybe, when he could afford it, he'd spend some time in a pub, where any company would be better than none. I didn't know whether he had access to his children now. His was probably a very bleak and solitary existence, suspended from duty and therefore excluded from the friendship circles he'd formed in the team, who were the only friends he ever had. Being suspended also meant he'd be *persona non grata* amongst other police officers. I wasn't even sure *I* should be here talking to him, but I could at least justify it by saying it was part of an ongoing investigation. I didn't know what the evidence was against him, but his suspension had to mean the IPCC had at least a credible *prima facie* case against him and, if that was substantiated, he'd soon be keeping Thornwyn company in prison.

Turley and I had never been friends in any meaningful sense, but we'd worked together a number of times and I'd initially respected him as a colleague because when I had first joined the team he'd been an effective police officer. I wondered whether his drinking had played any significant role in his being suspended, aside from any allegations he was part of what Smitherman had referred to as *the Fund*, money being collected from criminals by Thornwyn in exchange for allowing them to operate.

He returned and sat down again.

"What about Thornwyn's informer, Bernie?" I asked. "You know him?"

"Bernie the Buck? Is that little bastard still alive? Yeah, I know the scumbag." The venom in his voice was obvious.

"What do you know about him?"

"Thornwyn used to get intel from him about various things going on, and we made a few decent arrests off of what he gave us. Other than that, he's a slimy piece of dog shit. World'd be a better place if he was dead. Him *and* Thornwyn."

"Why's that?" I was curious.

"You remember, earlier this year, those weapons being nicked from that gun shop in Battersea?"

I nodded my agreement.

"Bernie was involved in that. He was in on the break-in."

"Bernie?" I was very doubtful. "Oh, come on."

"It's true." He was adamant. "Bernie and Thornwyn. Security was all over police on this because they thought the weapons were heading for the Middle East and would end up in the hands of terrorists. We were all grilled by the security boys but nothing came of it, or nothing I ever heard about. Funny thing is, nobody ever knew where they ended up." Turley found this amusing and he laughed loudly. "S'far as I know, they've never been recovered."

I remembered hearing about the weapons being stolen from what was said to be a secure storage facility. The word in police circles was it had to have been an inside job because removing them would have necessitated using a passcode to access the storage room. News of the theft of a sizeable weapons cache had never been given to the media as the public would expect at least an arrest and to know the guns had been recovered. Unrecovered stolen guns doing the rounds would not have been good news for the public to read about. Nobody had ever been arrested for the theft of the weapons.

"How does this involve Thornwyn?" I asked.

Turley sat forward in his seat and placed his now-empty glass on the coffee table. "I think he was involved in removing the weapons in the first place."

"Oh, come on." I was dubious. "Thornwyn? He's corrupt, but stealing weapons as well?"

"No, honestly, Rob. The word I got was, he helped Bernie steal the weapons and then told him to give us the wrong address to arrange for their disappearance."

"Huh? Why would he do that?"

"Because Bernie arranged for them to be sold on to whoever was buying them. Then he'd tell Thornwyn where they were and he'd have them all arrested." He stated this with a degree of certainty in his voice. "But it didn't happen like that, did it? The little shit gave Thornwyn the wrong address and, when we went to recover them and arrest the people involved, they'd all gone. We got fucked over, mate."

I looked straight at Turley. He had a determined expression on his face, like he had an important point to convey and wanted to be taken seriously. I paused for a moment.

"Thornwyn was involved in stealing weapons from a firm selling them so they could be sold on to criminals on the black market? You're sure about this?" I was still sceptical.

"Not so I'd swear to it, but it all makes sense. Bernie couldn't organise the theft of those weapons on his own, could he? He'd have to have someone help him. Thornwyn would have been able to get access to the weapons cache. Stands to reason, doesn't it?"

"How could he do that?"

"When the theft was reported to us, he told me he knew someone who worked for the firm where the guns had been stolen. Maybe that's how he was able to get hold of the password to get into the warehouse and get Bernie to steal them."

"Who did he know there?"

"Never said, but it'd have to be someone he knew well to give him a secure password, wouldn't it?" Turley was adamant.

I was still doubtful. I couldn't imagine why Thornwyn would be involved in stealing weaponry like this.

"Thornwyn incidentally let Bernie off for giving us a bum steer. He was taken in but he wasn't charged because of insufficient evidence," Turley said, sneering. "*And* no money was ever recovered from the selling of the weapons. Where did all *that* end up?"

I thought about what had been said. My scepticism was moving into overdrive. "You're telling me Thornwyn arranged for those weapons to be stolen and sold on to criminals and he used Bernie the Buck to cover his tracks?"

"That's what I heard, mate." He was adamant.

"Who from?"

"Who do you think?" His voice rose. "Thornwyn told me. We'd both had a few one night and he poured it all out, what he'd done. Quite proud of it as well, he was."

"He admitted his involvement in an arms theft to you?" I wanted to be clear about what Turley was claiming.

"Yup." He nodded solemnly.

"He say *why* he did this?" I enquired.

"Not to me, he didn't." He sat forward and picked up the bottle to pour another drink.

I leapt up and snatched it from his hand.

"Hey, what the fuck you doing?" He sounded like a child being punished for something he hadn't done, aggrieved at the injustice of it all.

I remained standing, looking down at him. I noticed how dirty and greasy his hair was.

"You're not bullshitting me, are you, Brian?" I said this calmly but forcefully, looking him right in the eyes. "'Cause if you're bullshitting me . . ."

I was tempted to pour the half-full bottle of vodka down the sink. He seemed to sense what I was thinking.

"No, honest to God, Rob, I'm not. That's what I heard, that's what he told me."

His eyes were pleading with me to give him his bottle back. He reminded me of a helpless puppy wanting a treat. I relented. He poured himself a drink and took a long gulp. He was a wreck. I wasn't sure how he'd stand up to the professional interrogators at the IPCC once they started on him.

He'd told me an intriguing story but I wasn't certain I believed it. Was Thornwyn really that duplicitous? Why would a CID commander be involved in the theft of firearms? What could he possibly gain from this?

"I mentioned Thornwyn blackmailing someone earlier," I said. "He was able to do so because of info he got from Bernie. Bernie pointed out the victim to him."

"Figures." He sat back in his chair. "Told you Bernie was a little shit, didn't I?"

We talked about a few other things and then I got up to leave. I probably wasn't going to learn anything more from

Turley but he'd given me a couple of things to think about, though I certainly didn't believe everything I'd heard. I thanked him for his help. He followed me to the door, then fixed me with a sheepish smile.

"You couldn't, er, do me a favour, could you, Rob, for old times' sake?" His voice had dropped somewhat and he wasn't quite looking at me as he asked. "I'm a bit flat and, well, you know how it is. Don't worry if you can't."

He looked longingly at me. I knew what he wanted and I sensed his acute embarrassment at asking. Against my better judgement I withdrew £20 from my wallet and gave it to him. He beamed and thanked me profusely, saying I was a hero and I'd saved his life. After I left I didn't doubt he'd be off down to the nearest off-licence to fortify himself with some decent brand name vodka. I left him to it.

I returned to the Yard. Smitherman saw me and asked me to come into his office. Happily he was sitting the right side of his desk. No one-to-one interrogation today.

"Just read your report about your chat with Commander Thornwyn," he said. "So, just to confirm, he *definitely* admitted blackmailing Paul Sampson." It was a statement rather than a question.

"Yeah, he did. Sampson stood down because Thornwyn pressured him to come out. Sampson wouldn't, so he resigned."

My disbelief as to this being the only factor involved must have registered on my face. Smitherman looked quizzically at me.

"You don't seem convinced."

"I'm not. I think Thornwyn's involved in something else which in some way contributed to Sampson killing himself."

"Why do you think this?"

I explained my belief that being homosexual was no longer a handicap to pursuing any career, and that even the Conservative Party had become more tolerant and inclusive, and had Sampson admitted to his sexuality and done so openly and honestly, he'd have been free of Thornwyn's blackmail demands. The fact he hadn't made me think he had resigned to keep the lid on something else. Smitherman asked what I thought it might be.

"I don't know, but I think it's something to do with the firm Bartolome Systems. I don't exactly know why yet, but I keep stumbling over this firm." I paused. "I'm also being followed by a PI who I'm almost certain's been hired by Bartolome," I said, almost casually.

"What?" Smitherman was stunned. He jolted forward as though he'd just had a minor electric shock.

I explained how I'd come to know this through following the person who'd been tailing me to Prevental's door and being told the woman'd been hired by a leading manufacturing firm, though they had claimed not to know why. I'd since followed the woman to the London offices of Bartolome but had received no explanation about her activities. I conveniently omitted any reference to meeting Richard Clements to ask about Sampson.

"Does Thornwyn have any connection to this firm?" Smitherman asked.

"No tangible one, so far as I know," I replied. For the moment I didn't tell Smitherman about Thornwyn being a shareholder in the firm. I wanted more information before I said this. Just buying shares *prima facie* proved nothing. "I've also discovered from someone who knew Sampson he didn't drink cognac or take super strong sleeping tablets but, when he was rushed into hospital, his stomach was pumped and that's what came out. The same person alluded to Sampson being murdered, though the post mortem ruled it as death through suicide."

"Where'd you hear this?" Smitherman's eyes narrowed.

"From one of my sources."

Smitherman looked thoughtful for a moment.

"My being followed started last Friday evening, not long

after I'd been to Belmarsh to speak to Thornwyn," I said. "This is what makes me think Thornwyn's involved with this firm somewhere along the line. You told me before I saw him that Sampson used to work for an arms manufacturer. I bet I can guess which firm it was." I smiled. I didn't tell him I already knew.

"So far as I know, Bartolome's not under suspicion for doing anything wrong, but I can ask a few questions, see if anything's known about them we should be aware of."

"Okay. Ask why they've put someone on my tail."

"They're quite an important firm in the defence world; you know that, don't you? We ought to be clear what we're looking for if we're suspecting them of something. Until then, back off a little. Wait until I hear something through official channels."

I then remembered something Thornwyn'd said in Belmarsh last Friday. "Can I ask you something?"

Smitherman nodded his assent.

"When I talked to Thornwyn, at the end of our conversation, he said I'd not been told what the bigger picture was. He seemed quite amused at this, as though that should have been the reason I was there. What did he mean by that?"

Smitherman nodded to himself a few times. "I'll just tell you this, for the moment. Commander Neville Thornwyn's being investigated for a number of things involving his work in CID, plus other things I can't go into at the moment. I was hoping he'd tell you himself last week, but clearly he didn't."

I looked straight at Smitherman. I took a stab in the dark. "Does this have anything to do with MI5?"

Smitherman remained silent, still nodding slightly to himself.

"So there is a bigger picture," I said. "This isn't just about his blackmailing an MP."

"For the moment, until other issues become clearer, that's all I can tell you." He said this in a tone suggesting I shouldn't ask anything else for the moment.

I left the office. I'd not told Smitherman about Brian Turley's assertion Thornwyn was involved in an unsolved arms robbery, partly because I wasn't sure about its veracity, given I'd been told this by a man who'd now taken up almost permanent residency inside a vodka bottle, but also because I wanted to know more about this before I said anything.

FIVE

Monday

SINCE TALKING TO SMITHERMAN, I'd spent the last few days catching up on some routine paperwork he'd been on at me to get done; I'd completed my account of the trial I'd wasted a day at, which was only a week late; I'd attended a routine albeit pointless department meeting about whatever it was (I didn't really pay any attention to it), which was ninety minutes of my life I'd never get back, and I'd immersed myself in a couple of ongoing investigations into the activities of a few known Islamist militant clerics who'd been accused in the tabloid press of radicalising their followers, familiarising myself with where they were. I had gone out on a couple of occasions with another detective to talk to a couple of his informers about this last thing and, given some of the language employed, was wondering whether a charge for *inciting racial hatred* would be appropriate.

I'd also had a couple of strenuous workouts in the gym, plus some unarmed combat training with my friend Mickey Corsley. He took training seriously and he'd unceremoniously put me on the canvas on two occasions, warning me about not concentrating and consequently dropping my guard. Just as well I'd been wearing a headguard as I'd still be hearing bells otherwise.

But, the previous Saturday morning in the office, during a quiet moment, I'd spent a little time looking up details of the weapons theft which had occurred a few months earlier. I'd been thinking about what Brian Turley had said last Tuesday and I was intrigued by the role Turley said Thornwyn had played in the theft of the weapons.

The weapons concerned, mainly Beretta 92 series

handguns, had been stolen from the shop premises of a company named Byzantium, located on Battersea Park Road, not too far from the park. Byzantium was a licensed seller of firearms to marksmen and shooting clubs. The weapons stolen had been stored in the warehouse behind the shop, in line with the current laws and regulations regarding the storing and selling of firearms, stating that stringent safety conditions had to be put in place *and* had to be inspected and approved by a senior police officer. These included determining those inside the firm who could have access to the firearms, which involved a police check as to their suitability to work with firearms, and the conditions under which the firearms should be stored. These security procedures had to be reviewed and updated on a regular basis to ensure compliance with the law, and any changes had to be approved by a senior police officer.

Accessing the warehouse where Byzantium stored its firearms meant having to go through to the back of the shop. There was no other entry point. Getting into the storeroom meant entering a passcode into a sophisticated computerised locking system, and the code was updated on a regular basis. There was also twenty-four-hour CCTV coverage. But, conveniently, on the night in question, the CCTV had gone on the blink a few hours prior to the robbery, as had the alarm system. The correct passcode had been entered and a number of handguns and rifles had been taken. Only three people working for Byzantium at that time would have known what the passcode would have been on this particular night, as it had been recently changed, but all could satisfactorily account for their movements that night. All three had been interviewed strenuously by police but nothing could be proven against any of them. The keypads had been dusted for fingerprints but, other than those of employees, none were discernible. In keeping with legal requirements, none of the three with passcode access had a criminal record and all had been vetted by the police. The weapons taken had never been recovered and no one had been arrested.

According to Turley, the theft had been arranged by Thornwyn and helped by Bernie the Buck. I was doubtful. Thornwyn had proved himself to be capable of many forms of criminal deception, but I wasn't convinced they would include stealing weapons from a reputable arms dealer. How could Thornwyn have arranged for the CCTV to be switched off? Would he really trust someone like Bernie for such a delicate operation? I'd thought about this over the weekend. Something wasn't making sense. I needed more information.

On a whim I called up the report about the theft of the weapons. Because of the sensitivity of the theft, Special Branch had taken an interest even though, as a robbery, officially it was a CID matter.

The facts were laid out in a straightforward manner and confirmed what I already knew. But I was more interested in the personnel involved. Who were the three persons who'd known the passcode for this particular evening? What did we know about them?

The first two were trusted employees who'd worked for Byzantium for several years. Neither had a criminal record and there was no suspicion against either man. Both had been questioned by police, had acceptable alibis and had been exonerated.

But I was intrigued by the third person, the general manager of the business, Edward Priestly. He was in his mid-fifties and, prior to employment with Byzantium, had been employed by Bartolome Systems for several years in a senior management capacity, though the reason why he'd left the firm wasn't given. He'd also been questioned by detectives about his movements that night and who he'd had contact with in the immediate period prior to the robbery, and, after an extensive trawl through his whereabouts on the evening of the robbery, police had been satisfied with his answers and he'd ultimately been eliminated from their enquiries. It was interesting to note the detective leading the investigation into the robbery had been Commander Neville Thornwyn. At this time police would have had no reason to consider Bartolome Systems in any context relating to the robbery, so the connection between Byzantium and Bartolome would not have seemed at all significant.

I was encountering Bartolome Systems a lot. Sampson had previously worked for them and had also been made a non-executive director upon becoming an MP. His father-in-law still worked for them as production director and Thornwyn had become a shareholder in the firm. I was also being tailed by a female PI who I was certain had been hired by Bartolome to follow me, though I didn't yet know why. I'd been largely deskbound, so I'd not seen Gillian Redmond behind me of late.

I decided to check details about Byzantium Ltd and went onto their website. It was all largely non-contentious: when the firm was established, what it sold, range of products, prices, pen portraits of the two directors of the firm, testimonials from satisfied customers and so on. I clicked onto the section headed *General Information* and ploughed my way through the dense corporate prose.

My eyes opened wide when I discovered Byzantium had been bought by Bartolome Systems four years previously and, whilst it still functioned as an independent trading entity in its own right, it was now a subsidiary of Bartolome Systems. Had Thornwyn been a Bartolome shareholder at the time he'd questioned Priestly?

This was becoming more intriguing by the minute. Businesswise, it was a rational decision. Bartolome produced weapons and Byzantium sold them, so operating under the same corporate umbrella was logical. But, as with everything else I'd heard of late, the connection was rather too cosy.

*

———◄○►———

Mid-afternoon I took a call on my mobile. It was Andy Harris.

"Mr Jack, I was drinking in the pub last night and these geezers come in looking for Bernie. They were looking to score stuff from him but he weren't around."

"Which pub?"

"Same one he always uses, by Chalk Farm tube station."

"By *stuff*, I'm guessing you mean ecstasy tabs."

"Yeah, that's it. That's what he deals."

I remembered Harris saying a week ago Bernie hadn't been around his usual haunts for a while now. The likes of Bernie the Buck weren't tourists. They didn't go on holiday; they were creatures of habit; they just hung around their patches and engaged in their usual unlawful activities, which, in Bernie's case, meant selling ecstasy tabs supplied by the Chackarti family.

"I've been to the pub a few times in the last week and I ain't seen hide nor hair of him. That's unusual, Mr Jack. He's always there, regular as clockwork. I asked the guy behind the bar if he'd seen him and he says no, he's not been in for a couple of weeks now. That's not like him at all. Do you reckon something's happened to him?" Harris almost sounded concerned for Bernie's welfare.

"I don't know, but thanks for the tip."

"I just thought you'd wanna know he don't seem to be around."

"Yeah, okay. Thanks. You still spending my money?"

"Got some more now, ain't I? Lots of punters in the market over the weekend. Got myself a few hundred, didn't I? Had some Kraut's wallet out of his bag when he was buying a coffee. Had four hundred and something in it. Lucky, eh?" He sounded pleased.

I ignored this comment. I was silently hoping, one day, one of his victims would catch him in the act and give him a slapping.

"Well, keep your ears open. You hear anything, I wanna know."

*

—<o>—

113

I brought Bernie's file up. His last known address was in a block of flats in Mansfield Road, close by Belsize Park tube station. I drove to his residence. His flat was on the third floor and the lift wasn't working. I rang the doorbell. No answer. I heard no sounds inside the flat.

Two women were walking along the narrow corridor so I showed them my ID, nodded to Bernie's flat and asked if they knew the man who lived there. One said she lived in the flat two doors along and knew him quite well. I asked if she'd seen him lately but she said he'd not been seen around for a while. I asked her if she knew where he might have gone. She said she didn't know, though she mentioned a pub in Chalk Farm and said that was where he spent a lot of time, and I might try in there.

I drove to the pub. For just after five in the afternoon, it was moderately crowded with drinkers and a few punters watching the late racing on TV and excitedly shouting for a particular horse named Raven's Beak. There was a man behind the counter, maybe early fifties, who looked like he might be the manager. He was. He had that bored expression that comes from doing barwork for any length of time, the look that says *I've seen it all before.*

"Looking for someone named Bernie Rayes. I know he uses this place quite a lot. You seen him lately?" I showed ID. As I did so, the man and woman drinking nearby picked up their glasses and moved away to a nearby table. A loud cheer erupted behind me and a group of drunks leapt to their feet, excitedly yelling and punching the air, so I assumed Raven's Beak had won its race and they were now quids in.

"No, not for a couple of weeks now. He's usually in here, regular like, but he's not been in for a while. Maybe he's got himself a new boozer." He shrugged.

"Unlikely. Where would his customers go to get their ecstasy when he's not here?" I asked facetiously. His face took on a shocked expression. "Any other dealers in here? They might know where Bernie is."

"What you on about?" He looked away sharply.

"Come on." I smiled knowingly at him. "You and I both know Bernie deals drugs out of this place."

He half-smiled.

"But, don't worry, he's not in trouble. I'm not drugs squad, though I'll bring them in if I don't get any answers." I stared directly at the manager. "I just need to ask him a few things about an unrelated matter."

Knowing I wasn't going to bust the pub brought relief to his face. "Someone else was also asking about Bernie recently, asking if I'd seen him lately, where he was and all that. He didn't show ID but I knew he was police. Couldn't help him either. This one was bloody angry he couldn't find Bernie."

"He's popular with all the wrong people," I said.

"Well, as I just said, he ain't been in for a coupla weeks now. That's the truth. Not like him at all. He usually spends a large part of his week in here."

I believed him. I thanked him for his help. I looked around the pub and considered asking around, but from the assorted clientele here I doubted I'd get a sensible answer. Most of them didn't even look intelligent or sober enough to tell me the right time.

I was about to leave when I saw the two drinkers who'd moved away from the bar. One was trying to turn his head away from me. This made me suspicious. I went over to the table. From the side I had an uncomfortable feeling I knew who he was.

"Evening, either of you two lovebirds want to buy the *War Cry*?" I asked.

They both turned to look at me. The woman shook her head. The other stared straight at me and I realised immediately I knew who it was.

Colin Addley.

Colin was Simon Addley's younger brother. Both at one time had been adherents to the philosophy of Red Heaven, a

Europe-based terrorist group responsible for several bombings over the past few years, including a couple in London. Both had been arrested late last year after Special Branch had foiled their attempt to place an IED near to the Albert Hall on the evening of Remembrance Saturday. Simon Addley had been tried and sentenced to twelve years in prison and was now in Belmarsh. Colin hadn't been charged because, after the arrests, I'd made the amazing discovery he was one of Smitherman's informants and had been keeping Special Branch in the loop concerning Red Heaven's activities, and so he was now at liberty. Simon, of course, didn't know this; he had assumed his brother was as fully committed to the cause as he was and was now incarcerated in prison somewhere.

I'd not seen Colin Addley since he'd been taken to Paddington Green police station after the arrests and I'd certainly not missed him. Simon, at least, was an intelligent guy, whereas his brother made two short planks look like a Mastermind contestant. If he had a brain he'd be truly dangerous.

I sat down at their table. Colin offered to buy me a beer. I thanked him but said no.

"Can we help you with something?" the woman asked. She was older than Colin, maybe mid to late thirties, with short, closely cropped dark hair, and was dressed in an oversized man's dark shirt and blue jeans. She wore round wire-rimmed glasses and big dangling gold-coloured earrings, and had piercing blue eyes which focused intently on me as she asked her question. "I know you're police, I can tell just looking at you. Colin's not done anything wrong. Why can't you people just leave him alone?"

"What are you, his mother?" I asked flippantly.

"No, I'm his spiritual guidance counsellor." She said this as though it was obvious. "Colin's a member of my group and I'm trying to help him to re-establish himself so as to be able to function as an independent autonomous human being after living in his brother's shadow for most of his life." She looked and sounded like she was in deadly earnest. "I'm trying to help Colin regain control over his identity and become more outer-directed in his aspirations so he can take back control of his own destiny in life and be whoever he wants to be."

I sniggered inwardly. I didn't think Colin Addley could even pronounce *autonomous*. It was a safe bet he couldn't spell it and an even safer one he couldn't explain what it meant, but I resisted the temptation to ask him to try.

"Colin came to me because he's troubled and confused and doesn't know what he wants or where he wants to go in his life." He was nodding his agreement as she spoke. "So through therapy and human interaction sessions with some aspects of his past life, like drinking in here, for instance, Colin is gradually coming out of himself and leaving his old self behind and discovering who he is and what he's capable of. He's acclimatising to changes really well so far." She looked at him like a mother speaking well of a child who'd just got a good school report.

When I'd seen Simon in prison after his sentence recently, he too had been shedding the outer skin of his previous life and finding his spiritual core through meditation. How serious the Addley brothers were about changing their mindsets I didn't know and, being honest, I didn't much care either. But if this was the way they wanted to go, then better that than being part of an organisation conspiring to commit a terrorist atrocity.

"Good for you, Colin," I said. I tried not to sound patronising.

"That's why I moved away from the bar. I recognised you, and you're a reminder of the past life I'm trying to escape from." He turned to the woman, who was now sitting alongside him. From the warm glow on her face, and the way she was cuddling up to him, I briefly wondered exactly what type of therapy she was giving him and whether it extended beyond formal boundaries. "This is the police officer who arrested me in the garage that night," he said.

"Oh, really?" She looked at me in amazement.

"Yeah, really. Him and his brother." I jutted my chin at him. "A real pair of pilgrims."

There was an awkward silence for a couple of moments.

"Well, given the role you played in his arrest, and the trauma it induced in him, Colin's handling your reappearance in his life remarkably well. I'm *really* proud of you, Colin." She leaned across, kissed his cheek and laid her head on his shoulder. He looked pleased. He held her hand and rested his head against the top of hers. It dawned on me that, as well as looking vacuous, he also looked extremely vulnerable. It was clear from the way she looked at him she really cared for him. Perhaps my scepticism was misguided and being with this woman was a good thing for him. Maybe she wasn't the flake I'd initially assumed she was.

"I know who you're looking for," he calmly stated.

The look of surprise on my face must have been all too real.

"You were asking about Bernie Rayes?" he asked.

I agreed I was.

"About two weeks ago, another bloke came in here looking for him. He wasn't here, no one knew where he was either. Bloke said he'd been to his flat and he wasn't there either. He asked around but no one could tell him anything."

"Who was asking about him?"

"Didn't show ID but said he was police. He said it was important he find Bernie Rayes."

"He say why?"

"No."

"Did you get a name?"

"No."

"What did he look like?"

He thought for a moment. "About your height, maybe a little taller. Thin. Dirty. Scruffy looking."

———◇———

"I remember him having really fuzzy eyes, almost like he was having problems adjusting to daylight," his therapist volunteered. "He'd also been drinking."

I thanked Colin for his help and, despite myself, I wished him a good life. His therapist gave him another kiss on the cheek as I stood up. He definitely wasn't getting one from me.

I left the pub. I'd recognised the description given. I knew exactly who he meant.

I rang the bell and a few seconds later the door opened. I didn't wait to be invited in. I barged past the man and went into his still horribly depressing bedsit.

"Fuck you think you're doing, McGraw?" Brian Turley said as he followed me into the room and closed the door. He tried to convey a stern, angry agitation at how I'd entered but didn't quite succeed. His voice was too slurred for this to have any meaningful impact and his eyes were wholly unfocused. He was under the influence.

"You didn't tell me everything when we spoke last week, did you?" I began. I spoke in a calm manner as I didn't want to alarm him. Not yet, anyway.

"What do you mean?" He was looking nervous.

"You didn't tell me you'd been looking for Bernie the Buck in Chalk Farm a couple of weeks back. You were suspended by then, weren't you? Why would you need to see Bernie? He wasn't anything to you."

He sat down on the settee. He picked up his drink and took a chug of it. He still looked a pathetic wretch, dirty and dishevelled. I could also smell body odour. To think, six years ago, this was the man I'd looked up to and respected when I'd first joined the team.

I remembered one occasion when he and I were attempting to arrest a couple of muggers we'd chased into a multi-storey car park. One had pulled a knife, waved it a few inches from my face and shouted obscenities, challenging me to *come and get sliced up*. Turley had instantly leapt at him, pinned him against a wall, kneed him forcefully in the groin and, at the same time, twisted his arm around, forcing him to drop the knife. When it was out of his hand, Turley had spun him around and punched him hard, dislocating the man's jaw. The victim had later claimed he'd been unarmed at the time his jaw was dislocated and his injury was a graphic example of police brutality. I'd claimed not to have seen what happened as I was arresting the other mugger, which'd been easy as he was so surprised by the punch, he'd meekly surrendered to police custody.

I'd been impressed by Turley's courage in tackling a desperate man brandishing a knife. Looking at him now, anyone waving a knife in his direction would probably cause him to soil his trousers.

I waited a few moments. He sighed.

"Yeah, you're right. I *was* looking for the little bastard. He owes me some money and I wanted it. Told you, didn't I, I'm skint."

"How'd he end up owing *you* anything?" I was surprised.

"From the weapons we took. He owed me my cut."

"*Your* cut?" I blurted out. "*You* were involved in stealing those weapons?"

He nodded, looking down at the floor. I was staggered by his admission. He'd said previously the robbery was down to Thornwyn and Bernie, but now he was admitting complicity.

"Does the IPCC know about this? Was this part of why you've been suspended?"

"No, I don't think so. It's not mentioned in any of the documents they've sent for me to look at before my hearing."

I shook my head sadly at the mess Turley'd landed himself in. "They find out about this, you know what it'll mean, don't you?"

He did; he didn't need me to tell him they'd hit him with everything they had and lengthy jail time would be as certain as day following night. He looked mournful, as though recovering from hearing bad news about a loved one.

"You planning to tell them, then?" he said in a way that was almost challenging. "That why you're here again?"

"Look, Brian," I said when I had recovered my poise, "why don't you tell me what this is all about, eh? I might even be able to help you."

He looked doubtful for a while. He looked at the bottle on the coffee table and picked up his empty glass.

I reached down and took the bottle away from his reach. "Preferably without any more of this for the moment, eh?"

He looked hurt, like he'd had his favourite toy taken away by his parents. He attempted to stand up. I pushed him back down on the couch. He got up again and threw a punch at me, which I saw coming twenty minutes before he threw it. I easily sidestepped it and pushed him back onto the couch, forcefully. He looked defeated.

"Don't be fucking stupid, Brian." I said this more in sorrow than anger. It was sad to see him like this. I sat down on the chair by the table, watching him trying to catch his breath.

"Okay, okay," he finally said. He was gasping. The exertion of throwing a punch had worn him out.

I waited whilst he gathered his thoughts.

He looked up. "I told you about the theft of those weapons from that gun shop's storeroom."

I knew what he was referring to. I nodded.

"Thornwyn organised it with the manager, Priestly. He gave him the passcode needed to enter the storeroom and arranged for the CCTV to conveniently be malfunctioning whilst me and Bernie went in and took the guns. That's why it was so easy."

"The shop manager was in on it?" I was incredulous.

"Yeah."

"What about Thornwyn?"

"Just me and Bernie went in. He wasn't there, he just arranged it."

"What did you do with the weapons?"

"They were sold on to someone in North London. Bernie took care of all that. I just helped him nick them."

"Who were they sold on to? Why'd they need these firearms?"

He paused for a moment to blow his nose. He looked and sounded like he had a cold coming on, or maybe it was the effects of a few minutes without alcohol. Either way he looked dreadful.

"I tell you, you promise you won't let on where you heard it from?" He looked concerned.

"You know I can't give any guarantees, but I won't tell anyone who doesn't need to know."

This seemed to satisfy him. He continued. "They were sold on to some Arab, don't know his name. He's supposed to be the leader of some Islamist group in North London who're planning to train up younger Arabs so, when they go off to fight in Syria or some other fucking pile of sand, they're already proficient in the use of firearms. That's what I was told."

"You sold guns to a terrorist? You out of your fucking mind?" I was angry at what I'd heard. How could he have been this stupid?

"We were assured they wouldn't be used in this country." He said this to make it sound like a justification for what had occurred.

"Oh, well, that makes it all right then, doesn't it? They won't be used in London, so you can arm them, no problem." My sarcasm was undisguised. "And you really believed that crap? I thought you were brighter than that, Brian."

"Don't matter what I believe, does it?" He shrugged, almost nonchalantly. "I just went along with it, didn't I? I mean, I don't care which group of fucking ragheads kill each other, s'long as they leave me alone."

"Why'd *you* get involved anyway? You planning to join them?"

"For the money," he instantly replied. "I was into the bookies for quite a few grand and helping Thornwyn do this got me out from under."

I didn't believe him. I knew he had a drink problem, but a gambling problem as well was a new one on me. Something about his tone and his body language suggested he wasn't being truthful with me.

"Why would a CID commander get involved in stealing guns and selling them on to some Arab for the reason you just gave? Doesn't make sense." I was bemused. "How would someone like Bernie even *know* about Arabs wanting guns?"

"I don't bloody know, do I?" He sounded indignant. He sat back in his chair and exhaled loudly. This seemed unreal. I looked at him for a moment.

"Look, Brian," I said softly. "This is doing my head in. Either you tell me the truth or I'm gonna blow the fucking whistle on you."

I tried not to look threatening but something in my tone produced an almost terrified expression on his face.

He breathed deeply a few times. "Can I have a drink first? You're making me nervous."

Against my better judgement I reluctantly acceded to his request. I poured him a small glass of vodka and he chugged it back in one gulp, almost like schnapps. He sighed and smiled.

"Thornwyn took me for a drink one night," he said. "Said he wanted to talk to me about something and it'd be worth my while. Bernie was there waiting."

"This was in Chalk Farm."

"Yeah. I wasn't aware he'd wanted Bernie there as well. Anyway, by the by, whilst we're drinking, Bernie tells Thornwyn he's got the buyer lined up for the guns and the other stuff from this place in Battersea. I wasn't certain what they were talking about. I kept thinking, *What's all this about guns?* so I asked what's going on. Thornwyn then tells me he's planning to remove some weapons from a gun shop in Battersea and he wants me to help him. Said it'd be a piece of piss as he'd have the passcode for the security system and we'll be able to go in because the CCTV won't be working."

"You ask how he knew that?"

"Yeah, I did. He said the manager of the shop was going to give him the passcode and arrange for CCTV and alarms to be offline for a few hours."

"The shop manager."

"That's what he said."

"So he really was involved."

"Up to his neck," Turley replied with certainty.

"What then?"

"I tell Thornwyn I don't want any part of it. I was shocked to hear him talking calmly about robbing a gun store. I mean, I knew he took money from shylocks and a few dealers; I'd helped him do that. It didn't bother me, taking money from people like that. All drug dealers are scum." He spat it out.

"Bernie's a drug dealer," I offered.

"Yeah, and I hate the bastard for it. But," he continued, "I told Thornwyn stealing weapons was a step too far." He paused to think for a moment. "Thornwyn then says, if I don't agree to help, he can make trouble for me. He knew I was in deep shit with a couple of bookies and said this was my chance to get myself on an even keel again. He kept on telling me how easy it'd be. No CCTV, no alarms, we'll have the passcode to get in, nobody'll ever suspect us, and so on." He stopped and looked me for a moment.

"You were really in debt with bookies?"

He nodded. His eyes said he was being truthful.

"So you went along with it," I stated.

"'S right. My debts with the bookies were close to ten grand by then, and I didn't want any hard cases coming after me. Not only that, my ex-wife was on at me for maintenance payments for the kids. I was fucking boracic, mate. But Thornwyn saying he'd clear these debts persuaded me." He looked at the vodka bottle. "So I help them rob the place. Bernie had arranged a van; we went in late at night, took what we went in to get and left. Manager turns up early for work next day, finds his stock's been diminished, some stuff missing, calls police in. He knew he'd be a suspect 'cause he's one of the few people there who'd know the passcode, but Thornwyn'd told him, *Get yourself a good alibi,* and that's what he did. He's also got no police record, so there was no reason to think he's involved in something like this. The fact it was Thornwyn interviewing him afterwards also helped him get away with it. Thornwyn wrote up the report stating there was insufficient evidence Priestly was involved, so he was eliminated from police enquiries. They went through the motions but it was all just for show, wasn't it?"

"How did he disable the CCTV? You can't just switch it off."

"I don't know. Somehow he got it to look like it was a temporary malfunction and it came back online a few hours later."

When I'd been reading the account of the robbery recently, I'd noticed police had surmised it was probably the work of some expert computer hacker and were concentrating their search on anyone whom they believed would have the nous necessary to disable a sophisticated CCTV security system and then time it to come back online soon afterwards, but so far with no luck. I wondered briefly how hard it'd been for police to swallow the line about a malfunction. CCTV only goes dead for a few hours but, in that time, the shop has its only ever theft of weaponry? I'd not have bought this had I been investigating it.

"You also know who this Arab was the weapons were sold to, don't you?" I wasn't really asking him. He'd acted stupidly but, even though he was now looking at the world through the bottom of an upturned vodka bottle, he wasn't so stupid as to be party to selling weapons to an unknown buyer. Even in his current liquidised state he'd want to know who they were going to.

He thought for a moment. "If I remember correctly, I think his name's Khaled al-Epouri, or some fucking raghead bloody name. I'm not sure if I've pronounced the name right."

"And how would someone like Bernie know him?"

"He didn't." He shook his head vigorously. "Thornwyn knew him. He arranged for them to meet up. This wasn't the first time this'd occurred, y'know."

"What, selling arms to this Arab guy?"

"Yeah."

"*Jesus*," I gasped. It took a few moments to recover from this.

I took out my police radio and called Special Branch. I requested details about someone named Khaled al-Epouri, believed to be living somewhere in North London. A minute later my call was returned.

"The person you asked about is almost certainly Khaled al-Ebouli, a Syrian national, got a place in Islington, lived in this country about eight years. He's a target and we keep an eye on him. He's known to be involved in promoting extremist causes in the Middle East. MI5 believes he's a talent spotter for the terrorist group Muearada, identifying those who he believes are ready to go out and fight for it. He helps radicalise them so they're more prepared to want to go. He's quite the religious rabble-rouser. You should hear some of his rhetoric; it's incendiary. We've transcripts of some of his talks; it's full of stuff about Western infidels and godless consumers and how people in the West believe in nothing. At least one person connected to him went to Syria, became a suicide bomber and took a few people with him. He gives his talks at various mosques and similar places about the evils of Western democracy and how he wants to see Muslims establish a caliphate in this country. He's also on record saying he wants to see Muslims judged using sharia law in the UK. He's a strong believer in a jihad and wants to see the Koran taught in all schools in the UK, regardless. Oh yeah, goes without saying he wants to see Israel wiped off the face of the Earth as well. He's quite the bogeyman in the press, particularly the tabloids, as you might imagine."

Thornwyn was supplying weapons to this joker? "What is he, a cleric?"

"No, nothing like that. He's an academic, a lecturer in history, specialising in Islamic studies, at Westminster University. Came over as a mature student to finish his dissertation and they offered him a lecturing post when he completed it; been there ever since. They get lots of Middle East students at Westminster and he's very popular with the department."

"Any record of him dealing in weapons or trying to buy them?"

"Nothing on our files indicating he does, but it's not been ruled out."

"He have connections to any other groups in this country?"

"None we know of."

"He ever been in trouble?"

"Not with the law. Only with those in the press who despise him and want him deported."

"Okay, thanks."

I summarised my conversation to Brian Turley, telling him what my office had told me about Khaled al-Ebouli.

"And you and Thornwyn were supplying arms to this creep." I stated this in such a way as to make it sound like an accusation. It was. "I hope it was worth what they didn't pay you."

He didn't reply. He sat back, looking more morose and

---

depressed than previously. My opening his eyes to what he'd been doing hadn't raised his spirits any.

There was a silence lasting probably only seven or eight seconds, but it felt much longer. Turley was looking down at the floor and tapping his fingers against his thighs.

"You gonna turn me in?" he asked, glumly.

"No. I've not enough information or evidence to do that. I'd need to know a lot more before I could do that. What I *am* gonna do is talk to Thornwyn and hear what he has to say. Before I do that, though, I need to check out a few other things."

Turley's eyes opened wide enough almost to fall from their sockets. He looked horrified.

"Don't worry, your name won't be mentioned," I reassured him. "If I can, I'll keep you out of this. I won't tell him I've spoken to you."

He looked longingly at the bottle next to my arm. I passed it to him as I stood up, and he poured himself a large drink, toasted me and drained it in one gulp.

"Oh, God, thanks, Rob. You're a pal, you know that?"

At this moment I didn't want to be his pal or even in the same room as him. I hurriedly left his flat.

What I'd not told Turley was that I intended to intensify my search for Bernie the Buck. People like Bernie tended to stay close to home, associate with the same people and do the same things they always did. I knew from my own experience they lacked the imagination to vary their day-to-day routines; they remained inside their circle of friends, which was why police were almost always able to find them in a relatively short period of time when they needed to.

Except this time. Bernie hadn't been seen for over two weeks now. He'd be a main source of drug money for the Chackarti family and there was no doubt they'd be missing him as well. I checked in with our technical people, gave them Bernie's mobile number and asked when this number had last registered any activity. The date given was nearly three weeks ago. Either Bernie was keeping a low profile somewhere, he'd got himself a new phone or he'd been taken out of circulation.

Using the siren to clear the way, I drove fast back to his flat in Mansfield Road. I banged on the door and opened his letterbox to listen out for sound. Something noxious regaled my nose. Something smelt unwholesome inside the flat and only one thing I knew gave off this smell.

I took a few steps back and charged at the door, hitting it hard with my left shoulder and throwing my entire weight against the side where the latch was. On the third charge the door crashed open and I was almost assaulted by the rancid smell of something or someone decomposing. Holding my hand across my nose I went into the main room and found someone lying face downwards on the floor, next to an overturned glass-topped coffee table. From the odour I guessed this person had been dead some while. There didn't appear to be any sign of a struggle and I couldn't see any obvious cause of death, but I didn't want to disturb a crime scene, so I used my police radio and called for assistance.

A squad car and an ambulance arrived four minutes later. Before they'd arrived I'd had a brief look around but had been careful not to touch anything. I identified myself to the DS in charge and explained how I'd come to be inside the flat.

The medics carefully turned the body over onto its back and then sprayed it with something to mitigate the repellent odour. From the facial structure and state of decomposition this person had to have been dead for at least a couple of weeks. I didn't recognise the victim.

I explained to the DS I was there looking for the flat's occupant.

He nodded towards the dead body. "Well, I know Bernie the Buck, and that ain't him. For one thing, he was never that good looking." He smiled at the other two officers, neither of whom knew who the deceased was either.

I asked to be informed of who the deceased was when he'd been identified. The DS agreed to that. I left quickly, glad to get back out into the open air again.

I was pulling out onto Haverstock Hill in the direction of the West End when my mobile phone sounded. It was Richard Clements.

"Rob, meant to call you weekend but life kept getting in the way. You asked if I could get you anything about Paul Sampson. I think you might be interested in hearing some of the things I've been told about him. When can you be available?"

I asked where he was. He was just leaving his office, so I told him I was on my way back to the Yard and I'd meet him in the Clarence in fifteen to twenty minutes, maybe less if I decided to switch on the siren. He seemed to know most pubs around political Westminster but I liked this particular one.

Fourteen minutes later I entered the Clarence. Clements was already there, sitting against the counter with a full pint. I didn't believe it was his first either, and the empty glass next to it confirmed my suspicion.

I'd gone off duty the moment I'd turned off the car engine, so I graciously allowed him to buy me a hideously expensive pint of Peroni as it was now 8.25 pm and I was thirsty.

"Let's talk over there." I picked up my beer and nodded to an unoccupied corner.

The thought struck me as I sat down that I felt more comfortable with Clements every time we met up. He was good company and I nearly always learnt something when we got together. He was well connected politically and beginning to make a name for himself in political journalism. The biggest issue I faced was ensuring my boss, his father-in-law, never found out a real friendship was developing here.

"You'll like this," Clements said. "A week last Saturday, I was in Trafalgar Square waiting for the demo to start, and I could have sworn I saw you walking fast through the square. I did a double take but whoever it was had gone. Didn't half look like you, though." He laughed.

I didn't bother explaining it probably was me as I was pursuing Gillian Redmond. "So, what have you found out?" Straight down to business.

"I've spoken to a couple of people in the know and heard a few things, but this is all off the record, right? You don't let on where it came from?"

"Only to your father-in-law." I grinned.

"Right, Paul Sampson," he began, looking very serious. "I talked to my friend on the *Guardian*, asked him what he knew about Paul Sampson. They'd done a few pieces about him, so I guessed he could help. He asked around amongst the people he knew and called me back. We met up and he introduced me to one of his contacts, and don't ask who either 'cause I'm not telling you."

I nodded my assent to that.

"Guy agrees to talk after my friend vouches for me, said I was reliable and I could be trusted to be discreet. This bloke works for one of the main Sundays, been a political reporter since before Lloyd George, knows *everyone* in the political establishment who's worth knowing as well as having good sources in the intelligence community. Even said he'd read some of my work and liked what I'd written." He grinned. "He said he knew Paul, known him since he became an MP. Used to talk to him regular in the House. Sampson was always available to talk about issues his paper was interested in. Thought he was a good constituency MP and all that. Sampson had a safe seat in Hertfordshire where they weigh the Tory vote rather than count it. This bloke wasn't at all surprised when he was put into the Government even

———◦———

131

though he'd not been an MP too long, as he's highly intelligent and well connected, and was expecting him to reach the Cabinet at some point."

"What did he mean, *well connected*?"

"Knows all the right people in the right places. Comes from a good family, married well, used to work for a prestigious arms company as a sales executive, father-in-law's a director of the same company, you know the kind of thing. The company he worked for, Bartolome Systems, is also a big contributor to Tory party funds. No surprise there."

"Married well?" I queried.

"Yeah. His wife's family's riddled with military people; uncle's a major-general, her dad's ex-military and her brother's currently a major in the army somewhere. She's got another relative who's the Lord Lieutenant of Hertfordshire, whatever the fuck one of those is," he sneered. "Her dad walked into a top job at Bartolome when he left the army. And they say the old boy network doesn't open doors anymore."

"Sampson stayed with Bartolome after becoming an MP, didn't he?"

"He did, yeah. When he became an MP, rather than lose him and his wide range of connections, they offered him a non-executive directorship. Someone with *MP* after his name and able to make connections for the company would be a bonus for the firm." He snorted with disdain. "It never ceases to amaze me there're still intelligent people out there who believe having *MP* after somebody's name is meaningful." He shook his head and laughed at his own cynicism.

As Clements spoke a thought flashed through my brain. Sampson had supposedly been blackmailed by Neville Thornwyn. I'd been told recently Thornwyn had been involved in a theft of weapons from a firm now owned by Bartolome Systems Ltd. Sampson had worked for this firm and been a non-executive director. Thornwyn was also a

———◉———

132

shareholder in the same firm. Could these all be linked in some way?

The look on my face must have suggested there was nothing at all contentious about what he was telling me. Clements recognised it.

"This is just background," he said. "There's some interesting political stuff as well, though."

"Like what?"

Clements leaned forward.

"Apparently, shortly before Sampson stood down from the House," he said softly, "this political reporter bloke and him met up for a spot of lunch. Sampson wanted somewhere private rather than their usual Westminster haunts, so they go someplace quiet."

"Why was this?"

"Sampson confided to this guy he's gay and has been living a double life for quite some time. He also said he was being blackmailed by someone, he didn't say who by and the guy doesn't know. Sampson was anxious about that but, just for good measure, he also said he'd been informed he was about to appear before the Parliamentary Intelligence and Security Committee and he was really worried."

This made me sit up and take notice. Smitherman had alluded to this. "Why's that?"

"The suspicion was he was involved in breaching the ban on selling weapons to certain organisations on the Government's proscribed hit list."

I knew what this list was. The British Government, like all others in a democracy, maintained a register of all organisations it had proscribed, meaning anyone joining or acting on behalf of these organisations was committing a criminal act just by so doing. This also meant UK firms were banned from doing business with such organisations because of their links to, or active supporting of, terrorism. Whilst the UK had a long and ignoble history of selling arms to nations where the record of promoting and enforcing human rights was suspect, to say the least, the official line was that the Government would only grant the necessary strategic export licences to reputable firms if it was certain the weapons or military equipment would not fall into terrorist hands, or the Government receiving them gave an undertaking not to use them on the civilian populace of their own nation. In reality the situation was very different. But, economically speaking, the sale of weaponry earned many billions for the UK revenue, which was why, despite the hand-wringing, governments of all political persuasions in the UK agreed to selling arms and military hardware.

"He worked for an arms manufacturer, though, didn't he?" I asked.

"True, but what he was suspected of had nothing to do with the official business of Bartolome Systems. Most of their business is with national governments. The committee was going to look into allegations made against Sampson of involvement in obtaining weapons and getting them into the hands of those who couldn't obtain them through the usual commercial channels."

"How'd he do that?"

"Story goes, he went to an arms fair in Abu Dhabi two years ago, ostensibly as one of the British Government's representatives, putting the case for why people shopping for their military hardware at this event should buy from firms in this country. He went with the S of S, the Secretary of State for Defence. At that time, before he was reshuffled across to the Home Office, he was Parliamentary Under-Secretary at Defence and involved in weapons procurement. Made sense, given his commercial background. But Sampson's also a director of Bartolome Systems, and the firm does business in the Middle East, so it couldn't hurt to have someone like him batting for them, could it? That's why Bartolome Systems were happy for him to go out there to the arms fair and, whilst there, see if he could put in a good word for them, rustle up a little business." He paused to drink some beer.

"Do I sense a *but* coming here?" I ventured.

"You do indeed. Leaving aside the fact it's a classic breach of the ministerial code of practice, lobbying for a private firm whilst on official Government business: at the arms fair, he gets linked up to people who're looking to acquire weapons but who can't get them in the normal way, if you get what I mean."

He raised his eyebrows to see if I did. I did.

"You mean groups involved in terrorism?"

"Correct. I mean, you're someone like al-Qaeda or Hamas, no Western business is gonna sell arms to you, is it? Not without getting all kinds of flak from their security services or their governments." He shrugged, almost indifferently. "So they have to get their weapons through other means. And one of these is to have an *in* with an arms company based outside their country. Someone who can get weapons for them but make it appear like it's all legitimate and above board; someone in a position to obtain the necessary licences to export such hardware and not raise any suspicions."

I thought about this for a couple of moments. "Sampson became the *in* for a terrorist group?" I wasn't sure I was going to like the answer Clements gave.

"So it would appear. He was doing business with a firm MI6 later confirmed was essentially a front for a terrorist organisation. Bartolome Systems gets duped by one of its own directors." He smiled broadly, lapping up the company's discomfort.

"Duped? What, you mean taken in?"

"Yup," he said, delightedly. "Through Sampson, Bartolome thought it was dealing with a reputable firm when it agreed in principle to supply weapons to them once the export licences were in place, but in reality it would have been supplying weapons which'd end up in the hands of a militant Islamist fundamentalist terrorist group. The company they dealt with was channelling anything they could acquire through an intermediary to a terrorist group. You know the group Muearada?"

I nodded. "I've heard of it."

"It fosters a global jihadist mentality. It's a very anti-Western group, known to have killed a few journalists and other Westerners it's encountered. This is the group behind the beheading of that American journalist last year. Anyone adhering to this lot is a committed jihadist, no question."

I was trying to take in how the director of a company like Bartolome Systems Ltd, a reputable UK arms manufacturer and a major player in the supply of military hardware and weaponry to the British Government, amongst others, could have been stung in so audacious a manner. Was Muearada that persuasive or was Sampson so negligent that he hadn't known whom he was dealing with? I thought about this for a few moments.

"How could Sampson be taken in like this? He'd worked for Bartolome for years. Surely he'd know the market and who his main competitors would have been," I ventured. "And if he didn't he'd have their bona fides ascertained first before they were sold anything."

"This guy thought that as well. But Sampson told him, and this is the key factor, Bartolome's teetering on the edge of bankruptcy; has been for a while. It's haemorrhaging money all over the place and so it was taking contracts anywhere it could get them. There was no *due diligence* check, evidently because Sampson was in Abu Dhabi representing Government. The firm Bartolome was dealing with through Sampson offered a contract worth close to twenty million, and Bartolome accepted what Sampson had negotiated for it. The Government's got lots of rollover contracts with Bartolome for continuous resupplying of equipment and armaments, and the firm would drop the military right in it if it went broke. So this capital injection would have been most useful, especially as they were going to pay upfront in one tranche."

It would indeed. Given how sensitive some of the military hardware that Bartolome supplied to the armed forces in the UK was, everything from missile guidance systems right down to flak jackets, for the company to go out of business would have been catastrophic for the armed forces and the Government.

If all this was correct, Sampson had much more to be concerned about than the financial aspirations of a venal police officer. MI6 would also have had him in their sights.

"So, what's happened since then?" I asked.

"It's all been hushed up. Can you imagine the embarrassment if this ever sees the light of day? When MI6 found out about it, they got it stopped. They slammed the lid on the whole thing and screwed it down tight. They made sure no strategic export licences were ever issued. No arms ever left the country and Bartolome's ended up scraping king-size dollops of egg off its chops." Clements was clearly pleased at the company's misfortune. "Couldn't have happened to a more deserving arms company."

I sipped some beer whilst taking in what Clements had told me. Paul Sampson's father-in-law was a director at Bartolome. Had he been a party to this decision?

"Did the board of directors know about this?" I asked.

"Preparations were being made for the agreement to go ahead, so you have to assume they did. You could hardly arrange for a sale of this magnitude behind their backs, could you?"

"And Bartolome's still in financial schtuck?"

"Not sure. I was told, behind the scenes, it's engaging in all kinds of financial restructuring trying to keep afloat." He drained his beer glass. "Bartolome's worried about this. If news of this gets out, and it hits the company's share price, that'd mean real trouble for the firm. Probably for Government as well."

I wasn't sure what I'd been expecting when I had arrived to meet Clements, but I'd not been expecting to hear this. Had Sampson been acting rashly, albeit with the best interests of the company in mind, or was there another agenda involved?

"And all this is on the level?" I asked.

"It is, yeah." Clements nodded his agreement. "Completely."

"*Really?*" I was sceptical.

"According to the guy I spoke to, that's what happened." Clements sipped his beer. "This guy's got good connections in the security services and he was told this by his contact inside MI6, someone he's liaised with for years. MI6'd received a tip-off from the CIA about arms and other hardware about to be sold by a British company being likely to end up with Muearada. They told this guy because news'll leak out sooner or later, some rumour or other about the company being in the shit or Sampson's role in it when he was still a Government minister. Everyone in politics and the media knows it's almost impossible to keep something like this quiet for too long. *Private Eye* probably already knows and is just waiting for the right time to publish it," he said, confidently, "so MI6 wanted to be sure, when news of this leaks out, it'll at least be reported by a journalist who knows the basic facts and whom it trusts to tell the story appropriately. It's classic news management; you anticipate something happening, so you prepare for it, and if it doesn't happen, you've at least covered your bases. He wouldn't have told me this unless his contact there had verified it." He was adamant.

"Which company was Sampson dealing with?"

"Company's called Endgame. It's based here, in London, though I don't know the address. Quite a shadowy firm, I'm told. I'm gonna try looking into it. Maybe there's something there we can write about."

I thought about what I'd heard for a few moments.

"One thing I don't get," I said. "Sampson was in Government when he went to Abu Dhabi. That means he'd travel with a sizeable entourage, a security detail, and quite possibly a couple of advisors, top civil servants who'd smooth the way in the initial negotiations with whichever host government they were dealing with. He wouldn't be going alone."

"Very likely," Clements agreed.

"Yet, somehow, Sampson ends up doing business with this Endgame firm. How'd he be able to negotiate with a firm like Endgame if he was there in a Government capacity?"

"You're asking *me*? I look like a fucking diplomat?" Clements laughed. "I've no idea but, however he did it, MI6 tumbled what he was doing. The issue was gonna go before the Intelligence and Security Committee as he was at the arms fair on Government business. I'm guessing it's to see if any other Government people were involved and whether there were any conflicts of interest. I wonder if the Defence Secretary knew about this," he mused.

I took stock of what I'd heard. "Sampson's now dead. What's the situation now?"

"That I don't know. This guy didn't say. I got the impression he doesn't know either. But it's obvious the spooks are gonna keep this buried if they can. Someone in Government involved with a firm like Endgame and Bartolome close to the financial rocks? What do you think?" he asked rhetorically.

It was difficult imagining Sampson having any sincere belief in the objectives of a group like Muearada. Yet it would appear he'd been involved in attempting to procure arms and other military hardware for them. It raised the question of whether he was acting alone in this or whether he was acting on behalf of someone else inside the world of arms procurement.

If what Clements had just told me was true, it would have

placed Sampson under an inordinate amount of pressure, especially if he intended to protest his innocence in the matter. Would he be able to *prove* he was innocent? Even though any investigation would have been behind closed doors, there was no guarantee some word of its deliberations wouldn't have been leaked to the media at some point in the proceedings. Given he was also being blackmailed by Neville Thornwyn about his sexuality, I could imagine Paul Sampson living the last period of his life experiencing very considerable anxiety.

What did Thornwyn know about this? Had he somehow been made aware of these allegations against Paul Sampson and been using them as leverage against him? Could this be why Sampson had refused to declare his sexuality in public?

I'd drifted off into my own world for a few moments.

"There's something else as well, Rob." Clements looked solemn. "This bloke doesn't believe Sampson committed suicide either."

"*What?*" This staggered me.

"Obviously he's no evidence to corroborate this view, but he's convinced Sampson's death had nothing to do with suicide. He doesn't believe Sampson was suicidal at all. He's convinced he was taken out to stop him talking if he ever went before the committee. That's partly why this guy agreed to talk to me; he was Sampson's friend and I got the impression he wants this out in the open when the time's right."

Geoffrey Tilling had also told me he believed Paul Sampson was murdered.

"*Holy Christ,*" I muttered. An ex-member of the Government eliminated. By whom? "I don't suppose this guy said who he suspects did it."

"He didn't, no, but it's a fairly easy guess, isn't it? Has to involve the security establishment in this country, doesn't it?"

There was a heavy silence between us for about ten

seconds whilst I assimilated everything I'd just heard. My head was spinning with notions of intrigue at the highest levels. Did we do state-sanctioned eliminations of those who the security service believed were threats to the security edifice of the nation? Clements would have no doubt. I wasn't sure.

"So, this any help to you, Rob?" Clements' voice brought me back to the present.

"Oh God, yeah, most definitely." I finished my beer. I wasn't sure how useful everything I'd heard was, but it was better knowing it than not knowing. I was pleased Geoffrey Tilling hadn't been listening to the last point Clements had made. "You're not planning to write about this, are you?" I asked.

"God, no. Not at the moment, anyway. I gave this guy my word we wouldn't, and I'm not gonna betray his confidence. When he gives me the all-clear, then the *Focus*'ll write something about it. What's Sampson done, anyway? Why are you looking into him?" Clements lapsed into political journalist mode.

"Tell you what." I smiled at him. "You don't ask and I won't lie to you." He'd know why I wasn't about to tell him, but I'd have been surprised if he'd not asked. "Suffice to say you'll know it when it happens."

His bus home wasn't expected for another twelve minutes, so I bought him another pint and told him how much I appreciated his help and that I definitely owed him a favour. I left him to sup it on his own.

Walking to the tube station, I wondered what I'd do or say if Smitherman ever looked me straight in the eye and asked if I'd seen his son-in-law recently and whether we passed information between each other. I respected him too much as a police officer and as a man for the idea of lying to him to be one I'd entertain. I just hoped he'd never ask.

SIX

Tuesday

I SAW A NOTE ON MY DESK asking me to call a DS Roberts. A number had been given. I was unsure who this officer was. I returned the call and he answered and identified himself as the DS I'd met yesterday in Bernie's flat.

"Thought you'd wanna know. The victim's been identified from his fingerprints. Name's Noel Partias. You know him?"

I said I didn't.

"Died from head injuries. Hit his head on something hard, probably that coffee table. The coroner thinks he might have survived if he'd got treated immediately. There were signs of a struggle, probably a fight from the bruises on his arms as they look like he was defending himself against attack. Had a couple of bruises on his face as well. Preliminary forensic investigation suggests he'd been dead a couple of weeks when you found him. You think Bernie could have done him?"

I replied saying, from what I knew of him, it was unlikely but couldn't be ruled out.

"We're naming him as the principal suspect. We're looking for him."

I immediately asked him to withhold naming Bernie as a suspect for the moment.

"Why's that?"

"Bernie's wanted by Special Branch for something unrelated to this, and he's gone into hiding. If he sees he's a murder suspect, it's likely he'll bury himself deeper. Look for him but don't name him, if that's okay with you? Also, don't name the victim, just say a body's been found and you're looking for next of kin. But, if you do find Bernie, I'd appreciate a call."

DS Roberts agreed that, for the moment, Bernie Rayes wouldn't be publically named as a murder suspect. I told Roberts I owed him a favour.

"Who's this Partias character anyway?" I asked. "You got anything on him?"

"I checked him out. A couple of convictions for assault and another for being caught in possession of stolen goods. Word is, though, he's a broker in the market for illegal firearms. I'm told by a few here who know him he arranges for the two parties to come together and he then takes a cut, but he's never been done for that. The whisper is he's being protected."

"Protected? By who?"

"Don't know."

"Thanks for this." I rang off.

With Thornwyn's help, Bernie had been involved in theft with Brian Turley. They'd stolen weaponry and, according to Turley, Bernie had the buyer lined up. Turley had mentioned the guns being bought by someone named Khaled al-Eloubi. Had Partias been the middle man, connecting Bernie to al-Eloubi? He'd been found dead in Bernie's flat, so it was logical to assume they knew each other. But who'd killed Partias and why? From what I'd learnt about Bernie the Buck I doubted he was capable of killing someone, but I couldn't rule it out definitively.

The even more worrying concern was al-Eloubi; he was a known jihadist with connections to the terrorist group Muearada. Weapons falling into his hands would almost certainly end up with those sworn to carry the jihad to the West at every opportunity. Were they for use in the UK, contrary to what Turley believed, or destined for further afield? As the death of Fusilier Lee Rigby had shown, committed jihadists could materialise anywhere and wreak a terrible revenge for what they perceived to be the West's crimes against Allah.

———◦———

There was also Thornwyn to consider. What was his role in all this? He'd provided the necessary intelligence for Turley and Bernie to steal weaponry and, if Turley was to be believed, had also cleared the shop manager during the post-robbery investigation. He also knew the weapons were destined for Khaled al-Eloubi.

Where did Paul Sampson fit into this pattern? I had to admit I didn't know. Clements had said Sampson had been duped into arranging to sell weapons to Endgame, an arms company, but the deal had been quashed by MI6 acting on a tip-off from the CIA.

Thornwyn was now in custody awaiting sentencing. I then remembered Smitherman telling me, when my going to talk to Thornwyn in Belmarsh was first mooted, that MI5 would almost certainly want to talk to him before the judge passed sentence. MI5 would need to ascertain how much of the national interest he'd harmed on top of his conviction for bribery and corruption, and this'd be reflected in whatever sentence was given to him.

Of the others, Turley had been suspended and was almost certain to be prosecuted for bribery and corruption at the very least, and Bernie the Buck was missing. Where did the deceased Noel Partias fit into this picture?

The only thing I knew for certain was Paul Sampson was dead, and if Clements' source was to be believed, it wasn't by his own hand either.

I entered the name *Endgame* into the computer's search engine to bring up their details. There was a file about the company but, when I clicked on the *open* button, a message in bright red lettering flashed continuously across the screen stating, *Restricted access only; permission to access denied.* I tried twice more, entering my password, but the same message appeared almost immediately. This suggested some involvement with MI5.

I typed the name *Noel Partias* and had better luck. He

was thirty-eight, Scottish and an ex-soldier. He was listed as being a mercenary, known to have fought in armed conflicts on two different continents. When not fighting for whatever cause, he was known to be involved in arms dealings and was suspected of involvement in at least two heists of weapons and military hardware in the Middle East.

What had begun just over eleven days ago with interviewing a disgraced CID commander about the resignation of a now deceased parliamentary under-secretary had morphed into something very different. Thornwyn had alluded to my not being told the big picture when I'd spoken to him, and Smitherman had been reluctant to expand on this when I'd talked to him last week.

Bizarrely, there was also the left-field issue of my being followed by Gillian Redmond, who I believed had been hired to tail me by Bartolome Systems. Where did *that* fit into the scheme of things?

I needed to make sense of all the pieces of information, and I realised I knew someone who could help.

She answered her mobile almost as soon as I'd finishing dialling her number. I asked if we could meet up as I wanted to sound her out about a case I was involved in. She agreed to meet for an early lunch. The thought of a few minutes in her company and looking at her across the table was a delightful one. My day was getting better.

Christine Simmons was an MI5 operative and only a heartbeat away from being the woman of my dreams. I'd first encountered her when she was undercover penetrating Red Heaven and we were both part of the operation to prevent a bomb being planted near to the Albert Hall. She'd shot and killed David Kader, a renegade MI5 agent who had supposedly also been undercover but was now known to have been acting for Red Heaven. She was drop-dead gorgeous but she'd been married quite recently to someone in MI5 who also worked for her boss, the loathsome Colonel

Peter Stimpson, so, sadly for me, my dreams were where she was likely to remain.

We were meeting in a little Italian place she knew by Pimlico tube station, so I decided to walk from the office. She arrived five minutes late and, when she saw me and smiled, I felt giddy and lightheaded, like a teenage boy waiting for his first girlfriend. Sitting opposite and staring across at her was likely to be the best part of my day. She had beautiful hair and for a second I briefly fantasised about what it'd be like to spend three weeks kissing her but then, just as quickly, told myself to behave.

We both had a cappuccino and shared antipasto salad and garlic bread. We had a brief chat about the new flat she and her new husband were buying in Lambeth as it was near to their office, and how much she was liking married life, which I tried not to let upset me.

"So, whatever happened about your friend Mendoccini? Police and security looked extensively for him, watching airports and all that, but he was never picked up. We've since learnt he's back in Italy. How'd he do that?" she wondered.

"I've no idea. I've not seen him since I chased him through Soho." The last part was true, but the other part wasn't. I knew *exactly* how he'd managed to escape because he'd called me from Italy soon after and told me how. But I wasn't going to let on I knew how he'd done it.

"The assumption is he got a lift out of the country from a lorry driver, though they aren't sure which port he went from. They're presuming it was Dover. So many lorries come and go across the Channel every day and searching them all would have been a nightmare. It would almost have meant instigating Operation Stack." She grinned.

"Sounds plausible." I maintained a neutral expression.

She stared at me quizzically for a moment, as if expecting me to say, *No, that's not quite how he got away,* but I kept a straight face. I couldn't explain why, but I didn't want the security people to know I knew exactly he'd left the country, though I'd absolutely no doubt I'd be in serious trouble if Stimpson discovered I knew how he'd escaped.

"Oh, well." She finally shrugged and took a large gulp of her cappuccino. "So, what did you wanna ask me?"

"I'm trying to find details about a company called Endgame but I've been denied access to anything about it on the Branch site, which makes me think there's an MI5 connection somewhere. Why else can't the Branch access a site?"

She smiled and nodded slightly whilst she thought. "Why do you need to know about Endgame?" she asked pleasantly.

After considering what I could tell her, I said I was looking into allegations of arms dealings and the company's name had come up on a couple of occasions. I said I believed it also involved Bartolome Systems, though I wasn't quite sure how just yet.

She finished some of her salad.

"You know what Stimpson'd say if he saw me with you," she said, semi-seriously, "and what he'd say if he knew what you were asking? He's not forgiven you for Mendoccini getting away. He still believes you didn't try hard enough to bring him in 'cause you two're old friends and he thinks you can't be trusted."

"I love him too," I retorted sarcastically. "Anyway, pardon my lapse into Latin, but *fuck* what he thinks."

Her face lit up as she laughed at my crudity. It'd been worth being crude just to see her smile.

"Good job Smitherman backs you up. I heard him telling Stimpson you're a first-class operative and he has full confidence in you," she said. Good for Smitherman. "Okay. I'll trust you to be discreet, and I realise you'd not be asking unless you had a good reason, so I'll just tell you this. MI5's aware of Endgame and what it does."

"Does this have anything to do with Paul Sampson's dealings with them being investigated by the Intelligence and Security Committee?"

"How did you know about *that*?" She looked amazed.

"Would you believe I asked someone and that's what they told me?" I smiled at her, but she was in work mode and didn't return it.

"Well, I don't know who told you, but that's classified material. Stimpson ever finds out you know about this, he'll go berserk. This is MI5 territory."

"So it's true, then? Sampson *was* about to be questioned by the committee when he took his own life." Richard Clements had clearly tapped into some top-secret information. Whoever he'd spoken to had been right in what he'd told him.

"Yes, it is," she finally agreed.

"My sources tell me he was supposedly dealing with Endgame, believing them to be reputable arms dealers when in fact they're a front company for Muearada."

"I can't comment on any of that. You shouldn't even know what you do. It's something MI5 are investigating. I shouldn't even be telling you this." She sounded concerned.

"You can trust me." I smiled at her. "Did you also know Sampson was being blackmailed?"

The look of shock and surprise on her face told me she'd not known about this. "Blackmailed? By who?"

"Before I tell you, did MI5 know he was gay, which was *why* he was being blackmailed? Someone had found out and, because Sampson didn't come out, they were squeezing him, so I'm wondering if it was just money he paid out for silence. Is this part of the reason for the investigation?"

"I don't know the full details. There'd been rumours he was gay but they'd never been substantiated. I just know some of his dealings from the final few months of his life were being investigated by the committee."

I tried imagining the strain Sampson must have been under in the period before he resigned and then just before he took his own life.

"Is there any reason to investigate Bartolome Systems?" I asked.

————◆◇◆————

"That I definitely can't talk about."

"So there is," I stated with certainty.

She drained her cappuccino and didn't reply. I sipped some more of mine.

"You know who was blackmailing Sampson?" Before I could answer she leapt in again. "Actually, no, don't tell me just yet. Let's see what comes out of the investigation. It may be nobody need know about it, if it's even true."

I paid the bill, overriding her desire to pay half. We left the restaurant together. On the corner of Vauxhall Bridge Road we stopped. She thanked me for lunch and said she was on her way back to the office and we should keep in touch concerning this case. I agreed we should without making it too obvious I wanted to see her again.

As she spoke, I looked over her shoulder and, out of the corner of my eye, I noticed a woman about fifty yards away, wearing a black lightweight jacket, white T-shirt and tight blue jeans, attempting to be inconspicuous whilst looking around at nothing and trying not to look in my direction. Gillian Redmond.

I shook hands with Christine and she walked away towards Vauxhall Bridge. I turned left and walked like I was in a hurry along the road leading towards Victoria station. If Redmond did the same, this would confirm she was on my tail again.

At the junction with Rochester Row I crossed over and turned right, heading north towards Victoria Street. I cast a furtive glance back as I crossed the road and could see her walking fast to keep up in case she lost me in the lunchtime crowds. Once around the corner I sprinted quickly to nearby Vane Street and ducked behind a parked van. Ten seconds later I saw her walk past. She'd quickened her pace and was anxiously looking around as I wasn't in sight. She looked behind but couldn't see me, so she kept walking on. I followed.

She stopped at the corner by Horseferry Road and looked

in both directions. She was about to cross over when I caught up with her.

"You sure I went that way?" I said evenly, standing behind her. She spun around and saw me smiling at her. She turned to walk away but I grabbed her arm and stopped her. "Ah, ah, sweetheart, either you tell me why you're following me or I'm arresting you and charging you with obstruction."

She struggled to try and break my grip. A builder waiting to cross the road saw what was happening, nodded to his friend and they came over.

"You alright, love? This bloke bothering you?" he asked, nodding at me with disdain whilst the other stood nearby.

I produced ID. "She's under arrest, guys. Nothing for you here. Move on," I said firmly.

As they walked away she stopped struggling. I released my grip. There was a stand-off of sorts for a moment. She was out of options and she knew it.

"Look, you're not under arrest, okay? But I wanna know why, every time I turn around, I'm tripping over you."

She realised she'd been caught out. I'd thought she was lousy at following me the first time I'd sussed her out eleven days back and saw no reason to change my mind now. If I were a client paying money for her services, I'd want a substantial refund.

"You don't tell me why you're on my case, I'm gonna go straight to Bartolome and make so much stink, you and them'll choke on it. I'll also get my boss to make inquiries with MI6, 'cause I know you used to work for them. He can make your life with your agency really uncomfortable. And I'll talk to my mate Gavin over at Prevental, see what he has to say about this."

At the mention of Gavin's name, her eyes opened wide in surprise.

"Gavin's an old friend; known him for years," I assured her. This wasn't strictly true but she didn't know that. "How'd you think I sussed you so quick?" I paused for a moment. "So, how badly do you want me to ruin your day?"

She took a few deep breaths and then sighed, almost exasperatedly. I waited.

"Is there somewhere we can talk?"

I agreed there probably was.

We walked further along and turned into Strutton Ground, and found an almost empty café. She didn't want to sit outside as a couple of tables still bore the residue from pigeons using them for target practice, so we took a table inside by the window. We both had an outrageously overpriced Earl Grey tea served in chipped cups.

Seeing her close up for the first time I could see she was a reasonably attractive woman but not in Christine Simmons' class. Few women were. I don't know why, but I noticed she was wearing a wedding ring. I looked directly at her across the small table. Somehow she seemed so much smaller sitting back against the chair.

"Before I say anything," she said, "I wanna thank you for helping my younger sister that time. She's really grateful for what you did. The whole family was."

"Huh? What're you talking about?" I was curious.

"About eighteen months ago my sister was taken hostage in a pub in Bayswater. Some scumbag held a knife to her throat. You helped get her out from under that. Thanks."

I thought for a moment, then realised what she was alluding to.

Louis and Paulie Phipps, being pursued by an assassin named Phil Gant, had taken refuge in a bar owned by my friend Mickey Corsley and had held Mickey, his wife and another woman hostage. The woman, Amanda Redmond, had only entered the bar looking for help to change a flat tyre. I'd been called in and helped get her away from the situation unscathed before Gant shot and killed the Phipps brothers. Now I was being followed by her older sister for reasons I hoped I was about to discover.

"She's your sister? Small world, eh?" I smiled. "No

---

problem, all part of the service. Glad she's alright. I hope she's none the worse for her experience."

"No, she's fine. We saw the pictures on the front of the evening paper, the two dead bodies. No one was ever arrested for that, were they?"

"No, whoever shot them was never identified." I didn't bother telling her I knew exactly who'd killed the Phipps brothers but couldn't prove it.

"When I was asked to follow you, your name sounded familiar, so I checked you out and found it was you who'd helped Amanda. Ironic, eh?" She almost smiled.

"Isn't it just?"

There was a five-second silence.

"So you're not denying you're following me," I began.

"What do you want to know?" she asked.

"First off, anything you tell me'll be in confidence, okay? I won't let on where I heard it from. Fair enough?"

She nodded.

"So, I wanna know why Bartolome Systems wants me followed. It *is* them you're working for, isn't it? How have I made it onto their hit list? Have I done something to upset them?" I asked directly.

She registered surprise at the question. She didn't say anything at first, marshalling her thoughts.

I waited a few seconds, then spoke again. "When I lost you the other Saturday coming from St James's Park, CCTV tracked you all the way to Prevental's HQ in Mayfair. I told you earlier, I know someone who works there. He told me they'd been approached by a leading manufacturer looking for someone to do some legwork for them. He wouldn't tell me who, though. I became suspicious when you were following me out of Berkhamsted next day. I'd been there talking to a woman whose deceased husband worked for Bartolome. You follow me back from there. I then track you coming out of your office in Chancery Lane, all the way to Bartolome's office in Holborn, and they confirmed they'd hired you, in a roundabout kind of way."

I paused and drank some tea.

"That'd explain how you'd *know* I was gonna be in Berkhamsted on the Sunday. The woman's father also works for Bartolome; he's a director, so he was probably instrumental in your being hired. I'm right, aren't I?" I grinned at her.

She sat in silence for a few moments, wondering whether to reply. I'd clearly caught her out. She grimaced for a moment, then appeared to relax.

"You'd been to see Paul Sampson's wife," she said.

"So? How's she of interest to you?"

She took a few deep breaths to compose herself.

"Okay." She looked serious. "A couple of weeks ago, we were contacted by Prevental, offering our agency a job, asked if we were interested. I went along to see them, hear what they were offering us."

"*Us* being DeeCee Inc.," I said.

"Yeah. Prevental introduced me to someone from Bartolome Systems. He said he had a delicate problem needing to be resolved and he thought, as we came highly recommended, we could help them resolve it."

"What did they want?"

"He didn't go into full details. He just said the company had been the victim of industrial espionage and had lost some vitally important documentation concerning weapons designs and blueprints, stuff like that which'd been stolen from their R&D department. He said there was nothing compromising in them. They were mainly just ideas; designers thinking out loud, blue sky thinking, what they could make if money were no object, how certain things could be improved or updated, plans for prototypes, that kind of thing. Nothing too specific. But what he was *really* worried about was the firm losing some highly sensitive financial information."

———◇———

153

"Like what?"

"Profit projections, cash flow forecasts for the next financial year. Confidential aspects of the firm's financial health and viability. These were taken from the chief accountant's office. He was particularly concerned about a bank letter which'd also gone missing, detailing how the firm was well over its overdraft limit and further lines of credit were unlikely unless the firm took steps to reduce its borrowings. He was worried about the impact on the company if this fell into unauthorised hands or if the media got hold of these details and published them. He said the company's share price'd collapse if they got into the press."

"So, how does this lead to you following me? *I* haven't got them," I said only part-flippantly, raising my eyebrows to emphasise the point.

"I'll come on to that in a moment." She was still looking serious. "The company's pretty certain it knows who's responsible for the theft of all this information but hasn't been able to definitively establish whether its suspect actually did take the documents. This person's one of only a very small number of people who'd have direct access to both the financial and the R&D documentation, so Bartolome decided to launch a private search for them. It got in touch with us. We've investigated and checked out everyone inside the company who'd have had access to one or both sets of information but so far have drawn a blank."

"Nothing personal, but why did Bartolome come to you? Why didn't it just go to the police? Something of this magnitude's clearly a police matter. They've specialists for this kind of investigation."

"As I just mentioned, the company wanted this kept under wraps. What it's lost is highly confidential and it wanted it kept that way. But, more importantly, it didn't want the police involved because it thought it might compromise the search for what's been lost."

"Huh? What do you mean?" I wasn't sure I understood.

"It was believed police were involved in this and the company didn't know how far this extended."

"*What?* Bartolome Systems thought the police were involved in stealing confidential information from the company?"

"No, just one policeman. Commander Neville Thornwyn."

It felt like a kick in the solar plexus. Thornwyn also involved in industrial espionage? I knew about his blackmailing of Paul Sampson and, through Turley, his involvement in the stealing of weapons from Byzantium and the possible connection to Khaled al-Ebouli. Both reprehensible enough on their own, but, if what Gillian Redmond was saying was true, this was simply staggering. Was this the bigger picture Smitherman had alluded to when I'd last spoken to him?

"Commander Thornwyn," I blurted out.

"Yes, your old skipper. That's who Bartolome thought was involved in stealing sensitive and confidential company information, and the company thinks he had help doing it."

"That's almost unbelievable," I stressed.

"Is it really?" she said in a challenging tone. "Bartolome believes he was working in conjunction with one of its employees to steal this information and use it to hold the company to ransom."

"Which employee?" Somehow I just knew which name was coming.

"Paul Sampson," she replied after a few seconds' pause.

"Paul Sampson?"

"Yeah. He's who I was alluding to just now when I mentioned it not being easy to ascertain exactly who was involved. Sampson took his own life recently but Bartolome still thinks he was working with Thornwyn in purloining this information."

"Bartolome really believes this?"

155

"That's right," she agreed. "It thinks one of its own non-executive directors was stealing confidential commercial information from it."

"Assuming what you say's true, why would he do this?"

"I've no idea, and I can't exactly ask him, can I?" A rare flash of humour. "I don't know the man, but the company believes it was him, so that's what I go along with until Bartolome tells me otherwise."

I knew Sampson had been blackmailed by Thornwyn. I'd no idea how much he was paying Thornwyn, but the thought dawned on me that Thornwyn had also been bringing in money from the scams he'd been running whilst in charge of the team I'd been a member of for a few years and, knowing him as I did, I could imagine the delight he'd take in knowing he could really stick his claws into a victim. So had Sampson been coerced into paying Thornwyn in company secrets to keep him quiet? As a director of Bartolome, albeit a non-executive one, and with a father-in-law who was also production director, with responsibility for R&D, how difficult would it have been for Paul Sampson to gain access to important and confidential material inside Bartolome Systems?

But, if there was already a tenuous connection between Khaled al-Ebouli and Thornwyn, did this involve secret information being traded as well?

"Sampson was known to be seen with Thornwyn several times in the period before he took his own life," Redmond said. "It was around this time the company became aware of the missing information. Sampson would have had access to it. Thornwyn's also now a convicted corrupt policeman."

I couldn't disagree with the last point.

"Besides, this is what the security service thinks as well. Bartolome's an important player in the defence industry and the Government was also concerned about all this information falling into the wrong hands. So we were asked to help look for what Bartolome'd lost."

I thought about what I'd heard for a few moments. "This is all very interesting, but how does all this lead to you following *me* around?"

"MI5 learnt Thornwyn had asked to see you just after he was convicted two weeks ago. His whole team was under suspicion for being corrupt, and I know at least two have been suspended pending further inquiries, *ergo* the suspicion you were in it with him. MI5 thought he might have been going to tell you where the documentation that'd been stolen was, so, through them, the decision was taken to have you followed. I was told to follow you, see who you met and where you went."

My eyes had opened wide in utter surprise. "*What?* They thought *I* was in it with Thornwyn?"

"That's why MI5 wanted you tailed." She nodded as she spoke. "It was they who contacted Bartolome when the concern about lost confidential information was first mooted. So Bartolome contacted Prevental, who, in turn, got in touch with us. The woman you were just talking to? Her boss is the one who was in contact with Prevental. He's also my uncle, which is how our agency got the job pushed our way. That should answer your question about why they'd use us. You know people in MI5."

I felt a mild nausea rise up in me, like I'd eaten something unwholesome.

"Your uncle being Peter Stimpson. Colonel Peter Stimpson." I said this calmly, so as not to make her realise I thought he was a pompous jackass.

"Yes, that's right." She smiled. "He's my mum's older brother. You know him, I believe."

"Yeah, our paths have crossed." I didn't mention it'd been unpleasant each time. "And he thinks *I'm* somehow part of this scheme to steal confidential plans from Bartolome Systems and blackmail the firm." I said this neutrally, trying to conceal my irritation.

"They had to be sure you weren't. So I was told to tail you, see where you went, who you spoke to. That kind of thing."

———◄◊►———

I spent a few moments thinking dark thoughts about Colonel Stimpson but didn't dwell on them as my mood would have turned very hostile. I continued. "They're sure it's Thornwyn?"

"It all points to him. Sampson was in the company's head office more than he usually was before doing what the company thinks he's done." She looked knowingly at me. "This coincided with the information going missing. As I said, he and Thornwyn were also seen together quite a lot during the same time. The belief is Sampson stole the information and passed it to Thornwyn, who's secreted it someplace safe. You going to see Thornwyn raised the suspicion you were also involved because he was supposed to be being kept isolated, yet one of his old team was allowed to go visit him . . ." Her voice tailed off, as if to say *you know what I mean*.

"I was *told* by my boss to go see him, see what he knew about another case we were working on. That's easily verifiable. I didn't even *know* about this and I'd not even *heard* of Bartolome Systems till last week." I emphasised the point.

She said nothing in response.

"Are you actually working for Bartolome Systems or MI5?" I asked.

"Let's just say MI5 has more than a passing interest in the case because of the strategic importance of Bartolome Systems. But, officially, I'm doing this for Bartolome."

"So, am I still a suspect?"

"I've not found anything, if that's what you're wondering. We've had you looked into but nothing's come up."

"That's not an answer."

She shrugged and sipped her Earl Grey.

"When you followed me from Berkhamsted, you were tipped off by Jeremy Godfrey, weren't you? I was there to talk to his daughter about her late husband and he was also present. He came outside with me when I left." I thought about when I'd left. "Yeah, of course, you'd see me and him

———◦———

158

together and you'd know which car you had to follow. That'd also explain how he knew my name. I'd not told him but he knew me, knew who I was."

She sat looking at me and didn't respond.

"He's the production director at Bartolome Systems. He'd know exactly what the significance of the missing documentation was. He was probably the one you spoke to at Prevental. His son-in-law's a suspect in this. Yeah, it was Godfrey who hired you." I stated this with certainty.

Her expression didn't change and she still didn't respond. It didn't matter. At least I now had some idea why she was following me. I wondered briefly whether she'd been behind me when I'd been to Bernie's flat or to talk to Turley.

Smitherman had told me, just after Thornwyn's conviction, that the team Thornwyn had been running when I'd first joined CID was tainted with corruption and everyone was likely to be investigated. Turley and John Paine had been suspended and Larry Jasper had transferred out before the shit had really hit the fan. Were Gillian Redmond's claims about my being suspected of involvement in the theft of Bartolome's information part of this?

"So, you satisfied now? You have any more questions for me?" she asked.

"Yeah, several, but just one for the moment. You still gonna be tailing me?"

She shrugged her shoulders, almost lazily. "Don't know."

"I see you behind me again," I said, standing up, "you know what'll happen."

"Is that a threat?" she said as I left the café. I didn't respond.

Bartolome Systems Ltd had its main production facility just outside Berkhamsted, in the heart of some quite delightfully leafy Hertfordshire countryside. It was set in the middle of what had once been an RAF base, and I could see what appeared to be an aircraft hangar, a series of Portakabins clustered around it and an ugly purpose-built five-storey office block clearly as I came off the A41 and drove along the winding lane leading to its car park. There was ten-foot-high chain link fencing, topped with barbed wire, running along the perimeter and I saw several signs stating that unauthorised entry onto the site was strictly prohibited and a criminal offence. I could see CCTV cameras every couple of hundred yards. There was a barrier at the entrance to the car park and, as I didn't possess a swipe card, I stopped by the sentry box and showed ID to the guard, who raised the barrier to admit me.

I pulled into the parking area reserved for senior managers and took great delight in parking in the space reserved for a Dereck Liddiart, whoever he might be. There was an expensive-looking BMW in Jeremy Godfrey's parking space. Walking towards the main building, I could see a man wearing some kind of uniform coming towards me.

"Oi, directors only. You can't park there," he said sternly as he approached me. "Visitors' car park's over there." He pointed across the car park.

I showed my ID. "You're quite sure about that?" I stared him down and he walked away.

I'd been angry after leaving Gillian Redmond, although the drive had calmed me down slightly. The belief I was some part of a scheme to rob Bartolome had stuck in my throat. Even worse, I was suspected of working with Thornwyn. But I'd been particularly aggrieved to learn MI5 was involved *and* I was being followed by someone related to Colonel Stimpson.

It wasn't rocket science. Bartolome loses confidential information; Thornwyn and Sampson are suspected of involvement; I once served under Thornwyn and, because he's corrupt and I once worked in his team, and because I visited him in Belmarsh, I must be involved as well, so I end up with the hapless Gillian Redmond on my tail. I'd decided to put my questions about this situation to Jeremy Godfrey himself.

I saw the sign requiring all visitors to the compound to *report to reception*, so I entered the main building. I showed ID at reception and asked for Jeremy Godfrey.

The woman behind the desk looked at me suspiciously. "I think he might be busy just now."

"Well, un-busy him," I suggested firmly. "Tell him it's very important I see him."

Still staring at me as though there was something growing out the side of my head, she made a call, listened, then hung up. I was informed I'd have to leave my mobile phone at reception as no cameras were allowed into the building for security reasons. I did.

"Take the lift to the fourth floor. You'll be met there," she said, handing me a visitor's lanyard which I slid into my pocket, much to her annoyance.

As the lift door opened I was met by a man who asked me to follow him. I did. He led me along the corridor and into what I assumed was Godfrey's office. It was sumptuous and well-furnished but also devoid of occupancy.

"He'll be here shortly," I was assured by my guide.

After taking in all the fixtures and fittings and trappings of the executive lifestyle, I was standing by the window, looking at the Hertfordshire countryside and seeing if I could spot my car in the car park, when the door behind me opened and, as Jeremy Godfrey entered the room, the other man left. Godfrey was holding a couple of files under his arm, which he dropped onto his desk.

"Bloody meetings," he muttered to himself. He then walked across to me and extended his right arm to shake hands. I reciprocated. "Jeremy Godfrey. We've met before, haven't we?"

"Yeah, at your daughter's house last week."

"That's right." He nodded his agreement and gestured for me to sit. I did.

—◇—

"So, what brings you up here to Bartolome HQ?" he began.

"I'd like to know why this company hired Gillian Redmond to have me followed," I said evenly. I sat back in this extremely comfortable chair.

"What do you mean?"

"I spoke to her earlier today. I'd already tailed her to your firm's London offices and the woman I spoke to refused to confirm or deny my claim, so when I caught Redmond earlier today I put it to her she was working for this firm. She confirmed this company hired her agency, DeeCee Inc., to tail me, but she wouldn't tell me why. So that's why I'm here. I'd like to know why."

He stared at me and nodded, like he was thinking. I waited five seconds.

"Are you denying it?" I asked.

"I'm not commenting on it, is what I'm doing."

"So you're agreeing with it."

He made no comment. I waited a few moments.

"How did you know who I was when I was at your daughter's house last weekend?"

"Martha must have told me," he said glibly. "How else would I have known? She said someone was coming to talk to her about Paul."

He was lying. She hadn't, because the first she knew about me was when I arrived at her door. I decided to jump straight in and ascertain his reaction to a few things I'd heard.

"So, are you any nearer to locating all those confidential documents from R&D you lost? I'm led to believe there's some sensitive stuff on them."

That got his attention. He looked at me with a surprised expression.

"What about the financial info, you any closer to retrieving that? It'd knock your share price down a bit if information about the company's precarious financial situation got into the press, wouldn't it?"

"How on earth do you know about all this?" he gasped as though drowning. "It's supposed to be top secret."

I didn't answer immediately. I was enjoying his discomfort. The fact of someone knowing the situation inside Bartolome was clearly a source of distress to him. I wasn't going to tell him it'd been Gillian Redmond. She was just following instructions in tailing me and, whilst I thought she couldn't even follow goldfish in a bowl successfully, I didn't want to drop her in it. She was just doing her job.

"How do you think? I'm a detective; I'm working a case and I've spoken to several people and heard things. I asked someone I trust in MI5 why I was being tailed working this case and was told what I've just told you. I can't get to grips with why my doing my job has led to Bartolome putting someone on my tail, so I'd like to know why. What am I supposed to have done to deserve your kind consideration?" Sarcasm abounded. "Or is it your belief I was involved in removing what your firm's lost?"

He sat quietly for a few moments, then he stood up quite abruptly. "I'm sorry, but I really can't talk to you about any of this. You know how important this company is to the UK's defence effort?"

"Colonel Stimpson tell you to say that, did he?" I smiled.

Fleetingly his expression changed. He was surprised to hear Stimpson's name, but a split second later he regained his composure. "I don't know who you mean. Now, you really will have to leave. I've nothing to say to you and I'm very busy today," he blustered.

I leaned forward slightly. "I hope you're not planning to follow your son-in-law into politics."

He looked confused. "Why's that?"

"Because you're a bloody poor liar, Jeremy, that's why." I laughed. "You ever wanna be a politician, you gotta learn to spin bullshit a lot better than you've just done."

"Are you calling me a liar?" He looked annoyed.

I didn't answer. I got up to leave, then stopped and turned

to face him again. "Oh, yeah, before I forget, you alluded to Paul Sampson being gay when I was at your daughter's house. Why're you so sure he was?"

"Because I *know* he was, that's why." He was on firmer ground now, more sure of the facts of the situation. He was back in control. "I could never put my finger on it, but there was always that *something* about him making me think he was homosexual. I think the modern vogue term is *gaydar*. I wanted to know, so I put someone on to keeping an eye on him. They followed him for a while and found he had a lovenest near London Bridge, sharing it with some senior civil servant. They'd been an item for some years, I was told."

He stopped for a moment. I wondered if he'd used Gillian Redmond.

"All those nights when he told my daughter he'd be in the House working late and would stay in his London flat," he sneered, "he was staying with his boyfriend." He spat out *boyfriend* like he was chewing something bitter. "*That's* what I meant when I told you to ask his boyfriend, because I knew he had one, you see? I knew he was leading a double life. This Geoffrey had even been to my house; came to a barbecue. He was introduced as a work colleague," he said, disbelievingly.

"Did Paul know you knew?" I asked.

"Too bloody right he did," he said firmly, chest thrusting outwards. "I went to his house soon afterwards when my daughter wasn't home and confronted him with what the PI I'd put on him had found. After we'd argued for a while, he eventually admitted it was all true. He said he loved this guy, Geoffrey whatever his bloody name was. I asked if he intended to leave my daughter but he said no, he was going to stay with her as he wanted to see my granddaughter grow up. I wasn't happy with that, and I told him so."

"What was his response?"

"Got quite annoyed. Told me to mind my own sodding business and leave his family alone. I told him it was to be my daughter or his manfriend, but he couldn't have both. I was insistent about that. My daughter's happiness is everything to me, Inspector, and I wasn't about to see her be played for a fool by my son-in-law."

I didn't mind being called *Inspector*, so I didn't correct him.

"I think I might also have said something about getting him kicked off the board of directors if he didn't make the right decision." He said this almost as an afterthought. "That really shook him up."

"So what then?"

"Nothing. He resigned a little while later and, well, you know what he did." He shrugged.

Paul Sampson must have spent the last year of his life experiencing the kind of existential angst I couldn't even begin to get a handle on. His public identity, a prominent Tory MP with a position in Government, a family man married with a small child, director at a large manufacturing company, the very exemplar of a modern Conservative Party success story, contrasted starkly with his private persona ... involved in a loving homosexual relationship with a senior civil servant, and with a part share in a flat in Borough where he took ecstasy and enjoyed the kind of liberated spiritual freedom his public life could never afford him. Small wonder Thornwyn's blackmailing had produced such pain in his life.

If only he and Tilling hadn't been so brazenly stupid in that car park.

"We think Paul was being blackmailed before he died," I said. "You know anything about that?"

"No, I don't." He shook his head. "Who's supposed to have been blackmailing him?"

"I don't know; that's what I'm trying to discover. That's why I was at your daughter's house last week, asking if she had any idea about it."

I was a better liar than he was. He bought my story.

Thanking him for his time, I left and began the drive back to London. I didn't see Gillian Redmond behind me. I again wondered if it had been her who'd been put on to following Paul Sampson.

I was cruising back along the A41, thinking about the past few hours. Gillian Redmond had confirmed Bartolome had put a tail on me, and I now knew why, and Jeremy Godfrey had refused to deny I was being tailed on his company's request because of the suspicion I was involved in the heist of confidential information from the company. It was dispiriting to know it was one of Stimpson's relatives who'd been following me. Even more dispiriting to know Stimpson had helped put them on to me.

What did Smitherman know about any of this? Stimpson had to have told him one of his team was under suspicion of being involved in the theft of confidential material from a manufacturer that supplied weaponry and military hardware to the British armed forces. It was just as well Christine Simmons had told me earlier I had Smitherman's full confidence.

I was idly thinking about what Gavin Dennison had said about freelancing for Prevental and wondering what I could earn there when my musing was interrupted by the chimes of my mobile phone. I laid it on the front passenger seat and put it on speaker. It was Andy Harris.

"Mr Jack, I'm just outside the pub in Chalk Farm with my lady friend, we're watching the racing . . ."

"Your lady friend?" *Harris has a girlfriend?* I was so surprised I almost veered across into the traffic in the fast lane. I was intensely curious as to what type of woman could look at Harris and see boyfriend material. Was she in full possession of her critical faculties?

"Yeah, we come here to watch the racing. The guy I put my bets on with drinks in here. Saves going to the bookies." He sounded pleased with the arrangement. "Anyway, I'm at the bar just now getting her another G&T – she can't half bloody put 'em away, you know – when I hears this bloke next to me talking to the landlord. The landlord was asking if he knew where Bernie was as he's Bernie's mate and Bernie ain't been seen in the pub for a while and there's been a couple of coppers coming round looking for him."

I refrained from telling Harris I'd been one of them.

"Bernie also has a bloody big tab at the bar which he ain't paid off yet and the landlord was saying he wants his money soon. This geezer next to me says he knows where Bernie is, he's staying with him 'cause there's some copper after him who's threatened to kill him, and he's scared, so he's lying low. This bloke was telling the landlord to let him know how much Bernie owed and he'll see it gets squared away."

This was positive news. After the past few hours I needed some. I was definitely interested.

"Andy, this is very important. Do you know who it was talking about Bernie?"

"He ain't a mate or anything but, yeah, I know who he is."

"Who is he?"

"He's known as Little Des. He's always round here."

"Where can I find this Little Des character?" I started to increase my speed.

"He's still here in the pub, ain't he?"

"I'm about fifteen to twenty minutes away from the pub, so keep an eye on this character but don't make it too obvious. I wanna talk to this bloke. It's very important I find Bernie."

"Okay, Mr Jack, I'll do that."

"Incidentally, is that *my* money you're gambling with?" I was indignant.

"Well, you know how it is, Mr Jack, you gotta speculate to accumulate, ain't ya?" He laughed inanely. I rang off, hit the siren and pulled out into the fast lane.

Twelve minutes later I pulled up in Prince of Wales Road, around the corner from the pub. I phoned Harris. He answered.

I leapt straight in. "Andy, don't speak, just listen. Is this guy still there? If he is, cough."

He coughed. He sounded like a seal with a sore throat.

"Okay, I'm gonna come in. Don't talk to me when you see me and don't take what's gonna happen personally."

"Huh, what—"

I rang off.

I went into the pub. There were some people gathered by the television watching the racing and a few solitary drinkers by the counter. I saw Harris and his lady friend sitting in the corner. My interest in knowing what kind of woman would want anything to do with Harris had to take second place for the moment, so I avoided looking at her.

"Harris, you slimy little bastard, I've been looking everywhere for you," I called out when I was about twenty feet away from him. As I approached his table he looked like a rabbit caught in oncoming headlights, unsure of exactly what was about to happen.

I grabbed his jacket collar and pulled him out of his seat and pushed him against the wall. I put my face close to his. "What did I tell you about nicking stuff from the market, eh? Didn't I tell you about that?" I prodded him a couple of times. "Didn't I tell you to stay away from there?" I said in a firm loud voice, then I quickly whispered, "Which one is he?"

"Yeah. Yeah, you did, I'm sorry," he stammered nervously, then he quietly said, "It's 'im by the bar, with the glasses."

"I tried getting that stall holder to press charges but he doesn't want to, so you're off the hook for now, but I find out you've been nicking again, Harris, I'm gonna shit all over you from a great height, you understand that?" I shoved him against the wall roughly.

"Yeah, yeah, I'm sorry," he mumbled meekly.

I turned and walked towards the door. Everyone in the pub was looking at me, including the man Harris had identified, so, in the few seconds it took me to leave the premises,

———◄◦►———

I was able to clock what he looked like. I felt mildly guilty about how I'd treated Andy, but it was all in a good cause. And he had been using my money to gamble. I returned to the car to wait.

The man left the pub not long afterwards. I saw him walking away and, from a safe distance, I followed him on foot. Why he was called Little Des was obvious as he was not much taller than five foot.

We walked along a couple of streets, then he turned left into Kentish Town Road and headed north. I crossed over occasionally so, if he was to turn, he'd not see the same person behind him, especially someone he'd just seen rousing a customer in a pub. But he had no reason to suspect he was being followed by anyone, so following him was easy.

I tailed him for fifteen minutes. By Kentish Town tube station, he went into a newsagent's and came out a minute later, then turned right into Islip Street. I ran to the corner and saw him cross over and stop outside a house. He produced a key and opened the door.

Noting the number, I took out my police radio and called it in, requesting a couple of uniforms to come to the address I'd given to affect an arrest. A few minutes later a squad car arrived and two uniforms got out. I identified myself.

"That house there," I said, nodding to where I'd seen the man I was following enter, "there's a guy called Bernie Rayes and Special Branch wants to talk to him, so I want you to go in and take him to the nearest police station. I'll join you there. Where's the nearest station to here, incidentally?"

"That way," one uniform said, pointing back to the main road, "just over there. Holmes Road."

"What's he supposed to have done anyway?" the other one asked.

"He's a known drug dealer. That'll do for starters."

"Okay, skipper." He nodded.

They went to the house and knocked. The door opened and, after talking to whoever had opened it for a few seconds, they entered. Several seconds later Bernie ran out the door and turned left. I crossed the road and chased after him. He was running haphazardly, arms swinging wildly like he was unused to running. As I drew closer to him I could hear him wheezing and gasping. He was unfit. We ran across a patch of grass and I rugby-tackled him, my left shoulder hitting his right thigh square on. I wrapped both arms around his legs and he hit the ground heavily. The two officers caught up, dragged him to his feet and put him into the back of the squad car for transport to the station.

"Good tackle, sir. You still play rugby?" one of the officers commented. He sounded impressed.

I returned to get my car from Chalk Farm. I was proud of the tackle considering I'd not played a competitive game of rugby for a decade. One up for muscle memory.

I showed ID at the station desk and asked to speak to a senior officer. A few moments later DS Roberts appeared. We recognised each other. He took me into a CID office.

"So, what's the Branch's interest in a toerag like Bernie the Buck?" He was bemused. "I know he sells drugs, but how does that rate the Branch's interest?"

I explained briefly about Bernie's involvement with Neville Thornwyn as an informant, though I didn't mention either blackmail or the stealing of weapons. I said, truthfully, that I believed he had information vital to a Branch enquiry. "So we're just tying up a few loose ends. Bernie can help us with that."

"Okay, you can have first crack at him, but I wanna talk to him about the dead body in his flat afterwards."

I agreed he could, though I was hoping I could ascertain who had killed Noel Partias before DS Roberts got involved.

I was taken to the interview room where Bernie was being held. Roberts and I entered the room, and the officer with Bernie left. I'd never been in this station before, but the interview room was as downbeat and unwelcoming as any I'd seen elsewhere. In fact this one was particularly grimy.

"Bernie, long time no see," Roberts said jovially. "This officer here would like a word with you, so you be a good boy and answer his questions. Alright? This isn't your first time in one of these rooms, so you know how it works."

After everything I'd been hearing about Bernie recently, it was almost an anti-climax to finally meet him. He was probably mid-forties, though he looked older than the picture I'd seen on his file, and was rapidly losing his hair. He was quite overweight, as evidenced by his bulbous face, which was how catching him had been easy, and his five o'clock shadow was prominent.

"I'm DS McGraw, Bernie, Special Branch. We met earlier." I grinned.

"And?" he replied sulkily. He was not impressed.

"*And*, when those two officers went to where you were staying, they were only gonna talk to you about possession of and distributing drugs, but, when they searched you just now, they found a knife in your pocket. That's not good, Bernie, you can go down just for carrying one of those, you know that? And you've already got form, so you'll go down for a five stretch if we press charges. That answer your question?"

He didn't respond. He sat looking morose, unsure of how his hideout with Little Des had been rumbled. His notion of safety in hiding had been shattered and he was probably wondering how it'd all turned sour for him.

"But, anyway, that's something the local boys'll deal with. Me? I've just dropped by to tell you something I know you'll wanna hear: Commander Thornwyn sends his regards and wants to thank you for all the help you gave him."

The mention of Thornwyn's name made him sit up and take notice.

"Yeah, I thought that name'd mean something to you." I smiled at him. He looked very worried. I let him worry for a few more seconds.

"Look, Bernie, I'm not gonna bullshit you." I leaned forward. "You may not know about me, but I know all about you: about you dealing ecstasy and selling it to Geoffrey Tilling and Paul Sampson. I know you sold them out to Thornwyn when you were arrested one time. He told me that. That's how he was able to squeeze Sampson for money. Blackmail him, in other words. You helped him with that, so that's a conspiracy to blackmail charge right there."

I stared straight at him as I spoke. He looked uncomfortable.

"I also know about you and Thornwyn and what you've been getting up to together. I know all about the weapons you were involved in stealing and those same weapons being sold on to Khaled al-Ebouli, an Islamist jihadist, no less. And all this on top of just being caught in possession of an offensive weapon. You're quite the saint, aren't you, Bernie? How'd Mother Teresa ever get by without your help?"

The look of shock on Bernie Rayes' face was such that I thought a heart attack was imminent, or at the very least a panic attack. I'd seen people in interview rooms turn puce when they'd realised there was no escape from what was known about them and the consequences of their actions were becoming apparent. Bernie couldn't deny anything because his expression had said it all. He put his hands on the table and lowered his head. He didn't move from this position for a few moments. For the moment I decided not to mention Noel Partias being found dead in his flat or Brian Turley being after him.

"Thornwyn tell you all this?" he finally said.

"No, the fairy godmother actually." I half-smiled at him. "Who do you think? He's sold you down the river, Bernie."

"I knew that bastard'd drop me in it someday." He shook his head resignedly. "He told me he'd look out for me, told me nothing would happen if I just did what he said. Him and that other fucking cop. Why did I believe that?"

"Good question; why *did* you believe him?"

"He was a DCI when I first knew him, then became a commander. He's a top cop, got a lot of clout. I figured if anyone could look out for me, it'd be someone like that. I've been giving him good tip-offs for years about various things."

"Well, he's sold you out, Bernie. How'd you think I got to know about everything I've just told you, through witchcraft?" Despite everything he'd done, I was going to try not to mention Turley's involvement, so I wasn't going to let on I knew him or had learnt most of this from him.

Bernie was looking ashen-faced, as though someone he loved had just died. He sat quietly for several seconds.

"Who's the other cop you were talking about?" I asked.

"Bloke called Turley. He's threatened to kill me." His voice rose slightly in indignation.

"Who's Turley?" I asked innocently.

"Used to be in Thornwyn's squad until he was suspended." His face broke out into an unexpected smile. "He's as bent as Thornwyn, got caught taking money, didn't he? Bribery and corruption," he said haughtily.

"So how does this lead to him threatening to kill *you*? Upset him, did you?" I was enjoying watching Bernie's discomfort.

"Why d'you think I was staying at Des's place? Turley thinks I've screwed him out of some money and he said he was gonna kill me for it, so I dropped outta sight for a while so he couldn't find me. He doesn't know Des, so I thought I'd be safe there for a while."

"You say he's a serving police officer, Bernie, so why would someone like him think a delightful fellow like you has, what was your phrase, *screwed him out of some money*?"

Bernie didn't appreciate my sarcasm, as was evident from his expression. "Bloody cops, you're all the same, all corrupt, all of you up to your necks in it." He looked straight at me. "Thornwyn's paying off lots of people; how much is he paying *you*, eh?" He sneered at me.

I immediately leaned forward and grabbed his left hand, which was on the edge of the table. I squeezed the first two fingers of his hand very hard and bent them back slightly. He registered a yelp of pain.

"Not the cleverest thing you've ever said, Bernie, and you say anything like that again, you won't be picking your nose with these fingers for a while." I released my grip. He grimaced from the ache in his fingers.

I was probably out of order doing what I'd done, but when the likes of Bernie Rayes accuse me of corruption, something snaps inside me and I react. Just as well there was no one else in the room when it happened.

But I took pity on him and called for the officer outside the door. I asked for two cups of tea or coffee. He went away. I let Bernie compose himself for a moment.

"Question for you, Bernie. You know what terrorism is?"

"Huh?"

"You even *heard* of it?"

"What're you talking about?" He looked as though I was speaking in Sanskrit.

"I'll spell it out for you, Bernie. You're a party to the selling of weaponry to a known Islamist jihadist, and those weapons'll probably be used to pursue an unlawful political aim. It's quite possible innocent British lives'll be lost as a result. You even helped steal them. You selling him those weapons means you've committed an act likely to further the aims of a proscribed terrorist organisation, and you've given aid and succour to Her Majesty's enemies." I spoke slowly and emphasised every word. "That's what they mean by *terrorism*, Bernie, and it means you're likely to go down for a goodly number of years. You're also a drug dealer and you were caught in possession of a nasty-looking knife. That's not good, mate." I shook my head solemnly.

He swallowed hard. At that moment the door opened and an officer arrived bearing a tray with two cups of tea. He placed them on the table and left. I took one. Bernie ignored his for the moment.

"What do you think a jury'll make of that, eh?" I sipped my tea. "You help steal weapons, they get sold on to an extreme Islamist fundamentalist and he and others use them to kill innocent people in this country. You think they'll like that and let you off?"

He didn't respond. From the lachrymose expression on his face I was wondering whether he was trying not to cry. His eyes were watering. He sniffed loudly. I let him stew for a few more seconds whilst I sipped more tea. He was scared.

"Look, Bernie, I'm not gonna lie to you. You're in deep shit, you know that? Stealing weapons and selling them on to someone whom the Government disapproves of is an extremely serious offence which could send you down for several years. That's if you're lucky. If we add the drug dealing on top, that's an even longer stretch. So there's only one way out of this for you," I said gently, "and that's to tell me everything you've been involved in."

He was trapped and he knew it. His only option was to cooperate. He looked forlorn.

"And if I do, what then?" He looked at me, almost pleadingly.

"It could be the difference between a *very* lengthy sentence and a not quite so lengthy sentence. That's the *only* choice you've got. You tell me your version of events and, if it checks out, we'll put in a good word for you and I'll dump it all on Thornwyn." Thornwyn was going down anyway, so what did it matter?

Bernie sighed and sat back in his chair. He waited a few seconds.

"It's Thornwyn; he got me involved," he said. "I don't know all the ins and outs of it, but he's involved in this plan to provide arms to some Arab in Islington."

"Was that what the robbery was for?"

———◀◦▶———

"Yeah. This Arab wanted weapons, so Thornwyn arranged for us to rob this gun shop. He knows the manager there, so he does it through him."

"This was just you and Thornwyn."

"It was me and this Turley character. We went in. We had the passcode, there was no CCTV switched on and no alarms, so it was piss-easy, you know what I mean?" He sounded pleased. "We wore plastic gloves so we didn't leave any fingerprints. We go in and we take the weapons Thornwyn'd pointed out to us."

I feigned shock. "This the same guy you mentioned earlier? Another police officer helped you?"

"Uh-huh." He nodded.

"What happened then?"

"We take them over to the bloke who's gonna sell them to this Arab. I never met the Arab; that was handled by the guy we gave them to."

I had the sudden feeling I knew who this was. "Would this be Noel Partias?"

"Yeah." He looked surprised at hearing the name. "How'd you know that?"

"So, who is this guy?" I didn't answer his question.

"He's something inside the Chackarti family. Thornwyn knows him. He's their weapons man, arranges for sales of guns and all that. You want to buy a gun, Partias is the man to see. He can get you pretty much anything you want."

Not anymore he can't, I cruelly thought. "So he sold them on to Khaled al-Ebouli."

Bernie looked vague.

"He's the jihadist I spoke about earlier. Known to be connected to Muearada. He's one of their main men in this country, Bernie. You know what Muearada are capable of?"

Bernie was now looking very worried.

"They're almost medieval in their barbarity. They chop the heads off their hostages. You remember the recent case about that American journalist beheaded in Syria? That's

Muearada's work. They kill non-believers. And you don't wanna know about what they do to drug dealers."

"I only helped with the robbery. I'm not a terrorist." He was sounding alarmed at what he'd heard. "I didn't know they were going where they ended up."

"You ever heard the phrase *ignorantia juris non excusat*?"

"Huh?"

"Didn't think you had. It's Latin, and it means *ignorance of the law is no excuse*." I said this slowly for maximum effect. "So, doesn't matter whether you knew or not who or where the guns were going to. Muearada's a proscribed organisation, which means they're officially on the Government's shitlist, to put it in your language, and you helping to supply them with arms isn't going to make you the flavour of the month with any jury, is it?"

He took a few deep breaths. If my intent had been to scare him, I'd succeeded.

"As a matter of interest, how much did they get sold for?" I asked.

"I dunno." He sounded indignant. "I never saw any money. Nor did Turley. He thought I'd cheated him, so when he came for his money and I'd not got it, he threatened to kill me if I'd not got it in a few days. He was serious as well, so I went and stayed with Little Des till Turley calmed down."

"So who got the money from the sale?"

He shrugged. "Dunno. I bloody didn't, I know that."

"Would Partias have it?"

"Might do. He took the weapons to this Arab bloke."

A thought flashed through my brain. Could it have been Turley who'd killed Partias? Could he have done this over a dispute about moneys owed? If it had been Turley, did he even know Partias had died? Did he think he'd just hit him a few times and left him on the floor?

I didn't mention Turley for the moment. "If Partias can get guns, why was the gun shop robbed?"

"I don't know, do I? I was just pressured into doing it."

This was something I'd have to put to Thornwyn.

"Let's go back a bit further," I said. "You know Paul Sampson? Yeah, 'course you do. He and his friend Geoffrey Tilling were your customers, weren't they?"

"Yeah, I know them. What about them?"

"Sampson's dead," I stated matter-of-factly.

"Yeah, I know. Topped himself, didn't he?" He smiled.

I fixed Bernie with an evil stare. "You think that's funny?"

His smile faded.

"You knew Thornwyn was blackmailing him, didn't you?" I asked.

"I didn't at first, but Thornwyn told me he was."

"He tell you why?"

"Yeah. Hated queers, didn't he, especially rich privileged queers, so when he found he had something on him, he milked him for all he could get. I collected it for him."

"*You* did?"

"Yeah. I'd meet Sampson, he'd give me an envelope full of cash. I passed it on to Thornwyn. I don't know how much it was either, before you ask."

"He always pay in cash?"

"Yeah."

"Where'd you meet him?"

"Different places near Parliament: a café, in a pub, a tube station. Wherever they arranged for me to go and meet him."

I nodded. I was imagining furtive meetings between the suave Paul Sampson and the pathetic wretch that was Bernie the Buck when he spoke again.

"Except that last time I met him. I had to go out of London."

"Where to?"

"Bloody Berkhamsted, up in Hertfordshire."

"Why'd you have to go there?" I had a feeling I knew what was coming.

"I had to go to the place he worked at as he wasn't coming into London that day. I thought I was going there just to collect a cash envelope but, while I was there, he gave me an A5 envelope as well as the money to give Thornwyn."

"He say what it was?"

"No." He shook his head. "I didn't ask either. It just felt like some sheets of paper and a couple of them little memory stick type things. I just drove straight back and gave them to Thornwyn. That's the last time I saw Sampson. He topped – I mean, sorry, he died soon after that."

"Did Thornwyn say what was in the envelope?"

"No. He seemed pleased to get it, though. Real chuffed, he was."

"You know what he did with it?"

"Nope. He just slipped me a few quid. That was it."

Didn't take a genius to realise what had occurred. Sampson had somehow managed to extricate Bartolome's designs and financial information and had spirited them out by using Bernie the Buck as his messenger. Bernie had then given them to Thornwyn, who had secreted them someplace, causing consternation inside the company and the very real fear of sensitive confidential information falling into the hands of competitors. Could this have been a reason why Paul Sampson had taken his own life?

What would Sampson have been thinking when he passed this envelope to Bernie? He'd worked for Bartolome for several years, his father-in-law still did and he'd be acutely aware of the significance of the firm to the UK's defence effort. Even when he'd been elected to Parliament, the company had offered him a seat on the board as a non-executive director, with a generous recompense of twice my annual salary just for attending half a dozen board meetings per annum. Smitherman had told me about the UK still supplying weaponry to countries whose regimes it disapproved of. I wondered if Bartolome was involved in supplying such weaponry. Had Thornwyn become aware of this?

179

Sampson had also been about to be questioned because of the suspicion he'd been involved in attempting to supply arms to a company known to be a front for Muearada. For him, this could have had damning consequences.

But what Thornwyn's interest in Bartolome's information would be was the question I couldn't get my head around. On their own, the disparate pieces of information he had would mean nothing, but to the right persons they could be of vital significance.

Any lingering fondness for my ex-boss Neville Thornwyn was disappearing as rapidly as bath water down a plughole. I resolved to ensure he answered for everything he'd done but had not been charged for. Whilst he'd not killed Paul Sampson himself, he was as culpable as if he had, and he was going to pay for this as well, one way or another.

"Thornwyn was arrested just afterwards, wasn't he, and he went down a couple of weeks back, didn't he?" Bernie happily said. "I ain't got him leaning on me to do things anymore, so I'm off the hook."

It was time for Bernie to learn the facts of life.

"Not quite. Noel Partias is dead, Bernie, did you know that?"

"Dead?" His eyes opened wide in surprise.

"Yeah, and what's worse for you, he was found dead in your flat."

"In *my flat?*"

"Yeah. I found him there when I was looking for you. The DS who came in with me wants to nail you to the floor about it when I'm finished in here."

"Oh, Christ, I didn't kill him, swear to God I didn't." His voice had risen an octave. He was worried and he was scared.

"Any idea who might have done?"

"Thornwyn?"

"Uh-uh." I shook my head. "He's been in custody the past few months, so it's unlikely to be him killed Partias."

"Could have been Turley," he suggested. "He was owed money as well. I couldn't take Partias but I bet Turley could."

I nodded. I didn't mention I'd already thought of that.

I left Bernie to fret anxiously whilst I found DS Roberts. The news of Partias being found dead in his flat had scared him.

"Wasn't him. He didn't kill Partias," I stated.

Roberts nodded. "Does he know who did?"

"No," I said, shaking my head, "but from what he's just told me I think I know who might have done, and it connects to something the Branch is pursuing, so we'll take this case now. Who'd have thought a twerp like Bernie'd ever be useful, eh?"

"Yeah. So what about him?" He nodded to the interview room. "I haven't gotta let the scrote go, have I?"

"No. He had a knife on him when he was brought in. Hold him on that for a while. He's given me some useful leads and I'm gonna follow them up. I'll be back to deal with him when I've checked something out."

Roberts agreed Bernie would be detained to help police with their inquiries. This was a practice frowned upon by the appeal courts, holding this to be an unlawful interference with the liberty of the subject, but just about every force did it. I had no qualms whatever when the person being detained was as guilty as sin, and Bernie was absolutely not without sin.

It'd been a long day but I still had one more thing to do. I called around to Andy Harris's flat on my way home. He was in. Psyching myself up for his wasteland I entered his flat, but, to my astonishment, the place was unrecognisable from the landfill it'd resembled recently. Everything had been tidied away and cleaned up. There were no clothes strewn about, no dirty crockery and no stale smells in the air. Every surface had been tidied and polished and there were empty fast-food boxes in the bin. Even Harris looked like he'd been brushed up and scrubbed. It was the tidiest I'd ever seen him look.

He was sitting next to the woman who'd turned his slum into something inhabitable, the place looking cleaner and tidier than I'd thought it was capable of ever being.

"Alright, who're you two and what've you done with Andy Harris?" I stared at both of them. He was looking loved-up and happy.

"This is my mate Mr Jack," he said to her. I was his mate? Harris thought of me as his mate? "Mr Jack, this is Stella."

I said hello to her. She was probably around mid-forties, pretty for her age, well turned out, and she looked like she could do so much better for herself. I wanted to ask her where she'd met Harris and in particular what on earth she could possibly see in an urban wretch like him, but I didn't want to spoil the moment for either of them.

"Hello." She stood up and we shook hands. Her voice was pure North London. "Andy's told me about you."

I frowned. "Only the good bits, I hope."

I apologised for how I'd roughed him up in the pub earlier and assured him it was done with the best of motives as I hadn't wanted anyone there thinking he was an informer.

"That's alright, Mr Jack, I ain't hurt. Made me a hero in the pub, it did, being turned over by the old Bill. Landlord gave me a free beer afterwards." He grinned.

I withdrew £20 from my wallet. His eyes lit up.

"Have a few more on me. And *don't* use it to gamble either."

"Money I bet earlier? I won £250 with it." He smiled, looking proud.

I left quickly before I snatched my £20 back.

SEVEN

Wednesday

I NOW HAD A GOOD IDEA of what Thornwyn had been engaged in. He'd put the squeeze on an MP and had ultimately involved him in taking sensitive confidential information from Bartolome Systems. The issue for me was, had Sampson taken this information voluntarily or under duress? He would have known the importance and the commercial sensitivity of what he'd taken, as well as the significance of it were it ever to become public. What would he have been thinking at the moment he handed the envelope to Bernie?

As well as being blackmailed, Sampson had been at odds with his father-in-law concerning his sexuality and had been threatened with losing his seat on the board, if Jeremy Godfrey was to be believed. Could this have been a factor in his helping to steal confidential information? Was he trying to get back at his father-in-law?

Thornwyn had also been the instigator of a robbery at a gun shop which had seen weapons being stolen and then sold on to a known jihadist based in the UK. The man who'd arranged the sale, Noel Partias, was now dead and I suspected I knew who'd killed him.

The reality now was that Thornwyn was in so deep he was likely to drown in this cesspool of intrigue he'd created. I wondered if MI5 know exactly what he'd been engaged in. More worryingly for me, did they still think I was part of it as well? I'd been concerned by Gillian Redmond's comments about Stimpson thinking I was part of whatever grand scheme Thornwyn had concocted relating to the theft of Bartolome's commercially sensitive information.

I needed to talk to Smitherman about what I now knew, as

I wasn't certain which end to approach this from. He wasn't in his office. I was told he was at a meeting the other side of the river, which was code for saying he was visiting Thames House, HQ of MI5. I left a message asking to see him when it was convenient.

Byzantium had its shop on the Battersea Park Road. I drove there and parked on double yellow lines fifty yards away. I looked in the shop window and saw a wide array of firearms, ranging from small-calibre handguns up to high-powered hunting rifles. It also sold a wide range of bullets, binoculars, flak jackets and many other essentials for the gun nut and the wannabe survivalists who assumed they had whatever it took to be Bear Grylls. It made me conscious of the fact I was armed as I entered the shop, with my service pistol resting neatly in its holster under my left shoulder.

After discovering Smitherman was unavailable, I'd decided I was going to unearth as much evidence as I could about Neville Thornwyn and then bury him up to his neck in it. One way to do this was to confront the person I now knew to be his accomplice, the manager of Byzantium, the man who'd smoothed the way to the guns being easily stolen. There could have been no robbery without his inside help.

At the counter I showed ID, emphasised I was Special Branch and asked for the manager, Edward Priestly. The assistant went to the back of the shop. I looked around and noticed CCTV cameras in the four corners of the shop. Convenient they had just happened not to be working on the night of the robbery.

A man approached and introduced himself as the manager. I told him we'd speak in his office.

Looking unhappy, he turned and I followed him into his small, oppressive and windowless office. There were pictures of handguns and other kinds of firearms on all four walls, many of which I didn't recognise. He sat down behind his desk but I remained standing. Experience had taught me that standing upright was an advantage when looking at a defendant who thought his bases were covered.

"I'd like to talk to you about the robbery you had here a few months back," I began. "You know the one I mean."

"Why's that?" He sounded displeased at having to go over it again. "I've already spoken to police about it. I've told them everything I know."

"Perhaps, but you spoke to CID. I'm with Special Branch and you haven't spoken to *us* about it. I wanna talk about it because we're interested in the security implications of the robbery. Our belief is the weapons taken that night have ended up with jihadists in North London and it's important we ascertain exactly how such weaponry might have ended up with these people."

He sighed. "Okay."

"You see, what we in the Branch don't get is the sheer coincidence of the CCTV not working *and* someone being able to enter these premises by using the appropriate passcode, which I'm told only a few people know about. It's also remarkable the alarms didn't sound when the thieves entered the place. I mean, the odds on your being eaten by a shark in the Thames must be greater than all those three occurring on the same night, wouldn't you say?"

"What are you implying?" His eyes narrowed.

"Not implying anything. I'm simply saying this was an amazing coincidence. What're the odds someone could just come here, punch in however many numbers or symbols they'd need and then, *bingo*, Aladdin's cave opens up for them?" I was being intentionally flippant. "We were told it'd take an expert hacker some time to crack the code to get into your storeroom, but whoever came in here that night did it in a heartbeat. Amazing, eh?"

"Police have investigated the robbery and they've accepted what you just said must have been what happened." He was trying to remain calm.

———◦———

"So I understand." I nodded. "But, you see, the thing is, Special Branch doesn't believe the story you've given to police, and we've good reason not to. You wanna know why?"

I stared directly at him. He was looking uncomfortable because he had no pre-prepared story. Thornwyn hadn't primed him for Special Branch involvement.

"It's because I've spoken to one of the guys who actually came in here that night and he's spilled his guts. Told us the whole story, he has." I paused for a few moments to build up the tension. "And he's named *you* as being involved."

"*Me?*" He was clearly trying to sound incredulous but didn't succeed.

"Yeah, you, Edward. We know the whole deal. I've spoken to the two guys who were here that night and they both tell more or less the same story, about being given a key to enter the shop, having the passcode to access the place where the weapons were stored and being able to do so undetected because CCTV was temporarily malfunctioning. They knew *exactly* where to go to get what they stole. I doubt they were in here even ten minutes."

He sat motionless for a few moments.

"You know what else is interesting about this?" I asked. "They've also both, independently, named the same person as being the brains behind the robbery that night."

"Who's that?"

"The very recently disgraced Commander Neville Thornwyn."

At the sound of Thornwyn's name, a look of shocked horror registered on his face. He couldn't have looked more surprised had he just seen his own daughter on stage, almost naked and wrapped around a pole.

I said nothing. I waited. Priestly knew there was no hiding place now. I was waiting for him to realise cooperating with me was his only chance to do himself some good.

"Thornwyn was behind this, wasn't he?" I asked. "The only way something like this could have happened was with inside help: yours. You gave him the passcode and blacked out the CCTV, didn't you?"

He didn't speak. He was looking at me but not seeing me. My story had shaken him up, which was my intention from the outset. It was now just a question of whether he played stupid or did the right thing.

I decided to prompt him. "CID believed your alibi for the night in question, didn't they?"

"Yes, they did." He nodded, looking hopeful.

"Okay. If you're so sure your alibi'll hold up, let's go see whoever it was alibied you. I'll tell him or her what I've just told you, but I'll also point out, if they're bullshitting me, that's a conspiracy to pervert the course of justice charge right there. But if they're telling the truth, they've nothing to worry about, have they? Neither have you."

He remained in his seat. I waited a few moments.

"You think whoever it is'll be prepared to go to prison for you when I whisper words like *obstruction of justice* to them? It's a serious offence to obstruct police in the execution of their duty, especially where terrorism's involved."

His eyes opened wide when he heard the word *terrorism*.

"When a jihadist uses weapons to achieve his objectives, that's what we in the trade call terrorism, in case you weren't aware of that, Edward," I said whilst watching him shuffling slightly in his seat. "Why d'you think jihadists want weapons? They're not for souvenirs; they want them to make some kind of political statement, and the ramifications aren't always palatable either."

I waited a few more moments for him to gather his thoughts. His certainty that any evidence trail wouldn't lead back to him had been shattered and he'd been caught out.

"So, what's it to be, Edward? You gonna tell me the truth about this or do I arrest you right here, right now, and have you charged with conspiracy to commit burglary, as well as being a party to supplying weapons to a terrorist? You know what you'd get for that?"

He sighed audibly. He was trapped in a corner and he knew it. He bowed his head slightly for a long few moments, then looked at me with a forlorn expression.

"Okay. You're right," he said. "Thornwyn was behind it."

"Tell me how it all came together that evening."

"He came to me one time, told me he was planning to rob this place. He wanted some of the weapons we were storing. I thought he was joking but he was in earnest. I asked why. He said someone needed firearms so he was gonna get them for whoever it was. I didn't think he was serious so I pointed out all the security we have here, the constant monitoring of CCTV, access to certain rooms only by a passcode which regularly changes, the alarm system and so on, thinking that'd deter him, but he said, no problem, you're going to help me do it. I told him I wasn't, but he said, if I didn't, he had enough evidence to prove I'd been defrauding Bartolome and he'd give it to the fraud squad."

"Was this a credible threat? *Had* you been stealing?"

He didn't reply. His breathing became more noticeable. Had he been strapped to a polygraph machine, the lines on the paper would have been wildly diverging.

"I know you used to work for them and had been there quite a lot of years. Is that why you left a senior management position to come here and run a shop selling guns?"

He thought about how to answer the question.

"I wasn't doing anything others there weren't doing," he protested.

"Look, I don't care what you did at Bartolome, my main concern's the robbery."

He looked like he was in pain. "Thornwyn said he had enough evidence of my activities at Bartolome over a number of years to have me put away, so he told me straight: help him out or face ruin."

"So you helped him," I said accusingly.

"What would you have done, eh? I didn't have any choice."

———◆———

"Keep telling yourself that, you might even believe it yourself one day."

He didn't like that comment, but I didn't care what he liked.

He continued. "He told me what night it'd be taking place. I know a bit about CCTV so I nobbled the computer, made it look like a malfunction, and I gave him the day's passcode." He shrugged. "You know what happened afterwards, don't you?"

"Yeah, I do. You reported the robbery next day and were investigated by the very man who you say coerced you into helping him, and he gave you a clean bill of health, didn't he, so you were in the clear."

He nodded.

"I know where the weapons ended up as well," I said. "That's why this goes beyond being just another robbery for CID to investigate. Did you consider what Thornwyn wanted the weapons for or where they might end up?"

He didn't reply.

"Thought not. Were any other employees here involved?"

"No, just me. They knew nothing about what was gonna happen. I didn't wanna get them into any trouble so I said nothing to them. They were all cleared by police."

"What did Thornwyn give you for your help, pieces of silver?" I asked in a sarcastic tone.

"He said he'd bury the evidence against me if I helped him out. I agreed." My allusion had gone over his head. "The thing I can't understand is how he would have got hold of it in the first place. How would Thornwyn have been able to access confidential information about me?" He sounded bewildered.

As he spoke, I realised where Thornwyn would have got it from: Paul Sampson. Sampson had probably been told to dig up the incriminating evidence against Priestly to use as leverage to get him to go along with the plan to rob the shop. Would Sampson have known what Thornwyn wanted this information for or would he just have gone along with it?

———◇———

I looked at Priestly and smiled. "*I* know how he did it, and if it's any consolation, you're not the only person Thornwyn was squeezing. That's how he was able to get the dirt on you."

"I know he's friends with the production director, Jeremy Godfrey, but I don't believe Jeremy would've spilled that kind of information to him." He looked puzzled.

"Thornwyn knows Godfrey?" I was surprised at hearing this.

"Yeah, they play golf together. They're members of the same golf club. Some place in Hertfordshire."

I'd not considered the likelihood of Thornwyn and Jeremy Godfrey knowing each other. This was something else to think about.

"That's how I first met Thornwyn, through Jeremy Godfrey," Priestly said.

"Interesting," I said, "but it wasn't him, that's not who I was thinking of. Someone else leaked that information to Thornwyn."

His eyes opened wide. "Who?"

"You don't need to know that." I shook my head. I was thinking, *could* it have been Jeremy Godfrey leaking information to Thornwyn? What would have been his motive for doing this? Did Thornwyn have something on *him* as well?

Priestly placed both hands on the desk and looked at me. "So, that's the story. What happens now?"

"I still have some other enquiries to pursue, but I'm officially cautioning you. You're not to talk about this to anyone, got that? You'll be taken in and charged soon. Anyone asks, I was here helping you update security procedures. Okay?"

He nodded. "I've cooperated fully with you. Will that count for anything?"

"That's up to whoever charges you." I hoped it counted for nothing.

Driving away, I was wondering what Priestly could have done whilst he was still working for Bartolome to make him fear Thornwyn disclosing the information he'd obtained. I made a note to ask Jeremy Godfrey when I went to pay him a return visit very soon. But first there was someone else to visit.

"Oh, fuck, what you want now?" he said as he opened the door to me. Brian Turley didn't appear overly pleased to see me again. I walked past him without waiting to be invited in.

His abode looked even more bleak and depressing now Andy Harris was living in a flat which was almost habitable. The curtains being pulled half-closed gave the room an even more downcast feel, and the clutter everywhere gave the impression of someone indifferent to his environment.

Turley followed me in and closed the door. To my surprise there was no glass of vodka on the table. I couldn't even see a bottle anywhere. He sat down in his usual place.

"I'm trying to cut down on my drinking," he said. He'd obviously seen me looking around his flat and he'd guessed what I was noticing the absence of. "I've been told by my union rep the IPCC are gonna start questioning me next week, so I'm trying to get my head straight, trying to lengthen the times between having a drink. I ain't strong enough to go cold turkey, so the longer I can go between drinks, the better."

"Good for you, mate," I said encouragingly. I meant it.

"I ain't had a drink today yet." He sounded proud. I looked at my watch. It was eleven twenty in the morning. "I'm trying to see if I can make it to dinner time without one."

I nodded. "That's good."

When I'd first encountered Turley on joining Thornwyn's squad, he had been a heavy drinker even then but had been able to function as an effective police officer. But within a year his effectiveness had gradually lessened as his drinking binges had become the stuff of squad legend. I remembered I'd once signed off on a report concerning a series of arrests made. The report was accurate in every detail, except for the part stating the arrests had been carried out by four detectives. Only I and two others had actually carried out the arrests. Turley had been too hungover to actively participate on an early morning series of arrests, so we'd covered up for him: a disciplinary offence and a possible suspension if it was ever made known, but this was the loyalty the team felt for each other. I didn't want to think about Smitherman's response if he ever discovered this.

"I was feeling quite positive till I saw you just now," he said resignedly. "Why do I think you've got bad news for me?"

I perched on the arm of an armchair. Moving all the clothing and magazines strewn across the seat seemed too much effort. "I'll come right to the point. You know someone named Noel Partias?"

"Don't think so," he said after a few moments' thinking.

"You sure about that?"

"Yeah, I'm sure. Who is he?"

"Who is he? He's the guy who took possession of the weapons you and Bernie the Buck stole from Byzantium. He was the go-between for your enterprising little gang and Khaled al-Ebouli, who was the recipient of the weapons."

"Oh, was that his name? Bernie took the weapons back to his flat and gave them to this bloke, who was gonna sell them on to this Arab and then we'd get paid off. I never knew the name of the bloke who took them. Didn't want to, either. All I knew about him was he was something in the Chackarti family, their weapons bloke or whatever."

"Did you know he's dead?"

"Bernie?"

"No, Partias. Found dead in Bernie's flat last week," I stated formally.

"Bernie killed him?"

I was looking intently at Turley's eyes to see how he was reacting. "No, not Bernie. Police think someone else did."

"How'd he die?"

"Hit his head on something, died from head injuries, lots of internal bleeding. He'd have probably survived if he'd been seen by the medics quicker. There was evidence suggesting he'd been in a fight beforehand, bruises on his forearms looking like he was trying to defend himself from being attacked. He'd also got contusions on his face, suggesting he'd been punched quite hard in the face at least twice. Don't know what his assailant looked like."

I was still staring at Turley as I spoke to check his reactions to what was being said. So far he didn't appear to be unduly perturbed.

"Any suspects?" he asked. "Anyone spoke to Bernie about it?"

"Yeah. It wasn't Bernie, but I've a pretty good suspect."

"Who?" he asked innocently.

I paused for several seconds, keeping eye contact with Turley.

"Did you think you'd got away with it, Brian?" I smiled at him.

"*What?* You think *I* did the bastard over?"

I didn't reply for a few moments. At last I nodded at him. "Here's what I think happened. You told me you'd been looking for Bernie in the pub he uses. You couldn't find him in the pub, so you went to his flat. He still wasn't there, but Partias was, so you two get involved in a dispute about money. You told me Bernie owed you the money you were promised for the robbery. You're both fired up, you argue and a fight starts, you smack Partias when he says he hasn't got your money. You hit him a few times and then leave. I don't think you meant to kill him, but he died from the head injuries he sustained hitting his head on or against something. Am I close to the truth?"

He slumped back in his chair, looking at the ceiling. He sat motionless for thirteen seconds, then looked up at me.

"Yeah, something like that," he admitted. "He said he'd not got any money, then after we'd argued about where the money was for a minute or so, he said something like why would Thornwyn even want to work with the likes of me, how could he trust some drunken excuse for a policeman? That *really* pissed me off, that did. No fucking Scotsman talks to me like that, so I belted him one, a good one, put him on the deck." He paused.

"And?"

"He got up, we struggled for a while, then I smacked him again, twice, and he went down. I kicked him in the balls twice whilst he was on the ground, asked him *how's that for a drunken copper*, called him a Scottish wanker and told him I wanted my fucking money soon or he'd get the same again. Then I left."

"So he was alive when you last saw him."

"He was groaning and holding his nuts, so I suppose he was."

"Well, he banged his head on something, 'cause that's why he died."

He closed his eyes and tilted his head backwards.

"Fuck," he sighed quietly. He looked down, nodding to himself for a few moments. "Anyone else know about this?"

"Police know he's dead. It was me who found him."

"You?"

"Yeah. I was looking for Bernie and went to his flat. Partias'd been dead about two weeks when I found his body. But what I've just told you, nobody knows. That's just how *I* think it went down. I've not spoken to anyone about this yet; it's just something I was thinking about when I was in the gym recently. This is just how I've pieced it all together from what I can ascertain about the situation."

"You still go to the gym?" He seemed more amazed by this than he was by my theory concerning the demise of Noel Partias.

"Yeah. How'd you think I stay so young and beautiful?" I grinned. He didn't.

"I don't. Not anymore. I haven't worked out for ages." He

shook his head, looking depressed. "My life's become a shitstorm of bad news, you know that?"

I didn't reply. What could I say, other than that I agreed with him and it was nobody's fault but his own?

"I didn't mean to kill him, Rob, honest to God I didn't." He was imploring me to believe him. "Yeah, I hit him a couple, but that's all. I wasn't gonna kill him."

Neither of us spoke for about ten seconds. The silence was heavy. Turley looked as though he was awaiting bad news from a cancer specialist after chemotherapy had failed.

"I never did find Bernie," he said. "I'd have kicked his fucking head in if I'd found him. God knows where he is."

"*I* know where he is."

Turley looked optimistic for a second. "Yeah? Where is the little bastard?"

"He's in custody; arrested yesterday. He more or less confirmed your story about how Thornwyn got the robbery organised when I spoke to him."

"*You* arrested him?"

"I did indeed," I said smugly.

"What you get him for?"

"Possession of an offensive weapon for starters. Said he was only carrying a knife because some crazy cop was threatening to kill him. I wonder whom that might be?" I fixed Turley with a benign stare. "He's being held in custody waiting for me to go back and talk to him."

Between the two of them I was now sure I more or less had the story of the night of the robbery at Byzantium. Bernie was an incorrigible lowlife, but it saddened me Turley had been involved. The corruption hearing was bad enough but robbing a gun shop, with the proceeds being placed with a jihadist Muslim, put Turley beyond the pale.

"So, what happens now? Am I nicked?" he asked quietly.

There was no easy way to tell him what I thought.

"You were right just now, Bri, you're in the shit. With what I now know about what Thornwyn's been up to, there's no doubt he's gonna offer up some sacrificial lambs if it'll get his liability reduced, and you and Bernie, I'm afraid, are those lambs. There's no CCTV evidence but it'll still be his word against you two. You're already suspended and, what with the IPCC hearing next week ..." I let the sentence tail off. He knew what I was alluding to.

Despite his stupidity, and the virtual certainty he was facing years in prison, I was surprised to find myself feeling sorry for Turley. When I'd joined Thornwyn's team nearly six and a half years back, he'd still just about been able to function as a productive police officer, and I had some good memories of the times we'd been out making arrests and of hearing some of his funny stories about times he'd been plastered, like the time he'd gone out on a bender and got, in his words, *royally mortal drunk*, but somehow driven back home and fallen asleep in the car in the garage. Next morning, when he'd come to, still under the influence, he'd driven into work still wearing the same clothes as the day before, including the puke-up down the front of his shirt which he'd failed to notice. What he'd also not realised was that, driving away, he'd been dragging his wheelie bin down the road, spilling rubbish everywhere. It was an amusing story and he'd dined out on that one for ages.

But his increasing reliance on the bottle had cost him his marriage, and his debts with his bookie had led him to help Thornwyn rob a weapons shop. There was also the fact he was already under suspension for aiding Thornwyn in acting in a corrupt manner whilst a police officer, plus the very real likelihood he'd be charged with the manslaughter of Noel Partias at the very least. I couldn't remember how old Turley was but I guessed somewhere around mid-forties, though he now looked older. The likelihood was that he'd be close to sixty when he emerged from prison, assuming he survived the ordeal, and he'd be unemployable and would have no police pension to collect as this'd be forfeited upon going inside.

"You know what? I was gonna ask you if you'd be a character witness for me when the IPCC starts its hearings. I'm allowed to have someone I worked alongside who could testify to my performance as a police officer. But I don't suppose you'd be interested now, would you?" He said this in a regretful tone.

"I'd have to take my union's advice on that one, plus I'd need to see Smitherman and talk to him about it," I replied evenly.

"That's a polite way of telling me to fuck off, ain't it, Rob?" He looked hurt for a moment, then laughed. "Actually, I don't blame you, mate. *I'd* tell someone like me to fuck off if they asked me to speak on their behalf."

There was nothing more to say. I stood up.

"You take care, Bri, look after yourself. Make sure you keep it up." I was referring to his abstaining from alcohol for longer periods.

He nodded. We fistbumped each other as I walked past on the way out. I wished him good luck.

"Thanks, mate."

I left him to think about the future. I didn't realise it then, but this was to be the last time I ever saw Brian Turley alive.

It was only just past one o'clock but so far I'd managed to break the story put forward by Byzantium's manager and got him to admit to his culpability in the robbery at his shop, and now I'd solved the riddle of who'd killed Noel Partias. Not too bad a morning's work. Maybe I could find Madeleine McCann before my shift was through.

Thinking about the robbery from Byzantium in the car, I knew the instigator was already in prison awaiting sentence for offences unrelated to this, Bernie was in custody and Turley was about to undergo an intensive interrogation from the IPCC. The weapons man, Noel Partias, was dead, and the shop manager had admitted his own complicity in the robbery. The weapons had been passed on to Khaled al-

Ebouli. I knew he worked in the History Department at Westminster University, so I drove back to the Yard, parked and walked to their central London campus.

The History Department was located north of Oxford Street on Regent Street, on the site of the old Regent Street Polytechnic. It was a large, impressive building with colourful posters in many of the front windows.

I entered the foyer and crossed the reception area. There were dozens of students milling around and talking excitedly. There was a wall nearby covered with notices advertising forthcoming events, including hustings for the student union president. The atmosphere felt vibrant and alive with excited young students and, for a brief moment, I was nostalgic for my student days at King's a decade ago.

At the enquiries desk I asked for Khaled al-Ebouli and was directed to his office on the third floor. I took the stairs and passed a number of students going down, a couple of whom looked at me suspiciously.

On the third floor I walked along the corridor and found the office I was looking for. The door was open and I tapped lightly on it. Khaled al-Ebouli was behind the desk typing on a laptop. He looked up and gestured for me to enter. I did. He nodded towards an empty chair. I sat down.

I knew I'd not get an admission or anything like that from him. My intent was simply to let him know he was on Special Branch's radar and we had him in our sights. I was interested in his reaction to what I was going to put to him.

"Are you a student on one of my courses? I don't recognise you." He looked up as he closed his laptop. He sported a thick black moustache and his hair was as black as coal and very thick. He looked austere and very serious and his eyes were like a viper's, betraying no feelings at all.

"No. I'm a King's boy myself." I produced ID and showed it to him. "DS McGraw, Special Branch. I'd like to ask you a few questions."

———◦———

He smiled ironically and sat back. "What do you want this time?" he asked in a neutral tone.

"This time? I've never met you before." I grinned at him. He didn't appreciate my attempt at humour. Was there even any place for humour in the world of the fanatical jihadist or would that constitute bourgeois distractionism? "You know a man named Noel Partias, I believe."

He thought for a moment. "Is he one of my students? I can't place the name."

"No, he's not a student. You bought something from him not too long ago and we have an interest in the merchandise involved."

"And what was this? What is it I'm supposed to have bought?" He adopted a challenging pose, leaning back in his chair.

"Let's not waste each other's time, eh, Khaled?" I stood up. "We both know you know who Noel Partias is and what he supplied you with. I know what they are, I know where they were stolen from and what you plan to do with them. I know about your jihadist views. I know you're involved with Muearada." I paused to let my words register. "Incidentally, Noel Partias died recently, and not from natural causes either. Were you aware of that?"

"I don't know the person you're talking about, so how am I to be aware of his death from whatever cause?" His English was good and he spoke almost fluently with little trace of any accent.

"Whatever. I'm just letting you know you're gonna be watched like a hawk from now on. I hope you like company, 'cause you're gonna get lots of it."

His expression didn't change. He sat looking nondescript, like he was in a waiting room calmly waiting for his appointment. "Have you finished threatening me?"

"You have a nice day." I left his office.

Strolling back to the Yard, I wasn't certain I'd achieved

anything from talking to Khaled al-Ebouli, but at least he now knew police were looking into him and his activities, if he'd not already known. I then decided it was time to look into Jeremy Godfrey more closely. I'd been surprised to hear he knew Neville Thornwyn. I was turning over in my mind how they intersected and I was sure I knew.

Before this, however, there was still Bernie the Buck to consider. He was now reaching the limit of the time period after which he'd have to be either charged or released from custody, and I certainly didn't want to risk losing him again.

I drove back to Kentish Town police station. DS Roberts was in his office.

Without going into specifics or too much detail I explained that Bernie had a connection to a Branch investigation and he was very likely to face serious charges relating to it and, whilst I wasn't yet in a position to arrest him for the offences concerned as I had a few more inquiries to make, I'd like him detained in custody as there was the very real possibility he'd hide again if he was released.

"No problem," Roberts said. He was clearly delighted at the prospect. He said he'd charge him with possession of an offensive weapon and conspiracy to supply and distribute dangerous drugs, and the local magistrates' court would order him to be remanded in custody for a week.

I was taken into an interview room to see Bernie. He was already in there, anxiously fidgeting and tapping his fingers on the table, nodding to some piece of music no one but he could hear.

"How much longer am I gonna be kept here?" he pleaded as I sat.

"Why's that, you got somewhere else you'd rather be?" I said nonchalantly. "They really like you here, Bernie, you know that? So much so, they're going to arrange for you to stay here for another week on an offensive weapons charge."

I was being deliberately facetious. I didn't like Bernie. I held him responsible for Paul Sampson being blackmailed by Neville Thornwyn, and for much of the intense psychological trauma Sampson had endured before taking his own life, because he'd sold Sampson out to save his own neck.

Bernie looked downcast at the thought of remaining in custody. He'd obviously thought this had been just a routine pull, the kind all working criminals in his position expect once in a while, almost like an occupational hazard. He was now discovering this wasn't the case.

"At the moment it's just this, and someone'll be in to charge you in a minute when I've gone, but it's gonna get much more serious for you. You've admitted receiving stolen documentation from Bartolome Systems, a major defence contractor, and you also burgled a gun shop and took weapons which ended up with a jihadist. I were you, Bernie," I said, standing up, "I'd learn to read, 'cause you're gonna get a lot of time to do it."

He stared at me like he'd not understood what I'd said. Perhaps he hadn't.

"Anyway, this is doing you a favour, mate," I said airily. "We haven't found Turley yet, and if he's after you, like you say he is, you're safer in custody, aren't you?"

He sighed resignedly. "So you say."

I left Bernie to his much-deserved misery, told DS Roberts I still owed him a favour and drove back to the Yard.

I phoned Bartolome's Berkhamsted site and asked to speak to Jeremy Godfrey. I didn't fancy a late afternoon drive to Berkhamsted on the off-chance he was there, so I was going to make an appointment to see him. I was put through to his secretary, who informed me Mr Godfrey was not in; he was at the firm's London office and probably wouldn't be back in his office today as he had meetings planned whilst in the City. Feeling pleased at not having to battle the early commuter traffic driving out of London, I thanked her for her time and rang off.

I took a taxi to High Holborn. When we reached Bartolome's office, I paid the driver and went into reception.

The same ginger-haired woman with the studs through her nose was behind the desk. The top two buttons of her cream-coloured blouse were undone, revealing her cleavage, and I could see the top edge of a tattoo over her left breast. Wincing at the thought of how painful having a tattoo in that place must have been, I showed ID and asked for Jeremy Godfrey. She replied he was in a meeting with senior managers which wasn't due to finish for probably another thirty minutes. I said I'd wait and walked across the foyer to where the armchairs were in the corner, under a large ornate mirror with what looked like gold trim all around. There were magazines and newspapers on a small table and I glanced at a copy of *Aircraft* magazine. It was full of technical specifications and aeronautical facts I couldn't begin to understand, so I looked at the pictures instead.

I'd been waiting twenty minutes when the ginger-haired woman approached and asked me to go through to the manager's office. I walked along the narrow corridor to the office I'd been in on my previous visit. Jeremy Godfrey was sitting where Diane Leander had sat when I'd last called. He looked up.

"I hope this won't take long, DS McGraw, I've a train to catch." He glanced at his watch.

"Depends, doesn't it?"

He looked like he didn't like that answer. I sat down.

"What did you want to ask me?" he asked.

"I think I can shed a little light on where your missing documentation might be and who took it."

"Oh, really?" He looked pleased. "That's good news."

"Yeah, but before I tell you, I wanna ask you something." He nodded his assent to this.

"Why did Edward Priestly leave Bartolome Systems?"

"Priestly? Is this relevant?"

"Yes, it is," I assured him. "He left a good position here to go manage a gun shop, and I'm curious why."

He didn't seem convinced, but he answered the question. "Edward was given the choice of resigning and walking away quietly or else facing prosecution and a likely prison sentence for what he'd done."

"Which was what?"

"Put in layman's terms, fiddling. He's a senior accountant and he'd been fiddling expenses and, over the years he worked for Bartolome, he'd milked thousands out of the company. I mean, there's nothing unusual about claiming slightly more in expenses; most businessmen do it at some point, but what he did went beyond any definition of acceptable theft."

Many firms operate a system of *acceptable theft*; it means firms recognise that pilfering of firm resources occurs but, so long as it stays within mildly acceptable limits, the firm will turn a blind eye. It's still theft, but firms recognise the impracticality of trying to enforce largely unenforceable rules, so they set limits and depend on the common sense of employees.

"Like what?" I asked.

"Claiming for hotels he never stayed in, taking non-existent clients to expensive restaurants, booking hire cars and charging them to the company whilst using his own car, things like that. On one occasion we even financed his family's bloody summer holiday with what he'd bilked us for." He sounded indignant at the effrontery.

Bartolome's board clearly wouldn't want the shareholders knowing about a top accountant getting away with cheating his employer for as long as it appeared he had, so knowledge concerning this would be restricted to those insiders who had a need to know, which would be a small number. "Who in the company would have known about what he'd done?"

"Very few; mainly the head accountant and a few directors. That's about it."

—◇—

"Nobody beyond the company?"

"Not unless Priestly told them himself." He was adamant. "How does this have anything to do with the documents we're missing? Are you saying he took them?"

"I'm coming to that. I'm asking about Priestly because he's become involved in something Special Branch is investigating, and he claims he was forced to do what he did because someone was holding the reason he left Bartolome over his head. But you've just said nobody outside the company would have known about why he left, and he's not likely to admit it himself, is he? So someone inside the company either was involved in what he did later or made sure someone outside the company knew his past. You follow?"

"I'm not sure I do." He looked puzzled. "What's Priestly supposed to have done?"

"For the moment that stays under wraps because there's national security implications involved. My concern here is how the person Priestly claims was blackmailing him got to know what he'd done to have to leave Bartolome."

Godfrey eyed me suspiciously. He had a sense of the way I was thinking and he was beginning to look concerned.

"The only way this blackmailer'd know is if someone told him," I stated neutrally. I waited a few moments before continuing, "And the person concerned just happens to be someone of your acquaintance. What a coincidence, eh?"

"Who's this, then?"

"Commander Neville Thornwyn."

"*Neville?*" He sounded surprised. Interesting he'd used his first name.

I nodded and waited for his reply. He hadn't replied five seconds later, so I continued.

"*You* told Thornwyn about why Priestly left this company, didn't you, and he used it against Priestly as leverage to get him to do something he wanted done. You denying this?"

He pursed his lips and looked out the window towards Southampton Row. He breathed out and looked like he

---

didn't know what to do next. I waited a few more seconds. I was about to ask him something else when he started talking.

"Neville approached me a few months ago, asked for a reference for Edward Priestly, asked if he was trustworthy and honest, would I feel comfortable recommending him for employ, things like that. He said Edward was being considered for a job and he was doing a background search to check his suitability. I didn't want information about what he'd done leaking out, so I told him, though I hid some of the excesses of what he'd done and I didn't give any figures. I generally gave him a good testimonial, probably better than he deserved, truth be told."

"Well, Jeremy, Neville, I'm afraid, was bullshitting you. Didn't it strike you as odd when he asked you for information about Edward Priestly?"

"No, I'm afraid it didn't," he said quietly.

"I mean, think about it. Since when does a CID commander get involved in doing a routine background check on someone's suitability for any job that's not involved in security? That just doesn't happen. Any inquiries are usually routed through personnel, not through the production director."

"Yes, I suppose so."

"You know why he asked you rather than the human resources department? Because you'd be more likely to tell him what he wanted to know, that's why. You and him were golfing chums, weren't you, so he could count on your indiscretion to leak information he had no business knowing." I wasn't sparing his feelings.

He sat silently, barely moving. He was absorbing everything I'd told him over the past few minutes and he didn't like what he'd heard. I let him stew for a few moments longer.

"You know what I'm wondering?" I asked. "I'm wondering whether you and Thornwyn were working together on this scheme to get Priestly to act for him. Makes sense, doesn't it?"

"What? You think I've something going on with Neville Thornwyn to go after Edward Priestly?" He sounded alarmed at my comment.

"Well, either you've been extremely gullible and naïve, giving Thornwyn information he wasn't entitled to, *or* you were reckless because you knew or were indifferent to what he was going to do with it, *or* you're in it with him. He asked and you gave him what he wanted, knowing what he'd do with it. There's no other way it can be," I said with certainty. "Which is it?"

As I looked at Godfrey I was reminded of Geoffrey Tilling's comment that Paul Sampson had been told by his father-in-law he'd lose access to his child if he were to come out and declare his homosexuality. I now believed it was true. This would have added to the enormous pressure Sampson had lived under for the last few months of his life. Just one more reason to despise Jeremy Godfrey.

"Neville Thornwyn's recent actions have threatened national security; were you aware of that?" I asked. "What he got Priestly to do has done an enormous favour to Islamist terrorism."

Godfrey looked at me with a bewildered expression. "What's Neville done? I saw he'd been convicted of taking bribes and acting corruptly, but how does that threaten national security?"

"Oh, he's done more than that, a lot more. Did you know he was also blackmailing your son-in-law?"

His eyes opened wide in genuine shock, like he'd just seen a ghost.

"It's true," I assured him. "He found out Paul was gay and used it against him when Paul refused to declare himself as homosexual. Thornwyn himself told me this just after he was convicted, and Paul's partner's also confirmed it. I don't know how much he took him for."

"Why'd he do this?"

"Because he could," I asserted. "Paul Sampson was a

sitting duck, wasn't he? He also had you on his case threatening to kick him off the board unless he chose his wife over his manfriend. You saying you really didn't know?"

"Yes, I didn't realise Paul was being blackmailed," he said softly.

"It's also our belief Thornwyn's responsible for the loss of the confidential information from this company."

Godfrey looked ashen-faced.

"We think he blackmailed Paul into giving it to someone else who, in turn, passed it over to Thornwyn." I wasn't going to name Bernie at this stage. "I'm going to see Thornwyn soon and ask him where he's stashed it, amongst other things."

"Paul gave away top-secret information about the company to a stranger?"

"Not quite a stranger. You know Thornwyn, don't you?"

Godfrey looked like he was struggling to breathe properly, shaken by what he was hearing. "Paul wouldn't do that. He's a loyal company man, for Christ's sake, he's not going to allow secret company information to be given away to anyone." He was trying to sound as though he was convinced of this point.

"Well, sorry to disabuse you of that notion, but it was definitely Paul. Thornwyn was using a go-between, and this person took the information to London and gave it to him."

"Thornwyn," he muttered as if trying to be sure of the name.

"Yeah." I nodded. "I've had this corroborated by the person Thornwyn used to collect the documents from Paul Sampson."

Godfrey closed his eyes for a moment. "This is unbelievable. I thought Neville was my friend. Why would he do this?" He was shaking his head slowly as he spoke, looking at me as if I was meant to agree with him.

"I used to think he was a police officer, but I'm beginning to doubt that," I replied cynically. "I've no idea why he'd be doing this, but what he's done has kicked over a hornet's nest and several people are trying not to be stung."

As I spoke I was conscious of the fact Thornwyn was on remand in Belmarsh, having been convicted on a range of offences pertaining to bribery and corruption but not for anything I'd discovered over the past couple of weeks. I resolved to make sure he answered for everything I'd discovered about him.

"So, what happens now?" Godfrey asked after he'd looked out the window for several seconds.

"Until I've spoken to Thornwyn and ascertained certain facts, there's nothing I can take you in for. *Prima facie*, it looks to me like you two are in this thing together. But for the moment all I have are suspicions and coincidences, and I can't take you in on those."

He looked very worried indeed. "You seriously believe I'm part of whatever it is Thornwyn's supposed to be doing?" His voice sounded strained of sincerity.

"I believe what facts and evidence tell me." I stood up. "For the moment there's nothing else, but after I've made some more inquiries and spoken to my boss, you and I will be talking again. Count on it."

I looked at him as I was preparing to leave. I didn't like what I saw. I think I understood at that point precisely why Richard Clements despised people like Jeremy Godfrey.

"What kind of pressure do you think Paul Sampson was under just before he took his own life?" I asked.

"How the hell would I know?" he snapped back. "I'm not a bloody psychologist. I don't know what he was thinking, do I?"

"If he had come out, would you and his wife have denied him access to his daughter? Are you that much of a homophobe?"

"That's a family matter, nothing to do with you."

"You think Paul might have been thinking about that when he took all this confidential information and gave it to Neville Thornwyn?" I asked.

It was apparent from his expression this was something Jeremy Godfrey hadn't considered. I waited a few moments for a reply, but none was given. I left him to ponder what I'd just said to him.

It was now late afternoon. I decided to walk back to the Yard. Thinking about all I'd heard from several people, I began putting a scenario together in my mind. I knew how the robbery at Byzantium had occurred; I knew who'd carried it out and with whose help. One of these persons was now in custody and the other in the process of pickling his liver. I now knew the shop manager had been pressured into cooperating by a threat of making known why he'd been required to leave his senior managerial post at Bartolome Systems. I knew who the weapons had been sold on to and by whom, with the seller now dead. I suspected I had a good idea why the recipient of the weapons would have wanted them as well.

I also knew Thornwyn had been involved in Bartolome Systems losing highly valuable and confidential information relating to the company, possibly by blackmailing Paul Sampson, but I didn't know what he might have done with it all. I couldn't understand why he would want this information either. This was something I was going to have to ask him.

Worryingly for me, I knew MI5 were thinking I was some part of Thornwyn's grand plan for the information taken from Bartolome. Establishing I had nothing to do with this was now an imperative.

I contacted the office. I was informed Smitherman was there but was in a meeting with the assistant commissioner. I said I'd grab him tomorrow.

It was just after nine in the evening and I was winding down with a cold beer. I'd arrived home late as I'd written up all the details of my interviews during the past couple of days, including my conversations with Jeremy Godfrey and Edward Priestly. I'd gone into detail about how Byzantium had been robbed, who by and where the weaponry had ended up, and had summarised my thinking about the issues involved, including everything I'd learnt about Paul Sampson and the pivotal role Neville Thornwyn seemed to have played in this situation. I pulled no punches with my hypothesis.

Curiously, though, I'd omitted any details concerning Brian Turley, both visiting him at his flat and discovering the personnel involved in robbing Byzantium through him, as well as his admission of assaulting and inadvertently causing the death of Noel Partias. Even as I was typing my notes up, I wasn't completely sure why I'd left these facts out.

The phone rang. I answered.

"Rob, apologies for disturbing you but you're needed back here." It was Smitherman.

"Why's that?" I was dismayed.

"You're wanted in an interrogation."

"Of whom?"

"Tell you when you get here."

"Okay, I'm on my way." I hung up. *Fuck it.*

I drove to the Yard in record time, using the siren to clear the way. I parked and went up to the Special Branch office. Smitherman was in his office, glancing at a report.

"Evening, DS McGraw. Apologies for the intrusion but you're needed on this. The person concerned has specifically asked to speak to you, says he won't talk to anyone else, so don't take your jacket off; you're off downstairs to interrogate a suspect soon."

"In connection with what?"

He looked up from what he was reading and paused for a second.

"Jeremy Godfrey was murdered a couple of hours ago. He was stabbed in the car park by Hemel Hempstead railway station."

My eyes opened wide in surprise.

Smitherman summarised the facts of the case. Godfrey had caught the 6.15 train from London Euston to Hemel Hempstead. In the car park outside he'd been involved in a fierce argument with another man, which had got quite vitriolic, and there had been lots of swearing. Godfrey had then pushed the other person away, and had been heard by a nearby witness to say something like, "*Get the fuck away from me and my family, you AIDS-ridden queer,*" whereupon the other man had produced a knife and stabbed Godfrey through the chest. The victim had died almost immediately. The assailant had then been seen calmly putting the knife back into his coat pocket, walking into the station and getting on the train to London Euston a few minutes later.

All this had been witnessed by several commuters who'd overheard what was said and had made statements to police. It'd initially been thought the victim had just been punched, but one man, going across to offer help, had noticed the victim had been stabbed and the alarm had been raised.

The whole incident had been captured on CCTV. The assailant had been identified and police had been to the man's home, arrested him and taken him into custody. He'd not even taken his coat off and had offered no resistance when told he was being arrested. The knife used in the attack had still been in the coat pocket. He'd even been heard to say, "What took you so long?" He was now being held in an interview room waiting for whatever happened next. Smitherman said it should be a straightforward case to wrap up.

"So who's the suspect?" I finally asked.

"Someone called Geoffrey Tilling."

Tilling was in quite an upbeat mood when I entered the room. The officer watching him said he'd been singing what sounded like an operatic tune quietly to himself. I told him to take Tilling's handcuffs off. The officer seemed doubtful about the wisdom of this action and asked if I was sure, reminding me the suspect had just killed someone, but he complied when I repeated my order. He left the room and I sat down opposite Tilling.

Tilling smiled broadly. "Hello, DS McGraw. I hope I've not put a dampener on any plans you had for this evening."

Compared to the two occasions I'd previously spoken to him, he sounded positively chipper, looking calm and unfazed even though he was about to be questioned about the circumstances preceding an unlawful killing.

He was wearing a lavender shirt underneath a floral waistcoat, which somehow seemed to match his designer stubble. His collar was open and I saw a silver crucifix on a chain around his neck. He looked much less distressed than when I'd last seen him almost two weeks back, somehow more alive in his own spirit, as though the weight of the world had been lifted from him. He didn't appear at all worried about being in an interrogation room.

I acknowledged his greeting. I asked if he wanted to speak to a lawyer before I began or have one present during this interrogation. He said he didn't and he didn't want to make any phone calls either. I then asked how he'd been coping since I'd last seen him.

"I'm okay, thanks. I'm holding my head up. I'm cherishing the times Paul and I had together rather than focusing on his loss. You know what they say, better to have loved and lost and all that." He shrugged.

This was at least a positive step forward compared to where he'd been when I'd first talked to him.

I waited a moment before speaking. "You've been arrested, so you know ..."

"Yeah, I know." He was still smiling at me. "Anything I say will be taken down and used in evidence against me, blah blah blah. They've told me all that."

I shrugged. "Okay, if you're certain, let's make a start."

I switched on the tape recorder, identified myself for the

record and said I was about to interview Geoffrey Tilling, who'd been arrested on suspicion of committing an act of murder, and who'd declined legal representation. Tilling stated his name, and then, slowly and carefully, he began explaining the events leading up to Godfrey's demise.

Tilling had recently realised Paul Sampson still had a valuable piece of jewellery at his family home which Tilling had loaned him several months previously, so he'd decided, after work, to go to Berkhamsted to ask for its return. He said he'd decided to go in person as he wasn't sure any letter would be answered and didn't want to talk on the phone.

Sitting on the train, he'd seen Jeremy Godfrey walking past. Godfrey had stopped, given him a look of total disgust and mouthed something at him which didn't appear to be friendly, though Tilling was unable to identify what he'd said. Tilling said he'd ignored him but, as the train had left Watford Junction and the carriage had emptied out, Godfrey had returned and sat opposite and asked if he was going to Berkhamsted. Tilling had replied he was and explained the purpose of his visit.

According to Tilling, Godfrey had then leaned forward and ordered him to "*Stay the fuck away from my family, you understand that? You go near my daughter's house and you'll regret it. The last thing she needs is the likes of you bothering her.*" His tone had been aggressive. He had then returned to his own seat.

Tilling then explained what happened next.

"As he walked away I felt something snap inside me. I can't explain it but every fibre of my being felt like it was on fire. I got really angry at what this arsehole had just said. It just kept going round and round in my head: *The likes of me? Just who does this bastard think he is?*" I noticed he was breathing slightly faster as he spoke. "My whole life I've had small-minded jerks like him flaunting their hetero moral superiority at me and thinking they're better than me because I'm gay and proud of it, so I thought, *Fuck letting him talk to me like that*, and I decided to make a stand. I followed him off the train at Hemel." His hands, which had been flat on the table, had formed into fists.

"So you were angry when you got off?"

"Angry? I was bloody *livid*." His voice rose slightly and his face was turning red as he emphasised the point. "I called out to him as he got to his car."

"What were you hoping to do when you confronted him?"

"Initially I was just gonna tell him I'm going to Paul's house to ask for the return of my property and he can go *fuck himself* if he thinks I'm gonna let him fuck my life over any more than he and his fucking family had already done." He nodded almost aggressively, his expression changing to one of pure hostility. His voice had hardened. "I was gonna challenge him to try stopping me going. I got right up in his face about it." He nodded again, looking pleased with himself.

"So, what happened next?"

"He got quite belligerent and we argued for a few moments, him telling me not to go there, but then ..." He paused. "You know what he said?"

"No."

"He asked, quite openly, did I know he was instrumental in Paul's dying? He told me, with Martha's assistance, he'd switched his pills for much stronger ones and she'd left the cognac there for him. They made Paul's death look like a suicide. He admitted quite openly they'd killed him."

His voice softened slightly and he began to choke up as he spoke. "He said he didn't want his granddaughter to have anything to do with her father, didn't want her raised by a couple of fairies. He wanted Paul out the way, so he and Martha made him drink the cognac and swallow a large handful of very strong sleeping pills until he blacked out. He was almost smiling as he said what they'd done. He then said it obviously couldn't have been a suicide as everyone who knew Paul would know he wasn't man enough to do anything like that."

Tilling paused for a few moments. He sniffed loudly a couple of times and dabbed his eyes with the sleeve of his shirt. "For a couple of seconds I was stunned. Still am. I couldn't believe what he'd said. I couldn't take it in, and I could feel myself shaking with rage and anger."

"Did you believe he was serious?"

"I did. You could see the delight in his face when he told me. He then pushed me away, said something like I had AIDS and told me to fuck off away from his family. At that point I just lost it completely and I lashed out with the knife."

"Did you already have the knife in your hand?"

"I don't remember." He was crying. "No, no, I didn't. It was in my jacket pocket. I just remember it being in my hand and thrusting it in his direction."

"You didn't target any part of his body?"

"No, I just lashed out blindly."

"Well, you got him straight through the heart, Geoffrey. He was probably dead before he hit the ground."

I looked at Tilling wiping his eyes for a few moments. That he was a man in pain was clear, despite his occasional attempt at bravado.

"I didn't mean to kill him. That's not what I got off the train for." He was sobbing quietly.

"Why'd you take a knife in the first place?" I asked. "You always walk around armed?"

He looked serious as he composed himself to answer the question. "I'd been to Paul's house once before and Godfrey was there. He'd threatened me, said something about *doing me in* if I ever came back. He said it in front of his daughter. I mean, look at the size of me compared to him. Physically, I've no chance against him, so I took the knife with me in case he was there again and came at me. I was just gonna wave it in his face, I wasn't gonna kill him or anything. To answer your earlier question, no, I don't usually go around carrying a knife, but I did so this evening in case Mr Ex-Army Macho Man decided to act out his homophobia and get violent."

He sat back in his seat, looking at odds with the world, trying to grasp the changed reality of the death of the man he'd loved. I wondered if the enormity of what he'd done had fully registered with him.

"I think I told you once I thought Paul had been murdered," he said. "Well, this proves I was right, doesn't it?"

He then sobbed for about half a minute, his head bowed and hands over his face and his whole body trembling. I was wishing a female officer could have been present. He stopped and wiped his eyes on his sleeve and apologised for crying. I told him he had nothing to apologise for.

I waited a few more moments.

"So, you're saying, for the record, you didn't set out this evening with the intention of killing Jeremy Godfrey," I stated.

"Correct," he said, sitting up straight, sounding a little more in control. "I was hoping he wouldn't be there. Martha Sampson may well be a fraud and a repulsive upper-middle-class Home Counties bitch, but she'd at least have been reasonable when I asked for my jewellery back. I'd no idea he was gonna be on the same train as me." He looked directly into my eyes, almost imploring me to believe him. "I'd have got another one if I'd known."

"If Godfrey was right, and she'd helped him switch the pills for stronger ones, how reasonable do you think she'd have been when you went to her house?"

He shrugged. We were both silent for a few moments. He nodded slightly, acknowledging I was probably right.

"You really need to talk to a lawyer, Geoffrey, because, if you're going to rely on the story you've just told me, you could be able to plead guilty to manslaughter." I was wondering whether Tilling might have the defence of *provo-*

cation available to him because he'd responded violently after being told by the victim about his part in the death of Paul Sampson, the man he'd loved. The legal question would be whether the response was proportionate to the provocation, or even whether Godfrey's words amounted to provocation, but that would be one for the lawyers to ascertain. I wasn't wholly certain as to Tilling's legal situation.

"Well, I killed him. I certainly didn't mean to, I just lashed out. Is that manslaughter?"

"If you admit killing Godfrey but deny any intent to do so, you could have the option of pleading guilty to manslaughter. If the Crown accepts this, there'll be no trial; it'll then just be a question of whatever the judge thinks is an appropriate sentence."

"And if they don't accept it?"

"You'll be charged with murder," I replied calmly. "It's then up to the jury. But, whatever, it's essential you take legal advice."

He nodded, resignedly. However, I had to point out the one reality of his situation which might well be the defining factor concerning his legal culpability.

"You were carrying a knife, though. That may well count against you, particularly at a time when the incidence of knife crime's increasing. You need to be aware of that. Celebrating knife culture may well be the done thing for rappers, but look how many of them die violent deaths. It'll be for the lawyers and whoever charges you as to whether the fact you had a knife on you at all is detrimental to your cause, so you need to be aware you could be staring at a murder charge."

"Yeah, I suppose," he said softly. He sat quietly for the next few seconds.

"Anything else you wish to say?" I asked.

He shook his head. I terminated the interview and switched off the tape machine. He then sat bolt upright. There was an expression which was hard to read on his face.

———◦———

217

"You know what? I'm not at all sorry he's dead." His voice sounded harder. "I mean, I didn't go out tonight wanting to kill him, but *he* came on to *me*. If he'd said nothing on the train, none of this would have happened. But what he said about Paul in the car park really upset me, so *fuck him*. At least there's one less homophobe on Earth tonight." He sounded choked as he finished. He couldn't maintain the hardened stance to its conclusion.

"Do yourself a favour, Geoffrey. Keep that thought to yourself. *Don't* repeat it in front of the lawyers and *definitely* don't say it in court."

I left him to think about where his life now was.

Smitherman had left to go home so I reported my conversation to the night duty officer, who then made the necessary arrangements to have Tilling held in custody overnight and arraigned before Horseferry Road magistrates' court tomorrow morning. Someone would also need to go and talk to Martha Sampson about the claims made by Tilling concerning her role in the death of her husband, though I was aware there was no corroborating evidence and, even if Jeremy Godfrey hadn't been killed, hearsay evidence was inadmissible in court. Given her father had also just been murdered, the next few hours for Martha Sampson would not be pleasant ones.

EIGHT

Thursday

SMITHERMAN WAS NOW FINALLY AVAILABLE, so I wandered up to his office. Today was bright and sunny with little breeze and hardly a cloud in the sky, so the view looking at the trees in St James's Park from his office window was delightful, and, despite having had little sleep last night after arriving home late, I was in a positive mood.

Smitherman looked up and gestured towards the chair. I sat. He looked pensive, like he was about to impart bad news. He took a deep breath. This didn't bode well. My good mood was on the edge.

"Before we begin I have to tell you something, and you won't like hearing it either. I've just received details about a fatal accident in West London shortly after midnight." His tone was solemn as he looked directly at me. "And it involves someone I believe you know."

"Fatal accident?" I asked nervously. I could feel my good mood beginning to dissolve.

"According to this report," he said, holding up a sheet of paper, "he walked straight out into the middle of a busy road without looking and was hit full on by a taxi. Died in hospital a couple of hours later."

"Who did?" I had a sinking feeling I knew what was about to be said.

"Brian Turley."

It felt like a punch in the stomach. My breathing became erratic as I tried to remain calm.

"I know you partnered with him in Thornwyn's squad and I'm led to believe you and he were friends. I'm sorry to have to break this to you, Rob."

I nodded to acknowledge what he'd said. I closed my eyes

---

for a few moments and breathed deeply, picturing Turley in my mind. I thought of what he had been when I'd joined Thornwyn's team and then of the last time I'd seen him in his flat a couple of days ago, trying to go a few hours without alcohol.

"Yeah. So, what actually happened?" I regained my composure.

"From what I understand he'd been drinking heavily all evening. He was drunk when he staggered out of the pub just after midnight onto the Uxbridge Road. A witness said he walked straight out into the road without looking. Traffic lights were on green and a taxi came round the corner from Wood Lane, couldn't stop in time. Hit him full on. He suffered massive head injuries. The hospital initially put him on life support, but it was futile."

Smitherman didn't embroider the situation. I felt a little moisture in my eyes. I took a few more deep breaths.

A fleeting thought raced through my brain. Had Turley done this intentionally? Was this his way of ending the unrelenting pressure he was under? I hoped not. The thought upset me and I tried to put it out of my mind.

"IPCC were due to begin questioning him next Monday morning about his time in Thornwyn's team. Saves them a job, doesn't it?" Smitherman's tone was less solemn now.

"He'd have gone down, you know," he said after a pause of a few seconds. "The weight of evidence against him was enormous. No way he'd have got out from under what they had on him. Did you know he had a six-figure sum in an account held under a fictitious name? Money he and the other one, John Paine, had amassed working with Thornwyn."

Smitherman wasn't sparing my feelings. I hadn't expected him to, either. Dirty police were anathema to him and, even though he was probably sorry for the way his life had ended, Smitherman would have no pity for Turley.

He waited a decent interval.

"I know he had a young family and it's sad for his kids to have to grow up without a father, but they were doing that anyway because he was divorced and was denied access." He waited a few more seconds before speaking again, with a degree of finality. "I know he was your friend, Rob, but in my opinion he was a disgrace to the uniform."

I knew Smitherman was probably correct but, despite it all, I liked Turley and he didn't deserve to die the way he did. I resolved not to mention his role in the death of Noel Partias.

"You okay? You wanna stop for a while?" Smitherman asked.

I was feeling dysfunctional after hearing about Turley but I replied I was fine to continue.

Smitherman again apologised for calling me in last night and said he was aware Tilling was in custody and due to be arraigned before the magistrates' court later this morning. "Why did he want to speak to you, anyway? How do you know him?"

I explained about Tilling being Paul Sampson's lover and how Thornwyn had been able to squeeze Sampson because one of his informants had sold ecstasy to them. I mentioned I'd spoken to Tilling twice previously concerning Sampson.

Smitherman nodded. "Obviously he'd know about the blackmail, but did he know about Sampson's passing confidential information to Thornwyn?"

"Never mentioned it. I don't think he did. Sampson bottled everything up, internalised it, didn't talk to anyone about what he was going through. He was under a lot of pressure."

I told Smitherman about my conversation with Godfrey and the ultimatum he'd given Paul Sampson, as well as the threat to have Sampson removed from Bartolome's board.

"All this as well as being blackmailed by Thornwyn about his sexuality," Smitherman said. "Can't have been much fun being Paul Sampson towards the end."

"Tilling said Godfrey told him he and Sampson's wife conspired to get Sampson to swallow all those pills and drink strong liquor he wasn't used to. That's why Tilling went for him."

"Maybe he did, but he's no longer with us, is he? Martha Sampson'll be questioned about it today but she'll almost certainly deny it, so it'll be Tilling's word against hers, won't it? Also, the coroner's verdict didn't say anything about those pills being forced down his throat. There was nothing to suggest any kind of struggle, and his body can't be exhumed because he was cremated. The verdict of suicide'll stand unless you can prove otherwise, and you know how difficult that'll be unless she admits to it?"

"So she gets away with it." I could hear the bitterness in my own voice.

"There's no proof she even did it, is there? But, anyway, for the moment that's not the main issue here. I've been reading your report. It's well detailed and seems to explain everything. I'll fill in the gaps in a moment."

What gaps? I thought.

He picked up a paper copy of my recent report. "First off, how did you know about the situation inside Bartolome Systems, about the missing materials and in particular their financial position?" He looked at me as he spoke. "This is *most* confidential. Not many people inside the firm know about it either."

"One of my sources told me."

Smitherman fixed me with a stern gaze. "If I said it was in the interests of national security, and I needed to know, would you tell me this person's name?"

I began to think of a reply. I certainly wasn't going to tell him I'd initially heard it from Richard Clements.

"Just as well I'm not saying that, then, isn't it?" He'd read the look on my face and he nearly smiled. "But I think your source is almost certainly someone inside the security service. The Government's particularly concerned at the possibility of Bartolome going under because the firm provides lots of specialised military hardware and weaponry to the armed forces, as well as to governments abroad. But you know what they're most concerned with? News getting out of Bartolome's role in supplying weapons to nations this country officially doesn't do business with. That's why I was concerned you knew about Bartolome's financial situation."

"Surely they can only export weapons and the like if they get the green light from Government? They'd need strategic export licenses and all that, wouldn't they?"

"You'd be forgiven for thinking that, wouldn't you?" Smitherman's look suggested he wasn't going to be drawn into responding to my comment.

"Anyway, I'll tell you who told me," I said. "It was Jeremy Godfrey. He told me when I first spoke to him in his office about the current state of the firm. Obviously they were concerned about the loss of all the confidential information relating to their finances, not to mention the R&D stuff they've also mislaid. That's how I found out."

It hadn't been Jeremy Godfrey, but I saw a convenient way of diverting Smitherman away from knowing who'd really told me. Godfrey, as a director of Bartolome, would have been *au fait* with the situation inside the firm, and my conversation with him had featured in the report Smitherman was holding. Besides, Godfrey was now dead and wouldn't be able to contradict my naming him as a source.

"Godfrey?" Smitherman sounded surprised. "Godfrey told you?"

"Yeah," I agreed. "He told me when I asked him why his firm had put a PI on my tail. He told me what they'd taken and explained it was important they retrieve the financial data because of the harm it'd do the company if it hit the press, not to mention the embarrassment to the Government. He told me they thought I was helping Thornwyn. That's why I was being tailed."

Smitherman puffed out his cheeks. "I hope to God my

son-in-law never hears about any of this," he said quietly. "I can just imagine what he'd do if he knew this."

I supressed a knowing grin.

"This has become a mare, Rob. What I'd thought was simply a case of a corrupt police officer blackmailing a Government minister about his sexuality has become something else entirely. But things have become a little clearer after the meeting I recently attended."

I was wondering what he meant by that, but he continued.

"According to what you've written," he said, nodding to my report, "it's your belief Thornwyn was directly involved in organising the robbery of those weapons from Byzantium and also having them sold on to some Islamist jihadist, Khaled al-Ebouli."

"So it seems," I agreed. "I heard this from one of the people involved, who's now in custody in Kentish Town. He gave them to the one found dead in his flat, Noel Partias, who I'm told is the weapons guy in the Chackartis. The guy in custody, Bernie Rayes, denies killing Partias. I've questioned him and I believe him."

"But we don't yet know who did it, do we?"

"Still looking into it."

I'd resolved not to say it was Brian Turley. I didn't want his memory besmirched any more than it was likely to be over the next period of time. No one else knew about it, so I wasn't going to draw attention to it. I was hatching a plan to keep his name out of things.

"And Thornwyn was assisted by the manager at Byzantium?" Smitherman asked.

"Yeah, but not willingly. Thornwyn has something on him and used it to get him to give up the passcode and switch off the alarm and CCTV. He's being brought in and is gonna be interrogated about it."

Smitherman was glancing at my report. "Thornwyn steals weapons which he helps get to some Islamist jihadist, and he also knows about the state Bartolome's in."

"Paul Sampson passed the requisite documentation on to Thornwyn. What we don't know is whether he was in it with Thornwyn or was pressured to do it. Hard to believe Sampson was acting voluntarily. I think Thornwyn coerced him into doing it. This is just one of the things I'm gonna ask Thornwyn when I see him, hopefully later today?" I looked at Smitherman, raising my eyebrows to indicate I was asking.

Smitherman shuffled through the papers on his desk, looking enigmatic. "At Thames House yesterday I met with Colonel Stimpson and someone from MI6, whose name I wasn't told."

At the sound of Stimpson's name I felt apprehensive. The feeling that somehow I was part of the reason for their meeting crossed my mind.

"Did you know your name was mentioned?" He smiled.

"Oh yeah?"

"Yes. They put me in the picture regarding what you've been investigating and what you've found out. I spoke to Colonel Stimpson again just recently," he said, nodding towards the phone, "to bring him up to speed concerning the content of your report."

"Does he still believe I'm working with Thornwyn to try and steal confidential information from Bartolome?" I asked, concerned. "That's what Godfrey alleged when I first spoke to him in his office. He said they'd put this PI on my tail because they'd heard from inside MI5 I was one of Thornwyn's team in what he was trying to do. Not hard to guess who their MI5 source was, is it? Especially as it was Stimpson's niece on my tail."

Smitherman chuckled to himself. "And this worries you, does it?" He was evidently trying to keep his voice neutral.

"Yeah, it does."

He fixed me with one of his inscrutable stares and, for a few moments, I couldn't tell what he might be thinking. I hoped I never had to play poker against Smitherman. He then smiled, sort of, and sat back in his chair.

———◄○►———

"You're part of my team because I have full confidence in your ability to do this job. You remember what I told you the other week, just after Thornwyn's trial? If I had *any* reason whatsoever to think you couldn't be trusted, I'd have you transferred out of the Branch," he stated formally, "and you know I'd do it, don't you?"

I nodded. "Yeah, I do."

"I told you the IPCC gave you the all-clear, didn't I? And after I spoke to Stimpson, even though he still believes you let Mendoccini escape too easily, he accepted you were nothing to do with whatever it is Thornwyn's been up to, so you don't need to worry about what he thinks."

I exhaled. I felt relieved. Tonight was going to be beer night after hearing this.

"So, does your meeting have any impact on that?" I nodded towards my report.

Smitherman looked thoughtful. "I can give you the broad outline, but the situation's complicated and I don't know the full story. Also there are some things I can't tell you, but, simply stated, Thornwyn had discovered Bartolome Systems was involved in selling weapons to places and regimes this country supposedly doesn't do business with. The supposition is he got this information from Jeremy Godfrey. They were known to be friends, and Godfrey would certainly know the situation inside the firm. Arms sales like these were the only thing keeping the company afloat."

"Government knew this, didn't it?"

"Of course it did. All governments for the past couple of decades have known this," he said, looking at me as though this was obvious to everyone, "and whilst they didn't exactly approve of it, they turned a blind eye to it. You know how strategically important a firm like Bartolome Systems is?" He paused momentarily. The question was rhetorical. "The reverberations if it ever went under, or if its current situation ever became known, or if it was known what they were doing, would be politically seismic. Not only would it be alarming, it'd also flag up a whole lot of questions certain people don't want to have to answer, and certainly not in public."

"And probably wouldn't if they were asked." My scepticism was evident.

"It won't come to that." He ignored my comment. "Bartolome's not going to be allowed to go under. There's some kind of rescue package being cobbled together as I speak. I don't know the financial ins and outs, or the amounts involved, but it'll put the company on a sounder financial footing. That's the important thing at present."

"Of course it is. What else could be as important?" My cynicism was there for Smitherman to see. He looked disappointed at my attitude.

"The *national interest*, DS McGraw. *That's* what important here." He emphasised both terms. "I don't like what's going on any more than you, but this has to be kept in proportion. There are reasons why this is being done. I don't know what they are either and, as I don't need to know, they don't tell me. But they assure me what's already been done and is being done is very much in the national interest, and I've accepted their assurances. So the case is pretty much wrapped up."

"In what sense?"

"A number of ways." He looked at me with an odd expression for a moment. "What I'm about to tell you *never* leaves this room, you understand? There are a few things you need to be aware of, given your recent investigations."

I nodded my consent. This was starting to sound ominous.

"It doesn't matter what Godfrey told Tilling about how Sampson really died," Smitherman said. "He was only half right. Yes, he was involved in killing him, but he had help and, no, not just his daughter. He was helped by MI5."

"*What?*"

"I mentioned the national interest just now, didn't I? Paul

Sampson was in the process of arranging an interview with a journalist he knew and trusted, where he was proposing to tell the whole story about arms sales to rogue nations and how the Government knew about this and how ashamed he was to be part of the whole deal. He was also going to tell this person about the state of Bartolome Systems and how near they were to financial calamity. He'd made contact with this writer and was going to give him one hell of a story. Between them they had it all worked out. The paper was going to get a major exclusive. He was going to tell him *everything*. Sampson wasn't just planning to rock the boat; he was going to turn the whole bloody thing over."

Smitherman paused to let what he'd said sink in. I'd heard what he'd said but was struggling to make any sense of it. He'd not mentioned the writer, but I assumed it was the person who'd spoken to Clements.

"A story like this would've gone viral in seconds. Every important paper in Europe and the USA would've run with it. Can you imagine the impact if this got onto the front pages of something like the *Washington Post*? Security here can't lean on papers in the USA like it can on papers over here and, even if it could, the paper'd just plead the first amendment. There'd have been questions in the Senate and congressional inquiries and all that. The propaganda victory to the enemies of this country would have been enormous." He waited a moment. "So it was decided: this interview can't be allowed to happen."

"By who?" I interrupted.

"People in a position to make such a decision, that's who." He was trying not to sound annoyed at my question. "It was known Sampson was suffering from depression and took pills to help him sleep, so ..." He shrugged.

"Godfrey and persons unknown shove a whole handful of pills down his throat and make him drink something he's not used to drinking. He passes out. His wife stays away for a few hours, time enough for the pills to do their stuff, and eventually Sampson lapses into a coma and dies. A friendly coroner rules it to be a suicide. Cremated soon afterwards. All very neat and tidy. The papers report a politician suffering from depression, which was why he took his own life," I said matter-of-factly, as though I was reciting ingredients in a recipe.

Smitherman didn't respond. He sat, nodding sagely.

"Didn't anyone query where he got the stronger pills from, or the cognac?"

Smitherman maintained a dignified silence.

"Was Sampson's wife fully in the picture about this?"

"That was never mentioned, and I didn't ask."

"Why didn't MI5 just lean on the writer, tell him not to do the interview? They could have had a word with the editor, asked him not to run with the story."

"Presumably they had their reasons for not doing so."

I didn't like what I'd heard. I thought about things for a moment. "Sampson was about to be investigated by the Intelligence and Security Committee, wasn't he? Why was that?"

"He was arranging to do business with a firm, Endgame, which was supposedly a front company funnelling arms to terrorists. The reality is, though, it *is* a front company, but one set up by MI5 to help it monitor the flow of weapons out of the country. You tried accessing its website a couple of days back, and it triggered an alarm in security. At the meeting yesterday MI5 wanted to know why you were attempting to do this. They weren't sure how you even knew about it. Knowledge about the existence of Endgame isn't exactly widespread. You seem to have some good sources, DS McGraw." Smitherman gave me a look suggesting he was either impressed with what I'd discovered or worried how I knew about it. It was hard to tell. This would also explain Christine Simmons' surprise when I'd asked her about Endgame. "Sampson was arranging to have arms sold to them. Security was of course all over this and took the appropriate steps to stop it, with a little help from the CIA."

"The CIA was involved?" I blurted out.

Smitherman looked at me as if to say, *Don't even ask*. I didn't.

I waited a moment. "So, what about the robbery at Byzantium? Where does that fit into all this?"

Smitherman almost smiled. "Thornwyn had found out about the arms sales, again it's assumed through Godfrey. He decides he wants to embarrass the company, so, as Byzantium sells guns and is part of the Bartolome group of companies, he arranges for the shop to be robbed and, through a middleman, to have the weapons sold on to some Muslim jihadist. He said, as we're already selling weapons over there, why not sell them to them over here? He wanted them to be used in this country to put pressure on the Government. The funny thing is, though, he arranges for this through an MI5 source."

"*Huh?* Who's this?"

"The man found dead in the flat."

"Noel Partias? He was MI5?"

"Not as such. He was a source, tipping them off about movements of weapons and things like that. That's why you going to see Khaled al-Ebouli was unnecessary, though a day's never wasted if you're upsetting someone like him. Partias had already told MI5, so they knew he had the weapons and were tracking them."

Turley had killed an MI5 man and hadn't known it.

"The security people believe two men entered the shop that night. You say one's in custody, but they don't yet know who the other one is. You've said Thornwyn's involved, but he's saying nothing unless he gets a deal, which he's not going to get," Smitherman said firmly. "So, when you go talk to the other one about the robbery, see if you can get out of him who he robbed the shop with. Offer him some kind of deal if he'll name his partner, but don't make it too generous. Partias would know, but we can't exactly ask him, can we?" He almost smiled at his attempt at a witticism.

"What's gonna happen to Thornwyn? And what about all that confidential information he purloined from Bartolome?"

"Another disgrace to the uniform." He snorted derisorily. "He's going down for a long time, that's an absolute certainty; mostly he'll be in solitary, and not just for his own protection either. He knows too much to be allowed free association with others. The stuff he's supposedly buried about the company, hoping to use for his own gain, is useless to him. He was going to give it back to Bartolome if they went public and admitted they were selling weapons to unfriendly nations. But, as I said earlier, the financial situation's being rectified and, should what was stolen ever come to light, it'll simply be denied. The bank's being brought onside. The other stuff's just designers' drawings and some rough ideas, nothing really; the company just didn't want them falling into competitors' hands." Smitherman exhaled. "Didn't want them knowing what the company's thinking." He looked pensive for a moment. "Thornwyn's role in all this will never be admitted or acknowledged. When he's sentenced soon, the media will simply portray him as a corrupt cop, though the full extent of his perfidy will, of course, never be known."

"I wanna see him again, ask him a few things before he's sentenced, preferably today if possible?" I raised my eyebrows.

Smitherman nodded. He dialled a number and asked whoever he spoke to on my behalf about visiting a prisoner being held in top security at Belmarsh. He hung up a minute later.

"No problem," he said.

To Belmarsh again. It was mid-morning but traffic was flowing steadily as I drove along the Plumstead Road. I'd been thinking about Paul Sampson and about Smitherman's assertion he'd been removed by MI5 to stop him talking publically about matters which would cause very consider-able embarrassment to governments going back two decades or more, and I could imagine the reluctance of any PM to stand up in the House and admit what Sampson had said was true. Governments rarely, if ever, talk about sensitive security matters at the dispatch box.

Nobody would ever know, now, what had triggered Sampson's fit of conscience and his desire to make public what he knew about arms sales to unfriendly nations. What I did know, however, was that Sampson's life had been weighed in the balance of the national interest and had been found to be expendable.

Smitherman, of course, had only given me the barest details. There was a whole lot more I didn't know about the situation and probably never would. But at least I now knew that whoever had spoken to Richard Clements, when he'd asked about Paul Sampson, had been telling the truth. Presumably it was this person Sampson had been planning to give the interview to. I briefly wondered whether he'd spilled so much detail to Richard Clements as a means of exacting revenge for the death of Paul Sampson, hoping Clements would eventually publish it.

Inadvertently, Clements was now in possession of facts that'd cause a political firestorm if he ever put them in print. I hoped for his own sake this wasn't what he was planning. I'd have to talk to him and advise him to keep what he knew under wraps. I certainly wasn't going to confirm the truth about Sampson's demise to him.

I also wanted to know who this person was he'd spoken to, but I knew it'd be futile asking. Clements had already named one of his sources to me a few months back and he'd made clear it was not a precedent.

After showing credentials at the front entrance to Belmarsh and passing through the security checks, and after attracting some dirty looks from a group of women and children as I walked past them to the front of the queue to be admitted, I was again escorted to the same block and taken to the same room where I'd previously spoken to Thornwyn. I saw the same prison officer who'd taken umbrage last time I'd visited standing by the door, and he fixed me with a dark glare as the door was opened. I nodded to him but he didn't return it. The escort then walked off, leaving just this one friendly prison officer to wait outside.

Thornwyn was already there. He'd been told to expect a visitor and he was looking very dapper in a smart white shirt and tie and crisply ironed dark suit trousers. He was sitting in one of the armchairs, glancing at a copy of the *Daily Telegraph*. He smiled when he saw me and stood up.

"DS McGraw, how are you?" He sounded as though he was pleased to see me. He extended his right hand to shake. Walking towards him, I extended my left hand whilst turning my body slightly rightwards and flexing the fingers on my right hand.

"'Allo, Nev," I said in an exaggerated thicko voice.

For a split second he looked bemused but, in that time, I launched myself at him and, with perfect timing and precision, as my friend Mickey Corsley had taught me, I hit him square on the jaw with an almighty right cross, possibly the best right cross ever thrown in Belmarsh. I put every ounce of strength and dislike of him into the punch. He was wholly unprepared for this assault and he staggered back one pace and dropped as though shot by a sniper. He waited three seconds, shook his head and tried getting up. I dragged him to his feet whilst he was still dazed and threw him towards the armchair he'd been sitting in. He crashed into it and knocked it over backwards, with him falling over the top of it. He let out a pained yell. I only discovered later the little finger on his left hand had been dislocated when he'd landed on the floor.

I heard a gasp behind me. The prison officer was open-mouthed at what he'd just seen, but, looking down at Thornwyn and then at me, he looked very pleased.

"Come on, Nev, off the floor, mate. You're making the place look untidy." I was still talking in an exaggerated thicko voice.

Between us, the prison officer and I pulled Thornwyn to his feet and pushed him down sharply onto the now righted chair.

"Sit there and shut up," I ordered in an authoritative tone.

"Tripped over his own feet, didn't he?" The officer winked at me as he walked out the room. At the door he looked back at Thornwyn. "You should be more careful, mate." He was laughing as he closed the door.

Thornwyn was rubbing his jaw with his right hand and looking at me with a *what the hell?* kind of expression. He was flexing the fingers on his left hand. He certainly wasn't looking pleased to see me now. He sat fuming for a few more seconds.

"Feel better now, do you?" he asked sourly.

"That's from Sampson and Tilling. They asked me to give you their best wishes." I sat opposite and pulled my chair closer until we were only a few feet apart.

I felt a very small twinge of conscience at assaulting a man now close to sixty, but it lasted barely two seconds. He'd deserved at least one good crack in the mouth. At least, as it was me, he knew it'd been given with love. Sort of.

"You tried to set me up, didn't you?" I asked. "You knew, when I came here that first time, it'd make MI5 think I was some part of what you were involved with. That's why you requested to see me, wasn't it? It hasn't worked. Stimpson's cleared me."

I wanted to hit him again. And again. But I resisted the desire. Hitting him the once had been cathartic. It was enough.

"You've got it all worked out, haven't you, Rob?" He was still rubbing his jaw and flexing the fingers on his left hand, looking in some discomfort doing so. I couldn't ascertain whether he sounded pleased or was being sarcastic.

I leaned forward.

"I'll make this short and sweet," I said quietly and firmly. "You *ever* mention Brian Turley in connection with the robbery at Byzantium to *anyone*, I'll come back and I'll spend all afternoon doing what I've just done. Fair enough? You understand?"

"Eh? What's Turley to you?" He sounded puzzled. "He's just a fucking drunk."

"Doesn't matter." I shook my head. "We have a deal? You're *not* gonna mention his name, *ever*, in any context. Right?"

He exhaled and looked directly at me, thinking about what I'd said. He waited a few moments.

"Okay, I'll not mention him. I'll keep him out of it. But you should be aware others know of his involvement. It's not just me."

"Not an issue. Bernie's in custody and Partias's dead, as is Jeremy Godfrey."

Thornwyn's eyes opened wide in disbelief. "*Dead?* Both of them?"

I nodded. "Yup. Neither of them from natural causes either."

"Bloody hell," he sighed. He looked shaken. Obviously news of their demise hadn't made it to this part of South-East London.

"Priestly's also confessed to his part in the robbery," I continued, ignoring his feelings, "and Bernie'll say nothing, not after I talk to him again. You can drop Bernie in it all you want, I don't much care what happens to him. You can say Bernie or Partias recruited someone to help him but you don't know who. Just leave Turley out of it. Understand?" I was emphatic. He could tell from my authoritative tone I was serious.

He nodded his agreement. "Alright," he said softly.

I stood up. I looked at him for a moment.

"You take care." I patted him on the shoulder. "Sorry about just now."

I meant it. Despite everything he'd done and was responsible for, there was still a very small part of me that recalled how fondly I regarded my time serving under Thornwyn when I'd been promoted to being a DC, and there was no doubt I'd learnt a considerable amount about the realities of policing and detective work in his team. I remembered a few of the arrests we'd been involved in and some of the squad's nights out in the West End. I recalled how chuffed I'd been the first time I'd made an arrest in his team. Afterwards he'd looked at the paperwork, smiled at me, shook my hand and said, "*Well done, DC McGraw. I'll make a bloody copper out of you yet.*"

I had no doubts that he deserved to be where he now was, given everything I knew he'd done, but it was sad such an illustrious career had come to this.

"I did a good job on you, didn't I?" He was smiling now.

I didn't respond. I left the room and saw the same prison officer waiting.

"Have to get that carpet looked at. Can't have our distinguished guests tripping over it and falling, now can we?" He was beaming, almost radiantly. "You've made my day."

I left Belmarsh and drove to Kentish Town police station. Bernie Rayes had been remanded in custody the day before after being charged with being in possession of a dangerous weapon, a knife, and also with conspiracy to supply and distribute dangerous drugs. Due to a shortage of prison places, he was being held in a police cell.

I had him brought to the interrogation room. I asked DS Roberts to turn off the tape recorder as I didn't want this conversation recorded for posterity.

I leapt straight in.

"Let me tell you how it's gonna be, Bernie, because your future depends on this. You're *not* gonna name Brian Turley as your accomplice for the Byzantium robbery, got that? You tell them you got a friend of a friend whose name you didn't catch to help you. Okay? Or you can say someone Partias or Thornwyn knew helped you out, whatever, I don't care which. You do that, I'll put in a word and see if we can get some time lopped off for you."

"Why can't I name Turley?" He was confused.

"It's part of the deal. You don't name him, and I'll guarantee you'll never have to worry about him coming after you. You'll be safe from his spiteful resentment about being shafted over the money you owe him. I'm protecting you, Bernie. He's a police officer. You really think he couldn't reach out and get to you in prison?"

Bernie looked doubtful. I said nothing for ten seconds.

"I'll put it like this. You name Turley and I'll see to it you get the book thrown at you for the robbery, plus I'll add conspiracy to any charges you receive. You remember what I said the other day about how long you could go down for? You're currently only on remand for the knife you were carrying, as well as drugs charges, but I can make things *so* much worse for you. You want that? You wanna go down for twenty years?"

He shook his head. He was scared, the response I'd wanted.

"Not only that, you'd still be on Turley's shitlist. You'll get a long sentence *and* you'll still have Turley coming after you. You really think he couldn't get you in prison? Do you wanna know how many assaults occur in prison because a con's pissed off someone on the force?"

I let him think for a few seconds. He now looked very worried.

"So, we're clear on what you're going to do?" I asked.

"Yeah," he eventually agreed. "I won't drop his name."

"You keep to that, I absolutely guarantee you'll be safe from Turley."

He looked relieved. I didn't mention he was as safe from Turley as it was possible to be.

"See? You *can* make a good decision when you try," I said.

Bernie didn't look convinced.

Leaving the interrogation room, I met with Roberts again and responded to his question by informing him we now knew who'd killed Noel Partias and Bernie'd helped in this, which might help when he was charged again after further inquiries were made.

I was unclear whether any prosecution would ever be brought against Bernie for the robbery at Byzantium. That would be for the spooks to determine. They knew who had the weapons and Bernie was likely to go down for possessing an offensive weapon anyway, so the exact situation was uncertain.

Late afternoon, I was at my desk typing up an account of my talks with Thornwyn and Bernie Rayes, and it was as well I wasn't doing this under oath as I'd omitted any reference to my threats to both men about mentioning Brian Turley. I'd also omitted any reference to assaulting Thornwyn.

I was going to considerable lengths to keep anyone from knowing Turley had been involved in an arms robbery which had seen stolen weapons end up with a known terrorist sympathiser. I knew MI5 knew where the weapons were and were tracking them. Turley's career had stalled due to his suspension but I didn't want his name besmirched any more than it was likely to be. I figured I owed him that much, though I wasn't completely sure I knew why. I was hoping, as he'd not been interrogated by the IPCC and had only been on suspension at the time of his death, that the reasons for the suspension would not be made public and his family would still qualify for death-in-service benefits and his pension, but that was for others to decide.

I filed the report and, a little later, was ready to leave when Smitherman saw me. He indicated he wanted a quick word in his office.

He informed me Geoffrey Tilling had been charged with murder and had been remanded in custody by Horseferry

---

Road magistrates' court to await crown court trial. His lawyer was going to try to plead guilty to manslaughter and this would be subject to discussion with prosecuting counsel. I was hoping they'd agree to it.

Smitherman then said Martha Sampson had been interviewed by two female detectives earlier this afternoon about Tilling's claim he'd heard Jeremy Godfrey say that he and his daughter had effectively killed her husband and made it appear to be a suicide. Predictably, she'd denied everything and had vehemently protested her innocence. She said she was still grieving for her father, who'd been murdered the previous evening, and how dare they choose now to come and doubt her story concerning her husband's suicide?

There was, of course, only Geoffrey Tilling's word, which was hearsay and inadmissible as evidence in court, so the truth would probably never be known. I was inclined to believe Tilling as I didn't doubt Godfrey was capable of such an act, and I'd also been told earlier Godfrey and someone from MI5 had been involved. Had Martha Sampson been involved as well? Did she help because she knew of her husband's true sexuality?

Smitherman hadn't read my report yet, so he asked how things had gone down. I explained that Bernie claimed he'd been helped by an accomplice whose name he didn't know, someone Partias or Thornwyn might have got to help him. I repeated Bernie's claim not to know who'd killed Partias. I mentioned my chat to Thornwyn and how I'd told him his little enterprise had failed, clueing him in about the deaths of Godfrey and Partias.

Smitherman sat in silence, nodding and staring at me for a few seconds.

"Were you aware that, just after you left Belmarsh earlier, Thornwyn went to see the prison governor about what he said was a serious matter?" he asked.

"About what? Wasn't I deferential enough?"

"Apparently, he claimed to have been assaulted by the

———◦———

detective who came to visit him. Quite irate, he was." He looked like he was trying not to smile. He then broke out into a broad grin. If I didn't know better, I'd have said he was laughing. "After you left, Thornwyn showed the governor a bruise on his chin, said his visitor had just done that to him. The governor duly reported his complaint and it's made its way to me as you're the detective who visited him, and I'm your superior officer."

He waited. He was clearly enjoying the moment.

"But, as I told the governor, it's just as well I don't believe any detective in Special Branch would act in so unprofessional a manner because, if one did, I'd have to suspend that person."

He fixed me with a knowing grin. I nodded.

"I told him that because there was also a prison officer in the room who said he saw what happened, and he made a statement to the governor saying he saw Thornwyn lose his footing, fall over and hit his chin on the side of the chair. He said he and the detective helped Thornwyn up. Oh, yeah, apparently Thornwyn also dislocated his little finger when he tripped up." Smitherman did not appear to be unhappy imparting this news.

"Should have been more careful, shouldn't he?" I replied in a neutral tone.

"Yes, he should." He nodded towards the door. I was dismissed. I got up and left.

Today, I'd learnt Stimpson was no longer after me, I'd ensured no black marks would go against Brian Turley's name and I'd put Thornwyn on the floor with a quite delicious right cross. And tomorrow I was off duty. Tonight would indeed be beer night. And it was.

NINE

Wednesday, nearly three weeks later

AFTER REVIEWING THE REPORTS prepared by probation officers and psychologists, and no doubt having heard from counsel representing MI5, His Honour Mr Justice Lincoln QC sentenced Commander Neville Thornwyn to twenty-two years in prison. Thornwyn was escorted back to Belmarsh to await the final decision as to where he'd serve out his sentence. Wherever it was, much of it would be spent in his own company. Even allowing for parole he'd be at least in his mid-seventies when he was finally released. I morbidly wondered whether he'd survive incarceration behind bars for such a lengthy period.

I was in court number one at the Old Bailey as he was escorted into the witness box by two prison officers. As the judge entered the courtroom and we all rose to our feet, I noticed the expression on Thornwyn's face. He was staring blankly at the bench as the judge took his seat.

The judge began with a lengthy reiteration of what Thornwyn had been convicted of, and expressed his horror at the scale of his crimes as well as the damage he'd inflicted on the good name and character of the British police. He then looked sternly at Thornwyn.

"Consequently, only a lengthy sentence can reflect the seriousness of the crimes committed and the harm caused to the reputation of the police by them. The public needs to be reassured that crimes of this magnitude will be punished accordingly, and this court will not shirk from doing its duty. You will go to prison for twenty-two years. Take the prisoner down."

Thornwyn had no expression on his face as the two prison officers led him down to the cells beneath the court to await transport back to Belmarsh. He could have been waiting for a bus for all the emotion he showed.

I had watched Thornwyn the whole time the judge was speaking. He had stood motionless, hands crossed together in front and looking directly at the judge. It was like watching the aftermath of a car crash, horrifically compelling in its starkness. A once proud, legendary senior police officer being addressed like a common criminal.

I thought back to the first time I'd met him when I'd been promoted to the rank of DC. He was a legend and I was looking forward to the challenge of being worthy of working under such an illustrious superior officer. He'd shaken my hand and told me what he expected of his officers and I'd replied with something anodyne, along the lines of how I hoped I'd reward his faith in me. The excitement I'd felt at meeting him for the first time had now given way to a sense of betrayal.

When sentence was passed his expression didn't change. It was as if the judge had just said good morning to him.

As he disappeared from view I realised his name would be forever associated with police corruption. His downfall, and the hubris accompanying it, would be taught in ethics classes for rookie police officers at Hendon Police College. It was a sad way for such a career to have ended. I was feeling confused as I left the court.

There was the usual unruly media scrum of television reporters, cameramen and journalists milling outside the court waiting to catch a glimpse of the van taking Thornwyn away, with uniforms attempting to keep them behind the barriers which would allow the van to leave unhindered. I wasn't sure why, but I waited across the road. A few minutes later there was an excited surge and the noise increased as the gates opened. A security van pulled out into the road and turned towards Newgate Street, heading towards Southwark Bridge and the road to Belmarsh. For a few moments there were dozens of camera flashes and some frantic shouting as the assembled throng tried to move forward whilst the van pulled away and then disappeared from view in the traffic.

I was about to leave when I heard a questioning voice behind me.

"You're not feeling sorry for him, are you, DS McGraw?" It was Smitherman.

"No, not at all." I hoped I was lying with sincerity in my voice.

"Bastard deserves every minute of the sentence," he said quietly, more to himself than to me. I nodded my agreement. He said he'd also been in court to see the sentence passed and was delighted Thornwyn had got such a lengthy spell inside, though he'd been hoping for at least thirty years. I wondered where he'd been sitting as I'd not seen him.

Then, to my equal surprise and horror, I heard another voice.

"Hello, Jack. What'd you think about that, then?" the voice said to Smitherman. I knew whose voice it was. Three seconds later the same voice addressed itself to me. "Oh, hi, Rob, didn't realise it was you. How you been?"

It was Richard Clements.

"Hi, Richard. Yeah, I'm good. You?"

"Yeah, fine." He was smiling. "Still writing for the *Focus*."

Smitherman, short-haired and in a crisply cut dark suit, pale blue shirt and tie, contrasted starkly with Clements, wearing black Levi jeans and a collarless navy blue cheese-cloth shirt. Clements' long hair wasn't in a ponytail. I'd have loved to have seen the expression on Smitherman's face had it been.

"Yes, of course, I forgot you two know each other," Smitherman said, pointing between the two of us. "You both went to King's, didn't you?"

"Yeah, we were in the same constitutional law group,

weren't we?" Clements said. I agreed we had been, plus a British politics set as well.

"We're about to meet my daughter and then go for lunch, DS McGraw. Would you like to join us?" Smitherman asked.

"No, I've got a few things I need to get done today. Thanks for the invite, though."

Smitherman hailed a taxi and Clements followed his father-in-law into the back of the cab. As he got in, Clements turned and nodded at me and I returned it. We both knew the score here. Neither of us wanted Smitherman sensing any degree of familiarity between us, and we definitely didn't want him knowing we were becoming good friends.

I watched the taxi drive away towards Ludgate Hill and speculated on whether, apart from them both loving the same woman, one as a father, the other as a husband, they actually had anything in common at all.